MW00465610

the bad boy's baby

a Hope Springs novel

CINDI
MADSEN

This book is a work of fiction. Names, characters, places, and incidents are the product of the author's imagination or are used fictitiously. Any resemblance to actual events, locales, or persons, living or dead, is coincidental.

Copyright © 2016 by Cindi Madsen. All rights reserved, including the right to reproduce, distribute, or transmit in any form or by any means. For information regarding subsidiary rights, please contact the Publisher.

Entangled Publishing, LLC
2614 South Timberline Road
Suite 109
Fort Collins, CO 80525
Visit our website at www.entangledpublishing.com.

Bliss is an imprint of Entangled Publishing, LLC. For more information on our titles, visit http://www.entangledpublishing.com/category/bliss

Edited by Stacy Abrams
Cover design by Louisa Maggio
Cover art from iStock

Manufactured in the United States of America

First Edition May 2016

*To the lovely people in my hometown of Sanford, Colorado,
who really do make quilts for newlywed couples and spring
into motion whenever anyone in town is in need.*

Chapter One

Ever notice that the world-changing days usually start like every other day, never letting on that they're about to grab onto the edge of your life, tip it totally upside down, and change every single thing?

This Monday had started much like any other, with bartering over the acceptable amount of time to wear a pink tutu, especially over pajamas, and trying to convince a two-year-old that the boring brown bits of Lucky Charms were just as delicious as the multicolored marshmallow shapes. Add in an outfit thrown together that might or might not match but definitely had a few drops of spilled coffee and a rainbow marshmallow smear and a mad dash out the door, and it was a typical Monday.

At least it was the usual for Emma Walker, and besides constantly feeling like she was forgetting something—and she most likely was—she'd been happier than she'd been in years, if sometimes a tad overwhelmed and more than a little desperate for adult conversation.

That was what happened when you were a single mother

of the cutest, most energetic two-year-old this side of the Mississippi, which was the bigger side of the country, for the record.

So when she pulled up to the transforming Mountain Ridge property, she downed the last of her now-cold coffee, took a deep breath, and then opened the door of the giant work truck that announced her exit with a loud, metal-on-metal screech. The door weighed about a hundred pounds and hated to be closed, so she shoved it hard and slammed her hip into it, telling it to stay.

Still, the beast of a truck was nicer than her car, which was classic in the uncool way that meant out-of-date, rusted, and often temperamental. It didn't handle the road to Mountain Ridge very well—she'd learned that the hard way, on day one of trying to prove she could take point on a job, only to end up high centered and stuck. It'd been mortifying, as well as a test in humility.

Nothing like telling your boss to go ahead and have his back surgery because you could definitely handle the job yourself, only to call and tell him you hadn't *quite* made it to the work site on account of being stuck. Luckily he'd taken pity, sent the crew to free her car, and then lent her the work truck for trips to and from the property. On top of taking on the bumpy road better than her car, the beast hauled more supplies.

Emma pulled out her trusty clipboard, the to-do list for the day already printed and color coded by priority, then stopped for a moment to bask in the fresh air and beautiful mountain backdrop, her thoughts on a sparkling lake a few hours' hike from here. She missed the days when she could so easily escape the world for a while, when all camping required was a small tent and a backpack full of food and essentials.

Days when she could go anywhere without three bags packed to the brim were gone, but she *was* planning on taking a camping trip once the weather grew a bit warmer. It was about time to introduce her daughter to one of her favorite activities. Although, for the first trip, she'd probably need to choose a different spot than Hope Springs Reservoir, because Zoey would definitely make a beeline toward the water, and two arms weren't nearly enough to hold that girl back.

As much as Emma wanted to head into the mountains for a day or two, the thought also exhausted her. The Mountain Ridge job involved a lot of planning and problem solving, as well as the construction of the cabins, and lately she'd been so busy—not to mention completely mentally and physically exhausted at the end of the day—that other things were falling through the cracks. She hadn't been to visit Grandma Bev in way too long, and she hoped that her grandmother was still taking her medications and eating healthy in Emma's absence, although she knew that was a long shot.

I've just got to get through this job, and then life will slow down a bit. Plus, I'll be able to use it for my portfolio, hopefully get a stellar reference or two, and land bigger jobs—the kind that'll help me better take care of Zoey, me, and Grandma Bev.

Moving to Laramie or Cheyenne for career opportunities was a double-edged sword. Jobs paid more, and there were definitely better opportunities to land positions where she'd get to focus more on the architecture part she'd gone to college for, but cost of living was higher.

Emma's blood pressure rose, the way it always did when she started trying to figure out how she was going to do it all, so she pushed her worries away to focus on the job here and now. God willing, it'd be the door the opportunities came knocking on, and then she'd decide which one to answer.

She walked up to what used to be the Mountain Ridge Bed and Breakfast but was becoming the Mountain Ridge Lodge, tucked her clipboard under her arm, and knocked on the bright yellow door. Every time she stood on this porch, she admired the new entryway and fresh lumber. Heath Brantley and his fiancée, Quinn Sakata, had been working hard to transform the once run-down property, and they were quickly becoming her favorite clients, even though she still experienced a pang of guilt every time she looked at Heath.

Quinn was even becoming a friend, too, along with her best friend, Sadie. They'd been inviting Emma along for their girls' nights. Dressing up in clothes that didn't have coffee, marshmallow smears, or paint on them, and getting away from her parental duties for a few hours every Friday had been helping her life feel more well-rounded and a little less lonely. The girls were also trying to set her up, but they hadn't found the right candidate yet, and in this tiny town where she'd known most everyone since forever, Emma doubted they ever would. She'd accepted that a relationship might not be in the cards for her—for at least a few more years, anyway.

That was okay. She had Zoey. That little girl gave the kind of unconditional love Emma had always wanted, and the love she had for her…well, it filled her up and was the reason she got out of bed every morning.

Just as Emma lifted her arm to knock again, the door swung open. She stepped back to avoid being in the way and opened her mouth to say hello, but then she noticed it wasn't Heath that'd come to the door.

Emma took another large step back, every cell in her body screaming at once as she stared up at the familiar face, hoping and praying her eyes were playing tricks on her.

She'd misjudged the edge of the porch, though, and her foot slipped, her center of gravity thrown. She flung out her arms, searching in vain for the rail, but before she could recover, Cam was right there, grabbing onto her wrist and tugging her closer to him.

Way, way too close. The rugged features that she'd admired so many times were still in full force, defined by a scruffy beard. His body had filled out even more since that night all those years ago, though, and back then the sight of him shirtless had been enough for her to completely lose her mind.

"Sorry," he said. "I didn't mean to…" He tipped his head to the side, his eyes narrowing as they roamed over her face. Her throat went dry as her flight response kicked in. Only his gaze and his grip on her wrist held her in place.

Maybe he won't remember me.

Wait. That'd be worse. I think. Oh, jeez, I don't know anymore.

Logically she'd known that she might see the father of her child again someday. But logic and seeing him were two different things, and the latter made her completely lose hold of the former.

One night. One night *ever* that she'd thrown caution to the wind and enjoyed a reckless night with a guy she'd crushed on from afar for years, and she'd managed to make the worst mess. Mostly because she'd been dumped the month before, her ex-boyfriend citing she was too boring—both in life and in the bedroom—and she'd been trying to prove she could be sexy and fun and the opposite of herself.

So she'd flirted with Cameron freaking Brantley, had *way* too much to drink, and ended up having a one-night stand with the town's bad boy hours before he'd deployed.

But she'd gotten an angelic little girl in return, and she'd never regret that.

"Hey," Cam said, his voice warmer now. "Emma, right?"

Her heart took off, beat after beat, although the fast pace made it hard to tell one from the other. It'd been torturous enough having to see Cam's brother on a regular basis now that he was back in Hope Springs for good, but it wasn't like she knew Heath, not really. Honestly, it wasn't like she knew Cameron Brantley, either, although thanks to their one-night stand three years ago, she knew all about the amazing things he could do with his tongue, and the memory threatened to make her overheat, despite the cool spring breeze.

Pull it together, Emma. She spotted her dropped clipboard on the edge of the porch and scooped it up, clinging to it like a lifeline.

"I didn't know you were…" She swallowed, waiting for him to fill in the blank. Was he back, back? Or just on leave? Why hadn't she heard about it?

"Just got back day before yesterday," he said.

"The army, right?"

He nodded. "I'm officially out, though, actually. Honorably discharged, so I could run the lodge with Heath and Quinn."

While she was happy for him, her stomach still clenched at the news. That meant she couldn't avoid him. It meant so much more, too, things she'd pushed so far to the background that she'd pretended she'd never have to deal with them. Heck, it'd been so long that she was pretty sure even the town had stopped making bets on who Zoey's father was. No one had guessed Cam, because none of them would ever think a girl like her could land a guy like him, even for a night.

The only reason she *had* involved him leaving on a long deployment, a lot of alcohol, and trying to prove she wasn't as boring as her ex claimed.

Cam's eyes lit on hers again, and she couldn't help but notice the irises that were somewhere between green and blue, to the point that she never knew which color to call them. Zoey had those same eyes, and they changed color depending on everything from what she wore to how tired she was. In fact, she saw so much of Cam in Zoey now that she stood face-to-face with him again, it surprised her no one had ever made the connection, especially his own family. With him back in town, people probably would notice.

Fear crawled through her at that thought, robbing her of

oxygen. So many complications. Such a big chance of future hurt—she could take it, she was a grown-up, and it was her failed attempts to contact Cam that'd landed her in her current messy situation. But her daughter…all the reasons she'd freaked out when she'd first found out she was going to have a baby with someone who'd made it clear he didn't want one came rushing back to her.

Before she could even think of what to say—or how much to say—Quinn and Heath came to the door. "Hey, Emma," Quinn said, bounding out and hugging her. "Sorry to keep you waiting. Things have been crazy around here. Cam came home a few days early." She slung her arm around him, and with the height difference, it might've been comical if Emma were in a laughing mood. Which she most certainly wouldn't be for a very, very long time.

Employing the shoving-away-to-be-worried-over-later skills she'd already used once today, she pushed everything else to the background. Later she'd analyze for hours and weigh pros and cons, but right now she needed to focus on the matter at hand so she wouldn't ruin all of the hard work she'd put into this job. "The guys should be here any minute, and then we'll get right to it."

Emma swept her gaze toward the road, hoping the guys would make a timely appearance, although her crew, while hard workers, was hardly ever what she'd call timely. They didn't take her as seriously as they should, either, despite the fact that she'd learned to state things instead of present them like an option, and she was working on raising her voice and becoming the kind of person who could stand in front of a room and take charge.

She glanced down and discreetly scratched at the dried multicolored marshmallow smear on her shirt, which probably didn't help the serious boss–type image she was going for. Boring and serious, yet not stern enough to be a boss—what a combo.

The cabins taking shape along the right side of the property proved that despite the bumpy start to calling the shots, she and the crew certainly got stuff done. *They're slowly getting used to my being in charge of a project after being the pushover administrative assistant/bookkeeper who answered the phone and gave them extra time to turn in their paperwork. I just have to keep proving myself.*

Those were her designs out there, too, even if her boss insisted on adding Pete, an architect from Salt Lake City, to the crew to approve her blueprints and check in on the progress from time to time.

Often it struck her as funny that she'd ended up working at a construction company. "Site manager" was such a broad term, though, and in her case, it meant she was good at dealing with vendors and keeping a tight budget and schedule, and that she was picky about how her blueprints were carried out. She didn't do a whole lot of constructing—not that she couldn't when needed—and this job was a good stepping-stone for her future architecture career.

And hopefully once she proved herself here, her boss would let her run more projects alone. The main problem she worried about after this job ended was demand. There weren't a whole lot of new buildings, industrial or residential, that went up in Hope Springs, and she had a family to take care of.

"Why don't we grab coffee while we wait," Quinn said, taking Emma's hand and tugging her inside instead of waiting for her to agree. Probably because she rarely said no to a cup of coffee. Lack of sleep combined with long days on the site required large amounts of caffeine.

Their footsteps echoed across the hardwood floor of the main room they'd put in to keep the bed-and-breakfast feel. They'd added a few rustic decorations, going for more of a country rustic than backwoods look. Emma was especially proud of the blend of styles, as Quinn and Heath had pretty much the opposite taste on every single thing. Architect and interior decorator were hardly the same thing, but in a town this small, you multitasked and faked it until you made it. When Quinn had asked if she could help decorate, she'd said she'd figure it out. Together, with a lot of help from magazines and online shopping, they had.

Quinn wound her dark hair into a bun and secured it on the top of her head. Her Japanese heritage and rock star style gave her a unique look that made her stand out from the crowd, especially in their town, and the girl definitely knew how to kick back and have fun. She was still learning how to deal with mountain critters and the inevitable renovation hiccups, but she'd kept her optimism high, which made her an easy client to work for.

She poured four mugs of coffee, her steady stream of conversation filling the air. When she bragged up Emma and all she'd done for the property, Cam looked her way again. Heat crept across Emma's cheeks, the attention making her squirm, and she ducked her head and tucked a strand of hair behind her ear.

"I've got a great crew, which makes it easy," she said, waving off the skills she'd just been feeling proud of. She knew she needed to stop downplaying what she did in order to give off the air of confidence it took for people to take her more seriously, but it was hard to change old habits.

The rumble of truck engines started low but grew, and Emma set down her mug. "Thanks for the coffee. I'd better go get to work so we can keep to our schedule."

With a quick nod, she rushed outside.

At least once she had her long to-do list and a crew to focus on, she could stop wondering what in the world she was going to do about the fact that everything in her life just got a hundred times more complicated.

• • •

Through the large front window, Cam watched Emma greet the group of guys who'd pulled in. Being home was…weird. For ten years, all he'd known was military life. Orders and missions and, honestly, a lot of violence.

Ever since Heath had mentioned the Mountain Ridge property was up for sale, all he could think about was getting home and running camping and hunting expeditions with his brother. Mostly what he wanted to do was forget all the bad crap he'd lived through the past decade and escape from everything and everyone, until he remembered who he was. Especially who he was without the military.

But now that he was here, he could hardly sleep or sit or stand still. He'd only been out for a couple of days, though, and he hoped that in time he'd adjust. The other thing he hadn't planned on was running into Emma. Years had passed since their last encounter—and man, had it been a hell of an encounter—and he wasn't exactly sure what to say to her.

The truth was, he didn't even know her. But their one amazing night together had played through his head several times in the past few years, even if the exact details were a bit blurry.

He'd been drinking at the Triple S with Heath, thinking about his upcoming deployment—and if he recalled right, ranting about Dad—and then he'd noticed her sitting a few stools down. Cam had remembered her from high school, the smart girl with the frizzy brown hair who had her hand up in every class, the right answer always on the tip of her tongue.

The girl had always intrigued him, his brain having a hard time wrapping around how someone could possibly be *that* into school. She was the sweet type of girl he knew to stay away from, because the townsfolk already blamed him and Heath for everything that went wrong, and he could only imagine the uproar it'd cause if he even dared to breathe her same air.

That night at the Triple S, though, she'd looked the same but different. Pretty in a classic way, her formerly frizzy hair transformed into sleek waves, her lips bright red and completely mesmerizing, and then there was the skirt that displayed a killer set of legs. And he'd decided he could risk offering the town's good girl a drink, since he was on his way out of Hope Springs anyway. Only she'd offered him one first, and he'd gone from intrigued to fascinated and became more so as the night went on.

Today she had her brown hair up in a messy bun and her makeup was minimal, but she was still pretty in a classic, down-to-earth way, and those tight jeans showed off the fact that she still had a killer set of legs.

His heart thumped as he watched her lift a clipboard and point, sending one group one way and the other group off in a different direction. He tried to remember how long it'd been.

Let's see…that was my third deployment, so right before my second tour in Afghanistan, and before I was stationed in Germany. He counted off the years on his fingers, trying to remember if Afghanistan had been a fifteen-month deployment or a year—all of them blurred together in one long streak, a lot of camo and desert and the feel of his rifle in his hands and dudes crammed into tight quarters.

Three years. Three years since I convinced the cute girl who knew everything to take shots with Heath and me, and then the night somehow ended with us having sex in my truck. His blood heated at the memory, and before he could remind himself that he should stay far away from good girl Emma Walker, he was out the door and down the porch steps, his toolbox in hand.

As he pushed through the door, Heath called out, "Wait up," and Cam slowed his pace so that his brother could catch up. Then they walked over to the cabin where he'd seen Emma and the second crew head, the one that was still just a frame.

But when he got there, Emma wasn't anywhere to be seen. He glanced back at the row of parked trucks, but the one she'd arrived in still sat in the driveway, the faded sign declaring it Hope Springs Construction missing enough of the P and E that it looked a bit like Ho Springs Construction. He laughed at that, then shook his head at his maturity level.

"Put us to work," Heath said, and Tom, a potbellied guy in a yellow hard hat, gave them instructions to start on the north wall.

The two of them started in on putting up the Sheetrock. Swinging the hammer and working up a sweat in the hot sun helped take a bite out of the antsy feeling Cam had been experiencing since arriving back in town, and he decided that keeping busy was the key to transitioning back into civilian life.

After the guys called lunch, he couldn't help looking around for Emma again. The sound of hammering, less noisy than what had been going on around him and coming from the next cabin over, caught his attention, and he wandered over to check it out.

Emma had parts spread all around her, the skeleton of a fireplace mantel taking shape inside.

"Lunchtime," he said, and she jumped, the hammer in her hands dropping to the floor with a *thunk*. He quickly picked up the hammer and extended it to her. "Sorry. I just scared you for the second time today."

"First time, actually. The other time…well, I expected the door to open, obviously, but…" She shook her head and then tucked that one strand behind her ear, like she'd done this morning.

"You didn't expect *me*."

Her chest rose and fell with a long exhale. Cam silently encouraged her to lift her big brown eyes so he could get another look into them—and so he could attempt to assure her that she had nothing to feel weird about—but he couldn't think of a way to say those actual words without it coming across as weird. Especially since it would be practically admitting that he'd been thinking about their night together since she showed up on the porch this morning.

What the hell am I doing? I should just leave her alone. The rarely used optimistic part of him argued that he was only trying to get back to normal small-town life, but nothing about this interaction felt normal. "Would you like me to help you?"

She winced, like that was the last thing she wanted. Apparently he completely failed at remembering how to do small talk. Or maybe he'd offended her.

"Not that you don't have it under control. I thought maybe you just pointed and gave the orders, but obviously you know what you're doing. I'm impressed."

"Yeah, give me a hammer and screwdriver and I can bang and screw with the best of them." Her face flushed pink, the brown eyes he'd wanted another look at flying wide.

"Trust me, I remember," he said, shutting his mouth too late to keep that thought from popping out.

She threw her hand over her mouth, but a laugh slipped out, and he couldn't help but laugh, too. "Oh my gosh. I'm going to go die now," she said, but then she laughed harder, and it triggered the memory of that night, when she'd been doing shots and started laughing at any and everything—the happy sound had warmed him from the inside out, the noise carrying off his worries as it drifted into the air, just like it did now.

She put her fingertips to her forehead and shook her

head. "What I meant to say was that pouring the concrete and framework are a bit out of my league, but…" She shook her head again. "I'm the queen of saying the wrong thing, and this is just…"

Cam put his hand on his chest. "No, I said the wrong thing. Sorry. I think I was trying so hard to not mention that night that it sort of backfired. I'm usually good at keeping my thoughts inside."

Her gaze had snapped to his when he said "that night," and he suddenly couldn't swallow.

She winced and glanced away. "Look, I—"

"Emma. There you are." The guy who'd arrived about an hour ago, looking more suited to an office than a job site, stepped through the doorway. He got a silly grin on his face as he looked at Emma, and it made Cam wonder if they were more than coworkers.

His gut pinched, a sensation that felt suspiciously like jealousy.

Of course she's involved with someone else, someone who's actually suited for her. Not like she and I were even ever involved, anyway. "I'll catch you later," Cam said, backing away.

Really, it was for the best. His head was nowhere close to a place where he could go out on a date and pretend that everything he'd experienced during his last mission didn't follow after him.

Chapter Two

Emma hadn't had another chance to talk to Cam since Pete, who'd arrived in town from Salt Lake for the week, had interrupted to ask if they'd received the tile to complete the next phase of the remaining kitchens yet.

Okay, that was a lie. She'd purposely kept busy and stayed out of the radius of both Brantley boys, her emotions such a mess that she'd put one of the mantel logs on raw side out and had to unfasten it and start over.

As she walked up the sidewalk to Happy Hearts Day Care, she let herself wonder what more Cam would've said if they hadn't been interrupted. The words, "Trust me, I remember," and the way he'd said them ran through her head on a continuous loop throughout the day. What would he have followed that up with?

Not that it mattered, because she should've stopped any conversation and…what? Just blurted out that he had a daughter? That *they* had a daughter.

The guilt that she'd pushed to the background broke through every barrier she'd erected and slammed into her full force, crushing her lungs in the process. Fear came right on its heels, even stronger than this morning. The most important thing in her life was Zoey. Keeping her safe and happy and taken care of, and most of all, making her feel wanted.

Suddenly she didn't know how to do all that, not with Cam Brantley back in Hope Springs.

She knocked on the door, and the second she stepped inside, Zoey yelled, "Mommy!" and ran over and hugged her legs. Emma picked her up and kissed one of her chubby cheeks, hugging her even tighter than usual.

Tanya told her the highlights of the day, along with the fact that Zoey hadn't eaten her lunch very well. When playing was an option, getting her to sit down and eat was a challenge that involved a mix of bartering and discipline. Plus ketchup. Zoey would eat almost anything with ketchup, including carrots and green beans. Emma had felt like quite the genius when she'd discovered she could actually trick her two-year-old into eating veggies.

The things she was proud of these days. Three years ago she'd been counting down the days until she could move to the city and become a big-time architect, one who designed homes that'd be featured in magazines. Of being the person people called, whether for new homes or remodel projects, and having a reputation for getting things done quickly and efficiently while sticking to a budget.

Once she found out she was pregnant, those plans were postponed. She'd barely graduated college, and had planned on taking the summer for a mini-breather and for applying for jobs. That got pushed back until she had time to recover from having a baby.

Right when she'd decided it was time to finally make the move to a big city and go after the career she'd trained for, Grandma Bev had mixed up her meds—probably added a bit of alcohol, too, although she still denied it—and fell and broke her leg. She claimed she was fine, and even proudly showed off her hot-pink cast around town, but Emma still worried about her. Grandma Bev had been the one to take care of Emma after her parents' ugly, drawn-out divorce, and she couldn't leave her to recover alone.

Then she'd been so busy balancing a new baby and her job, all while trying to get Grandma to slow down enough to let her leg actually heal. And when the only job offers Emma received were unpaid internships, it was hard to justify leaving. No doubt the internships built skills and would look great on a résumé, but she needed money more than experience at that point, so she'd asked her boss at Hope Springs Construction about taking on more responsibility and ways to move up. Each year she'd gained more responsibilities and another title until this opportunity with Mountain Ridge came up.

This was her chance to get her career back on track, but with Cam Brantley now in the picture, everything she'd worked for was suddenly at risk. He'd be so upset once he found out about Zoey, and she couldn't blame him. While she'd like to use her couple of failed attempts to contact him as an excuse, she knew she should've tried harder, regardless of already knowing how he felt about having a kid.

Will he fire me from the Mountain Ridge job? Just make finishing it hell? What if I can't even use those beautiful cabins in my portfolio? All that work, only to be thrown away…

During the drive home she played out the likely scenarios, trying to come up with a game plan for each one. But the short trip was hardly long enough, and she had a feeling she'd never feel prepared for what the next few days might bring.

On her way into the house from the garage, she nearly tripped on the giant rocking horse that Zoey must've moved in an attempt to reach the package of cookies on the counter.

After making a quick dinner and doing the dishes, Emma settled onto the couch with Zoey for what had to be their thousandth viewing of *Frozen*.

Thirty minutes from the end, Zoey's eyelids grew heavy, and she quickly lost the battle to stay awake. Emma ran her fingers through her daughter's fine blond curls and whispered, "I don't know what to do."

Her gaze moved to the stack of bills on top of the TV—the envelopes seemed to breed like bunnies. She could hardly keep up with her own bills, and while Grandma Bev kept telling her not to worry about her, Emma did. Each year another medication got added to the weekly pillbox, and she knew they weren't cheap. Once she landed a job that made more money, Grandma would have to stop refusing her help and suck it up and deal with the fact that she was going to pay some of her expenses, like it or not.

The image of her tackling her surprisingly spry seventy-year-old grandmother and trying to force her to take money made her giggle, but honestly it was probably what it'd take for the stubborn woman to let her help. After all, Beverly Harris was invincible—according to her—and they were still involved in their ten-year battle over reducing fried foods to try to keep her cholesterol and blood pressure under control.

Zoey stirred when Emma turned off the movie, and she adjusted her grip, stood, and carried her into her room and laid her in bed.

Emma slipped off the tutu and decided the jammies could handle one more night, even if it was the third day and night she'd worn the outfit.

By the time she made it back to the couch, exhaustion tugged at her, but if she crawled into bed, tomorrow would start that much sooner, and she wanted to relax with a non-Disney show, perhaps some mindless television where the hero was ripped and occasionally shirtless, as it was the only action she got these days.

Unless you count Cam Brantley saving me from falling

backward down the porch steps, his warm hand on my wrist, his body definitely ripped under that T-shirt.

She scolded herself for even thinking it when everything about Cam only brought a hundred complications, but her mind wouldn't stop spinning, his image from today crashing into past ones, namely that one fateful night.

When she closed her eyes, she found herself back at Seth's Steak and Saloon—or the Triple S, as the locals called it—hair done in pin curls, wearing a dress that was tighter and shorter than she usually wore, along with bright red lipstick and a new, fiery attitude.

All because Ricky told me I was boring before he dumped me. How stupid. That night, Cam Brantley had paid attention to her for the first time *ever*—and okay, part of that was because she'd been literally sitting three feet away—and she'd thought the sexy new look must be working.

At first he'd barely glanced her way, and then he'd gone right back to talking to Heath. They were discussing their father and their half brother, and she couldn't help eavesdropping—not that they seemed to be trying to keep their voices low enough to avoid being overheard.

"Of course he's ignoring the kid," Cam had said. "He didn't even raise us. Now he's got another son with a woman half his age. The best thing that could happen to that kid is for Dad to stay far, far away."

"But Oliver's mom isn't exactly stable, either," Heath had said. "I'll try to take care of him when I can, but I'm probably not much better than Dad."

"You'd be way better than Dad. I'm the one who's a mess. Which is why I don't want kids."

"You might change your mind someday," Heath said.

"No, I won't. If there's one thing I can guarantee, it's that I won't ever put a kid through what we had to go through. The best way to make sure that happens is to never have a kid. Hell, if Dad and Mom never had me, they never would've gotten married, and think of how much better off the world would be."

Emma had winced at that. Yes, it was a harsh thought, but it was one she knew all too well. She'd been the reason her parents married as well. Whenever things were bad between them—which was pretty much always, and they hid it less and less as she got older—Dad would bring it up. How Mom had to go and get herself pregnant, even though obviously she hadn't gotten *herself* pregnant. How he would give anything not to be trapped with her, with a kid.

Mom just let him talk to her like that, and Emma could see that every time he said something harsh, it stripped away a little more of her self-esteem. It hadn't exactly made Emma feel great about herself, either.

"Hey," Cam had said, turning fully toward her. "It's Emma, right?"

She'd nodded.

"You were in a few of my classes, and you always had all the answers. Do you still?"

The fact that he was staring at her, his gaze slowly moving over her body, made her heart skip a couple of beats. She'd crushed on him so hard in school, the bad boy she should know better than to want. She'd always thought he had a rough exterior but a deep soul. Whatever that meant. She gestured to the heavy-on-the-vodka drink she'd asked for and attempted a flirty grin, telling herself she wasn't boring. She had on red lipstick and a short skirt, dang it, and Cam Brantley had noticed.

"I do," she said, then she asked Seth Jr. to pour Cam a shot—and to put it on her tab, telling herself it was such a nonboring, ballsy move.

"You do," he said, reaching for the tiny glass she slid his way. She got a little lost in the motion when he tipped it to his full lips, and she wondered what those lips would feel like against hers.

He slid the cup back toward Seth, asked him to refill it and pour Emma one, too—on his tab this time.

As she'd passed the shot glass back to Cam, he wrapped his fingers around it, catching hers, too, and an electric current traveled up from their touch and settled in her chest. "What should we drink to?" he asked.

"Oh, I…" Honestly, she'd planned on dumping the shot into her drink when he wasn't looking and maybe only taking another sip or two, since she was already feeling buzzed. But then she realized that Carefree and Exciting Emma tipped back shots, no worrying about things like too drunk or hangovers. "To living in the moment."

Cam grinned. "I'll definitely drink to that." He clinked his cup against hers and they downed the shots.

As soon as she blinked the stinging tears from her eyes, she leaned toward him, one arm on the bar, and flirted like she'd never flirted before. She couldn't remember how many shots had followed. Only that she'd laughed a lot, and then Cam said something about getting out of there, taking her hand instead of waiting for an answer, and she'd blindly followed.

Once they'd reached the nearly empty parking lot, he slid an arm around her waist, pulled her to him, and kissed her. The alcohol haze lifted a bit, every inch of her body coming alive as he worked magic with his lips, the soft brush of them followed by the stubble on his chin.

She threw herself fully into the kiss, wrapping her arms around him and rolling her tongue over his. Somewhere along the way, they'd ended up in his truck. She protested his driving, because obviously they were way too drunk, and he'd tossed the keys to the floor, saying he didn't plan on going anywhere for a while. Then he brushed his fingertips across her collarbone, eliciting a shiver and spreading goose bumps across her skin.

Another protest about making out in the truck was on the tip of her tongue, but they were in the back corner, where the tree branches hung down and created fair cover, and his windows were tinted black.

Then he kissed her again, like it was the end of the world and he planned on making every last second count.

Parts of the night were so fuzzy and parts were so sharp.

She distinctly remembered his ripped torso and running her fingers across his pecs and abs, awed at the way the muscles dipped and curved. She'd also traced the tattoo on his chest, although she couldn't recall what it was now, only that it stood out from the ones on his arms. She definitely remembered when he'd slid his hands up her thighs. She even remembered the sex that followed, blips of kisses and his name on her lips. But she couldn't for the life of her remember the condom, although she'd sworn he'd pulled one out at one point.

With that last memory—or missing memory, as it were— her eyes popped open and she was transported from his truck and the past into her messy living room, the TV currently playing a show no one was watching.

He said he didn't want a kid—he couldn't have been any clearer about it.

Still, right after she found out she was pregnant, she'd googled how to find military members' email addresses. One site said there was a standard format for the army using the first name and last name, but that if there were more than one person with the same name, there'd be numbers added. Hoping he was the only one with the name, she'd sent an email to test the waters that said, "Hi, this is Emma Walker from Hope Springs. Are you the Cameron Brantley from there?"

But it'd bounced back, message undeliverable, and without knowing things like his unit or regiment, finding his real email address without involving a lot of people—including contacting the Department of Defense—was impossible.

For a couple of months, she'd left it alone. But halfway through her pregnancy, when everyone was asking about the father and she'd blurted out he didn't want to be involved so please stop asking, she'd experienced another bout of guilt, even as she'd told herself it was true.

So she'd sucked it up and decided to ask his father, despite being scared of the guy. A bad reputation was one thing, but she'd witnessed a few of Rod Brantley's drunken disturbances firsthand. She went into his auto repair shop, thinking it'd be a safe place to approach him. He was yelling at one of his employees about a mistake he'd made on a car, his face red with anger, and she'd panicked and fled.

Then she asked herself why she was trying so hard to contact a guy who didn't want a kid in the first place.

It was easy to think she'd done him a favor by not telling him, because he didn't want kids and she didn't want to experience what her mother had, a guy telling her how much he regretted being with her. How much he resented having to deal with a kid—which was also something she felt very strongly about protecting Zoey from.

While Cam's opinion on having kids probably hadn't changed, there was a big difference between telling herself he'd moved on and was pretty much unreachable so she was justified in never telling him, and seeing him every day and holding it back.

She tried to convince herself that it'd be selfish to tell him just to rid herself of guilt, but it became painfully clear that he had a right to know…

And she was going to have to find a way to tell him.

Chapter Three

This was the moment Cam had been looking forward to least. The closer he, Heath, and Quinn got to his childhood home, the tighter his nerves stretched.

To calm himself, his mind searched for a serene image. Over the years, he'd often imagined sitting at the edge of a clear blue lake, complete with mountain backdrop, to control his temper and keep the bad memories away.

But the image that popped into his head now had nothing to do with nature. No, this one belonged to a woman who had brown eyes, a warm laugh, and had said that she could "screw and bang with the best of them."

He bit back a grin. He'd wanted to talk to her more, but she'd kept to the outskirts this afternoon, and every time he'd moved into her orbit, she'd gone off on another job, into another cabin, that Pete guy who'd interrupted them earlier in the day trailing after her.

Cam didn't care if they were together—well, he *shouldn't* care. Ever since he'd seen Emma, though, he couldn't stop thinking about her lips and the way she'd kissed him all those years ago. She'd surprised him, and he was so rarely surprised by people.

Just forget about it, Brantley. She's out of your league, even if she was drunk enough one night to forget it, and it's not like you're looking for a relationship anyway.

Because relationships required trust, and all the ones he'd been in only proved women always had another agenda. There was a lot of trying to manipulate feelings involved, not to mention the trap questions that led to fights, and after the last one, he'd pretty much given up ever having another.

He trusted his gut, his brother, and his platoon—more specifically, the other nine soldiers who'd been in his squad.

Nine, until that last mission. Now there were only eight of them left, and seven with him gone… Cam pushed away those thoughts and concentrated on the reason he'd started this line of thinking in the first place.

Sure, Emma seemed like the trustworthy type, but that didn't change his stance on relationships, and he had other things to focus on. Get the lodge running, along with the hiking and hunting tours, and escape to the mountains as often as possible—those were the main goals. Well, and ensure Mountain Ridge was successful enough that he and his brother could make a living. While the army had given him a place to channel his anger, he'd lost a bit of himself with each mission, and the last one had made him question everything, including whether his squad was better off without him.

While he knew he'd never get back to the person he used to be, he wanted to get back to someone who didn't always think about exit strategies or how many ways he could kill a possible threat.

Like right now, with the truck pulling up in front of the run-down three-bedroom bungalow where he'd grown up, the urge to bolt consumed him. Open door, tuck and roll, run down the street. As an exit strategy, not too complicated, but those always worked the best, unless enemy gunfire was involved.

Judging from the look Heath gave him across the cab, he understood. "Dad really is doing pretty well. He's trying, Cam."

"Is he still drinking?"

Heath's hesitation said everything.

"He's trying to cut back," Quinn said. Then she turned to Heath. "Does he know about…?"

Great. More crap to face? Cam's nerves stretched that much tighter, seconds from snapping.

"He's trying to make it work with Oliver's mom, too," Heath said.

"The stripper who's half his age?"

"She's not a stripper anymore," Heath said, like that made it so much better.

"Can't we just stay at the lodge and pretend our father doesn't live in the same town?"

Quinn put her hand on Cam's arm. "He's been talking about you coming home for weeks. He's been so excited about it, and like Heath said, he really is trying to get his life back in order and make amends."

"He likes Quinn, too. She doesn't put up with his crap, and I honestly think our relationship is what gave him the push he needed to try to change." Heath opened his door, tugging Quinn out with him.

His brother's happiness made him happy, but Cam was pretty sure it also made Heath overly optimistic. Cam got a kick out of Quinn, too. She was this tiny firecracker whose swearing rivaled some of the guys he'd served with, and she said whatever thought popped into her head. Working together was going to be fun, which was good, because Heath would be hitting the road with his band, Dixie Rush, to promote their album's release before too long, and then it'd be the two of them trying to keep things running—he hoped they'd be busy enough to make it a challenge, too. He needed challenging and busy.

What he didn't need was to lose the bit of calm he'd managed to obtain since he'd arrived in Hope Springs, and he was afraid tonight might just undo it all.

With a sigh, he pushed out of the truck. This house, his dad—they were the main reasons he'd jumped at deployment after deployment and volunteered to be stationed in another country.

As soon as his father opened the door, Cam was transported back in time, to the days before he'd been big enough to stand up for himself. It was another reason he'd been so angry when he'd found out Dad had another kid. Cam had worked so hard to keep Heath protected from Dad's temper and drunken rage episodes, and it'd been such a relief once both of them were big enough to take being cussed out and told how useless they were and push back if he turned violent. Or the always fun days when they needed to be strong enough to carry his drunk ass out of the Triple S after he drank too much and started yet another fight there.

By the time he found out about Oliver, though, Cam had already committed himself to the army, and he felt guilty over how relieved he'd been to have an excuse to get him out of raising another kid, the way he'd pretty much raised Heath after Mom left them alone to deal with Dad.

A mom who'd abandoned her kids, a drunk and disorderly dad, and two boys who were forever in trouble, whether they'd committed the crimes or not—that was the Brantley family legacy in this town.

Hopefully the lodge will help change that, too.

Dad wrapped his arms around Cam and hugged him, patting him hard on the back. Cam knew he should say something about being glad to see him, but he couldn't muster up the lie. He'd spent most of his life resenting him, and time away hadn't magically fixed it.

"Cam!" Oliver ran into the room, his shoelaces flying behind him. He held his hand up for a high five and Cam smacked his palm. He barely knew his half brother, but the kid always greeted him like he was some kind of rock star.

"Hey, Ollie." In every email the kid sent, it was questions about the military, from type of guns to vehicles to missions, or baseball. Cam chose the safer subject. "How's baseball?"

Oliver launched into an overly detailed account of his last baseball game, then explained that he was trying out basketball now, but he didn't like it much. His mom, Sheena, came into the room, they exchanged slightly awkward hellos, then they all sat around the table to eat takeout fried chicken, a weird mesh of a family.

Afterward, Dad cornered Cam. "Glad to have you back, son."

"I'm happy to be back and working on the lodge."

"Well, I hope you boys find enough customers to keep the place running, but if you don't, you'll always have a job at the auto shop. I always figured my sons would take it over."

While he'd never minded mechanic work, the garage was just one more place where he'd heard that he wasn't doing anything right and had to suffer from Dad's temper. "You might as well sell the place once you decide to retire. If the lodge thing doesn't work out, I won't be sticking around." Cam turned to escape the kitchen.

"Son," Dad said, catching his arm. "Look, I've already talked to Heath and apologized for screwing up when it came to you two. I tried to push you so you'd have a better life than me, but I know now that I pushed too hard."

Cam eyed Dad's hand—the one that'd caught him this same way dozens of times before the yelling started, and Dad let go, a smart move on his part.

"I didn't know what I was doing, and once your mom left…" Dad rubbed the back of his neck. "Despite me, you turned out real good. I'm proud of you—of both you boys."

"Pride's nice and all, but I'm not sure if it's enough to make up for all the *pushing*." Cam remembered having bruises from the pushing that was a lot more like being thrown around. Dad didn't always get violent when he drank, but the bad nights were especially bad, and whenever he got like that, Cam would sometimes egg him on, just so he'd focus on him and leave Heath alone.

His biggest fear, one that he kept to himself, was that the fact he'd enjoyed most of his missions and took pride at how good he was at taking out the enemy meant he had that same tendency toward violence. That last mission probably proved his fears, too, although he hadn't enjoyed it, especially not the price his men had paid.

The antsy sensation took over again, and the need for air overwhelmed him. "Dinner was nice. Sheena seems nice enough, too, but do us all a favor and wear a condom," Cam said. "The last thing you need is another kid to screw up."

Chapter Four

At the end of the day, Cam wiped his brow with his forearm and then made his way over to the cabin he'd seen Emma disappear into. Yesterday he'd thought she might be avoiding him. Today there was no thinking about it—he'd raised his hand in a wave and she'd ducked her head and rushed away.

All he wanted to do was let her know that he was willing to forget the past and never speak of it again so they could work together without things turning awkward. That was it.

Well, that wasn't exactly true, because he couldn't forget their past—and he didn't want to—but he *could* refrain from talking about it.

Despite the fact that he'd perfected moving noiselessly, he stepped hard on each porch step, announcing his arrival so he wouldn't scare her again. He even knocked on the open door before stepping inside.

Emma sat in the center of the room, stacks of paper spread all around her. Her brown waves were pulled into a ponytail, with a few loose strands framing her face. The end of the pen tapped her mouth, drawing his attention to the full bottom lip, and a swirl of lust tumbled through him.

He remembered sucking on that lip, and the way she'd responded, arching her hips into his, and he found himself craving another nip. Which made him forget the reason he'd come in here in the first place.

"Paperwork," she said, unfolding her legs and pushing to her feet. "It never ends."

"You'd rather be…how'd you put it? Banging and screwing with the best of them?"

She laughed and brought her hand up to her forehead. "You're never going to let me live that down, are you?"

"Probably not."

"I'm so glad that I made such a good impression about my *construction* skills."

"Right." He flashed her a smile. "Construction. And Quinn and Heath tell me that you designed the cabins, too. I'm impressed."

Her face lit up. "Thanks. I'm rather proud of them. It's easy to be inspired when the cabins are going up in such a beautiful place. I've always thought this was one of the prettiest spots in Hope Springs, and I wanted the buildings to fit in with the natural beauty, not detract from it. And I wanted every cabin to have a spectacular view and give people that feeling of escaping the world. If I did my job right, they'll be planning their next trip here before they even leave."

He found himself drifting closer with every word, and he couldn't agree more. This place was beautiful, and the cabin designs made him feel like he was at home, whether looking at them from the inside or standing outside looking in. It felt like the world couldn't touch him here. "They'd be crazy not to want to come back."

He noticed a black smudge on the corner of her mouth. "Um…" He gestured to it. "You've got some ink."

Emma reached up, wiping the wrong side, and without

thinking, he stepped forward and swiped the pad of his thumb over the black drop. Her mouth dropped open, a shallow breath escaping from it, and her eyes lifted to his. Then she took a quick step back and rubbed the spot until only a hint of the smudge remained.

He'd gotten so caught up in how easy it was to talk and joke with her, he'd forgotten that he'd come in here with a purpose. "I hope that you don't feel awkward because of what happened all those years ago."

She shrugged. "It happens, right? I mean, not to me. Well, not usually. Or *ever*. But obviously, it did. That, uh, once. I'm fine with it, though. Really."

Yeah, he could tell by the way she wasn't looking at him anymore. "We have to work together for the next month or so, and I just don't want you to think you have to avoid me the whole time."

"I wasn't—" At his raised eyebrow, she cut herself off. "It's not why you think."

Ah. The shadow. "Pete? Is he your boyfriend?"

She shook her head. "He's more like…my comanager, I guess. Since this is the first project where I'm taking point, and he's completed a lot of projects like this, we're working closely together. I'm trying to make a name for myself with this job and hoping that I can use the experience to get a position at an architecture firm. Possibly even in Laramie or Cheyenne, where there'd be more design opportunities and I could make more money."

His gut sank at that, even though he wasn't looking for anything steady with Emma. "Guess everyone tries to leave, right?"

"You did."

No use in denying that, he supposed. "I did. I wasn't sure I'd ever come back, either. If it wasn't for Heath, I probably would be off to Afghanistan again."

"Is that an option still? You deploying?"

Did she sound upset or hopeful? He couldn't tell. "Just to the mountains. I plan on heading up with nothing but the pack on my back as often as possible, whether with a tour or not."

"I'm jealous. I used to head up there for days at a time. Just me, my tent, a good book, the occasional fire… My mom was sure I was going to get eaten by a bear."

The longing in her voice made it clear that she wasn't one of those women who claimed to love the mountains and camping but wanted to leave the second you set up camp and a bug showed up. He could picture her by the fire, a book in hand, the glow from the flames dancing across her pretty features, and he found himself wanting to be there next to her. They could chat, she could laugh some more…

"We should head into the hills some time." Was it so bad to want to be friends with Emma, regardless of their past? There was something calming about her presence, and they obviously shared a few hobbies. "I could use help figuring out exactly what trails and sites I want to use for the tours."

"Oh." She retreated to herself again, hugging her arms around her middle. "As much fun as that sounds, I'm afraid I'll have to pass. Those trips are a thing of the past for me. At least for a while." She bit her lip and glanced down. Then she sighed, one of those sighs that carried so much weight it made it clear that whatever followed would be bad. "I…this is… man, this is hard. I've thought of every possible outcome, and I know… But…"

He wanted to put his hands on her shoulders, look into her eyes, and tell her to just spit it out, but he had a feeling that'd only freak her out. Maybe people still viewed him as scary here—they certainly hadn't been his biggest fans when he and his brother were teens and out causing a bit of trouble, and she'd probably heard a ton of gossip about him and his family. Hell, his dad had knocked up a stripper. Who was apparently getting her real estate license now, so they could be an almost normal family.

"Cam, I have a daughter," Emma said, all in a rush. "She turned two a few months ago. It's why I haven't been to the mountains for more than a picnic or a quick fishing trip in a long, long time."

Wow. A kid. Being involved with a single mom in any shape or form was another thing entirely, and he understood now why she'd hesitated. "I didn't realize. So…a two-year-old. You must be busy."

"You have no idea."

"Just you? Or are you…married? Divorced?"

The laugh that slipped out wasn't her usual warm laugh. This one was hollow and almost sarcastic. "No. Never been married. I'm a single mom, and I'm fine with being that, I swear I am. The most important thing in my life is my daughter, and I can take care of myself. I just need you to know that."

"Okay," he said, confusion setting in. He understood that having a kid made life more complicated. Maybe his offer had come out more like asking her out on a camping date. And maybe he would have been more okay with that than he'd thought he would be, but of course the news about her having a kid changed everything—he definitely wasn't ready for complicated of any kind, dating or friends. Casual fun was probably a no go when you were a parent, and honestly the thought had him itching to get away from the entire awkward situation as fast as he could.

"Well, you have a good night. I'll talk to you tomorrow." He started toward the door, resolving again to keep his head down and focus on the lodge, the way he was supposed to, no more thinking about the intriguing woman he'd spent an amazing night with so long ago.

"Cam?"

He slowly turned back, a pang going through him at the vulnerability working its way across Emma's features. He didn't know why he felt everything so much more strongly around her. The war between wanting to soothe her and wanting to rush away before he started to care more than he should was giving him internal whiplash.

"That night at the Triple S…when we were in your truck…" She couldn't seem to decide what to do with her hands. One second she was wringing them together, then she moved one to rub the side of her neck. "Do you remember…?" Red crept across her skin, and she tucked that strand of hair behind her ear.

"Of course I remember—we established that yesterday, I thought." And again a few minutes ago, when he told her he didn't want things to be awkward between them because of it.

"What I mean is, do you happen to remember if…?" She brought her hand up to her mouth and bit on her thumbnail. "I thought you pulled out a condom, I just don't remember… if you actually put it on?"

He frowned. "I'm always sa—" Cold crept across his skin, and his internal organs turned to lead. She wasn't implying that he might… How old did she say her kid was? "Wait. You're not saying…"

"I am. That's the night I got pregnant. Cam, Zoey's yours."

Chapter Five

Emma's words hung in the air, taking up all the space from one end of the unfurnished cabin to the other.

She'd run through several scenarios in her head of how this would play out, every one ending in him yelling at her.

Instead, Cam stumbled back a few steps, like her words had shot him in the chest. He reached back for the empty bed frame and sat down on it, his mouth slack.

She didn't know why she hadn't factored in shock. After all, when she'd lifted the pregnancy test and looked back and forth from the box to the result window, confirming she was, in fact, pregnant, she'd stumbled back against the wall, slid down it until her butt hit the floor, and stared at that damn stick for about five minutes before she'd believed it. Then the tears had come, fast and furious.

Cam scrubbed a hand over his face, and she thought he'd reached the acceptance stage, but then he jerked up his head. "Are you sure she's mine?"

A sharp twinge shot through her chest. Of course he'd doubt it—she wished it didn't hurt, but it did. "I'm sure. My boyfriend had dumped me a month before that night in the bar, and we hadn't had sex for a month before that. There was no one after you, either. I did the math a bunch of times—and I'm good at math. The details of that night are a bit fuzzy, but I've come to the conclusion that either you never put on the condom, or we're the one percent who it didn't work for."

Cam stared at her, those eyes so much like Zoey's, but unlike their daughter's, his were completely unreadable.

The back of her throat tightened, making her have to work for every word. "I don't want you to feel obligated—I know you didn't want kids, and I can take care of her. I can keep going on how we've been going. I just…well, I thought you should know."

"You thought I should know?" The words came out edged in ice, and she flinched—she shouldn't have told him. He obviously didn't want to know.

"Look, if you don't want to meet Zoey and be part of her life, that's your choice. You're missing out, but again, that's completely your choice."

"Choice?" He laughed, and like the laugh she'd given after he'd asked if she'd been married, it wasn't the happy kind of laughter. "You didn't give me a choice. I should've *known*—past tense. How could you have not told me when you found out you were pregnant?"

Her heart thundered, and sweat pricked her forehead, the reaction she always had when dealing with any kind of conflict—she hated conflict and usually avoided it at all costs, but she'd gotten herself into this mess, no avoiding it now. "You were several countries away. I didn't even know how to contact you."

He stood and advanced on her, and fear spiked. She backed up, but he kept on coming. "You get my information from my dad, or my brother. You… *Damn it!* You find a way!"

When he raised his arm, she flinched, but he only ran a

hand through his hair. His eyebrows drew together, offense pinching his features. "I'm not…I'm not going to hit you."

Tears gathered in her eyes. "I don't know—it's not like I know you. Your brother just moved back, like, six months ago, and I've been sick with guilt over not saying anything. But what was I supposed to do? Write you and say, oh, hey, remember me, the girl you slept with because you were drunk and getting ready to deploy and I was there? Well, now I'm having your kid."

"Yes."

Emma gritted her teeth, resolved to keep the tears from spilling down her cheeks. "You're right. I did try to find your email address, but I should've tried harder. I…" She almost went into how she'd attempted to talk to his dad, but she didn't want to insult his family right now, and in the end, it was still an excuse. So she went with the truth. "I was scared. I'm still scared, every day. I'm sorry, because I know I did this all wrong. But I was trying to protect my daughter."

"Our daughter," he said, his gaze boring into her. "According to you."

"Yes. Our daughter." Despite her best efforts, her tears spilled over and ran warm trails down her cheeks. "I can't change the past, but now you know. That also scares me, more than anything ever has, because Zoey—she's my world."

Cam stepped back again, his head shaking over and over, and she couldn't take it anymore. As hard as it'd been, she'd told him, and now he'd have to figure out what he wanted to do about it. But she couldn't stand there in the suffocating, tension-filled room any longer. So she swallowed the lump in her throat and walked out of the cabin.

She meant to calmly walk away, but before she knew it, she was in the truck and peeling out, headed away from Mountain Ridge.

One thing was for sure. No one would call her life boring

now.

. . .

The headache working its way across Cam's forehead pounded harder, in time to his rapidly hammering heart, beating out rational thought. He'd made it out of the cabin in time to see Emma's taillights through a cloud of dirt. Anger and shock had formed a toxic combination, and he knew he needed to release some of it before he spat out any harsh words or made a decision he'd regret.

So he'd ducked into the cabin he'd been working on earlier in the day, picked up some drywall and a package of nails, and hammered for all he was worth. The first few he'd gone too hard, driving the nail so deep that he'd left circular hammer imprints.

Still the anger came in waves, so he kept at it.

How stupid was I, thinking she was trustworthy. Thinking that she was different from other women.

She should've told me yesterday.

No, she should've told me years ago, instead of just springing it on me and claiming she doesn't expect anything.

He swung and swung, until his shoulder screamed with each movement.

"Cam?" Heath walked in, his arm around Quinn. "We appreciate your enthusiasm about finishing these up as soon as possible, but it's time for dinner."

He just shook his head. Once again his temper whispered that he was just like Dad, and now he didn't have missions and taking out bad guys as an outlet. How could he be a father? Why had he ever thought going back to civilian life would be good for him?

Coming back home to the slow pace of Hope Springs was supposed to be calming. Supposed to help heal the broken part of him.

Then again, he wasn't supposed to have a kid. *A two-year-old daughter.* He swung the hammer again, this time missing the stud completely and bashing a hole in the drywall. The broken plaster bits rained down on his forearms, the dust clinging to the hairs there and turning them white.

"Cameron." Heath put his hand on his shoulder, and when Cam glanced at his brother, worry hung heavy on his features. "What's going on?"

Cam tossed the hammer aside, the loud *thunk* slightly satisfying. He sucked in a deep breath and let it out. "Emma. I need to talk to her. Where does she live?"

Quinn walked over, slow and calm, like life hadn't suddenly stopped making sense. "Look, Cam, Emma's awesome, and obviously she's very pretty, too, but her life is super complicated. She's a single mom, and I'm not sure that you and she would be a good idea."

It was way too late for good ideas now. "Heath, did I ever tell you that I slept with Emma the night before I deployed?"

Heath's jaw dropped, which he took to mean no.

"Holy shitballs," Quinn said. "I *so* didn't see that coming."

Cam kept his eyes on his brother's. "Have you seen her little girl?"

He nodded. "Yeah, I've seen her around town a couple of times. She's a cute kid. Lots of blond curly hair, always wearing a ballet skirt."

"Tell me something…" His heart thumped hard in his chest. One beat, then two, then three. "Does she look anything like me?"

Chapter Six

"But what about pizza?" Emma asked Zoey.

Zoey held up the box of mac and cheese. "Cheese."

"Pizza has cheese, and you love pizza, remember?" She loved to pick off the cheese and leave the tomato sauce and crust, anyway.

Zoey's eyebrows drew together and she held the box of mac and cheese higher. Nothing made you feel more in control of life than losing an argument with a two-year-old.

With a sigh, Emma gave up and took the box from Zoey's pudgy fingers. This day had beaten everything out of her, and she didn't have it in her to debate the merits of pizza versus neon-orange noodles anymore. She figured she'd just have one of those disgusting microwave dinners—the ones she'd bought when she'd decided she needed to eat healthier, and the "lean" on the package and mini section for vegetables had lulled her into a false sense of healthiness. As usual, she'd pick at it and end up eating the other half of the macaroni straight from the pot.

She'd just poured a pot full of water when the doorbell

rang. She walked over and looked through the window on the door, and her stomach fell right to her toes. Since Zoey was busy with the dollhouse in the corner of the living room, Emma stepped outside quickly, pulling the door shut behind her.

"Cam. Hey."

"I want to see her," he said.

A clashing mixture of relief and fear tumbled through Emma. "It's my job as her mom to protect her, and more than anything, I want her to feel loved and wanted. I have to be careful about pulling people into her life."

The muscles around Cam's jaw tightened, and she put her hand on his arm. "I'm not saying you can't see her—I want you to. I'm just trying to figure out the best ground rules to keep us all safer." His gaze moved to her hand, and she dropped it, working to keep her composure. "At least until you spend a bit of time with her and decide what kind of a role you want to play in her life."

Cam slowly nodded. "I guess that makes sense."

Emma glanced through the window of the front door. Zoey was still busy with the dollhouse. "We were about to have dinner. If we go out…well, then the entire town will be talking."

"I'd rather not do this in front of everyone."

"I agree. I could order a pizza?"

He nodded again. "That's fine. I just want to see her."

At least he'd decided that much. Now hope jumped into the mix of emotions—hope that Zoey could have a dad who cared about her and that they could work out some kind of arrangement, even though fear edged every beat of her heart at the thought of it going wrong. "For now, we'll just introduce you as my friend Cam. Is that okay?"

Cam shrugged, and it was odd to see the massive, all-man dude on her porch looking so unsure of himself. If the situation weren't so awkward and difficult, it'd be endearing.

Okay, maybe it was endearing anyway. Emma took a deep breath and walked inside, holding the door open for Cam. Zoey glanced up, tossed her doll aside, and ran over. She wrapped her arms around Emma's legs, clinging to them.

"She's a little shy when you first meet her," Emma said to Cam, then she reached down, scooped her daughter into her arms, and hugged her tightly. "Zoey, this is my friend Cam. Cam, Zoey."

. . .

In the field, Cam never froze. He reacted, and he reacted quickly, not letting himself second-guess anything, because it could mean the difference between life and death. But here he was now, frozen in place by a two-year-old.

The cutest little two-year-old girl he'd ever seen. She had Emma's curly hair, although it was blond, not brown, and she had Emma's nose. But the eyes…they were a Brantley family trait. Her face shape was his, as was the slight dimple in the chin. There was something that hinted at Mom, too, although he couldn't pick out what. Part of him had still doubted she was his until this moment, but all of that faded as he looked at her.

"Hi," he said, not knowing what else to say. She curled into Emma, her pink ballet skirt crumpling. But then she peeked at him and gave him a small smile, and his heart cracked right there. He had no idea what to do about the fact that he had a daughter.

But something inside him had told him he'd regret it if he didn't at least see her. If only he knew how to act now that he had.

Emma bounced her higher on her hip. "Zoey, I'm going to order some pizza and—"

"Cheese!" she said, adamantly shaking her head.

"I was going to say, and I'm going to finish making you mac and cheese." Emma tapped Zoey's nose and then glanced at him. "It's all she eats right now. That and L-U-C-K-Y C-H-A-R-M-S. I do make her eat veggies and fruit once in a while, though, I swear."

She seemed worried he'd judge her. He had no idea how to take care of a kid, and Zoey looked healthy to him. Healthy and happy.

Emma asked about pizza toppings, he assured her whatever was fine, and then she gestured to the couch. "Make yourself at home."

Cam sat on the small couch and glanced around the room. Pink toys sat in every corner, and there was a pile of large Legos in the middle of the room. Besides the toys, the house was clean, although dated and a little run-down. Nothing major, just a few cracks in the overly textured walls, peeling eighties linoleum in the entryway, and brown swirl carpet that'd seen its fair share of use.

He'd grown up about like this—if you added a thin layer of dirt, Dad's stacks of magazines circling the room, and an empty six-pack of beer on the table—so he knew that you could live in these conditions, but he wasn't sure Emma was as fine as she claimed, especially financially.

His defenses prickled at the timing of it all, her telling him only *after* he and Heath had acquired the property that'd taken their savings, as well as a portion of Quinn's. He certainly didn't have spare cash sitting around, but if the lodge did well…

Movement from near the kitchen caught his attention. Zoey peeked out at him and then ducked back around the corner. The minutes ticked by, slow and yet fast, his head still spinning as he tried to grasp the fact that he had a kid, and then the pizza guy showed up.

They ate in the kitchen, mostly in silence, but afterward, Zoey tugged on the leg of his jeans and led him over to the dollhouse in the corner of the living room. She handed him a doll and then began playing. When he just stood there, the doll dangling from his hand, she grabbed that hand, showed him how to play—clearly thinking he didn't get it—and then sang to herself.

This was so freaking weird. It felt like he'd fallen into a dream, or someone else's life, and part of him wanted to wake up, even as he felt a strange pull in his gut toward the little girl in front of him.

After a few minutes he found himself making voices for the doll, struggling to interpret what Zoey said, and sitting on the floor with his legs crossed. Occasionally he'd glance at Emma, who smiled encouragingly, even though he was sure he was getting everything wrong. There was a hint of nervousness in every move Emma made, too, which only added to the pressure building inside him.

When Zoey had a meltdown over a dress not going onto the doll the way she wanted, Emma came over and picked her up. "That means it's bedtime."

"Uh-uh," Zoey said, but Emma carried her into the hall, rocking and humming low, and Zoey dropped her head on her shoulder. Cam didn't know if he should follow or just stand there and wait, and finally he settled on picking up toys, since it was something he felt semiqualified for.

Several minutes later, Emma returned, her arms now empty. She looked at him, he looked back, and he could tell she had as little clue about what to say as he did.

"I…I want to be in her life," he finally said. He didn't know how to be a dad, but he couldn't walk away and pretend he'd never met her now. It didn't sit right with him, especially after he'd experienced parental abandonment. He'd probably screw up a lot, but he doubted saying that would inspire a lot of confidence in Emma. He figured he should be as truthful as possible, though. "I'm not sure how big of a role I can play, but I won't leave her to wonder why I don't want to be in her life."

He could practically see the wheels in Emma's mind turning as she processed everything he'd said.

"Okay." She hugged her arms around herself like she'd done earlier and nodded. "Next time, we'll tell her you're her dad."

"Will she be okay with that?"

A small smile touched Emma's lips. "I'm sure she will. Little kids are pretty resilient, and they adjust faster than most adults. I'm sure it'll be easier now than if she were older. She hasn't quite realized it's not normal for her to not know her daddy."

He took a couple of steps toward her. "If I hadn't come back? Would you have ever told me?"

Emma bit her lip. "Probably not. I heard you that night in the bar. You said you didn't want kids. That you'd never change your mind—you sounded so sure that I truly figured it was for the best if you simply didn't know, and with you so far away anyway…"

"I never planned to have any, it's true. My dad…" He thought about the days after Mom walked out on them, leaving him and Heath to fend for themselves. It didn't go very well, not when Dad's drinking only got worse. "Let's just say I didn't want to turn into him. I have no idea how to be a dad."

"I had no idea how to be a mom. Some days I feel like I still don't know how, actually, and that I'll never figure it out." She reached out like she was going to touch his arm again, and he didn't realize how much he wanted her to until she dropped her hand before contact. "I'm sorry, Cam, I am. I didn't expect my life to turn out like this. But I wouldn't change it, not now that I have her."

The anger he'd felt earlier moved to the background. He was still upset she hadn't told him, but he couldn't hold onto it after spending the past few hours with her and Zoey. "Well, now that I'm here and I know, I guess we both have a lot of things to figure out. Like…" He gulped, because the words still seemed so strange, and thinking about all the details that'd need to be ironed out made him realize how much his life was about to change. "Child support and that kind of thing."

"We're okay. Like I said, I didn't tell you so you'd feel obligated."

Yeah, we'll see. He did feel obligated, too, but it was more than a sense of duty. It wasn't something he'd experienced before, so he didn't know how to describe it. Still, his goals of the lodge and of adjusting to normal life had just become that much more important. "This week we'll figure out the best plan of attack, and then we'll put it into action."

"How much trouble would I be in if I saluted you and said, 'Yes, sir'?"

He cracked a smile, something he definitely hadn't expected after she'd dropped the bomb this afternoon. "Feel free to follow all my orders," he said, and she rolled her eyes.

Then everything that'd happened and all it meant came rushing back in. He could deal with a truce and helping out with Zoey, but he still didn't completely trust Emma, and he wasn't sure he ever could.

"See you tomorrow," he said, heading toward the door.

"See you tomorrow," she echoed, and he told himself not to feel sorry for the sadness that'd crept into her voice.

But the tiniest part of him still did.

Chapter Seven

Wow, he did a great job of leveling the road, Emma thought as she pulled up to the cabin nearest the lodge. When she'd left work, Cam had been in a tractor, dragging the road from the turnoff to the Mountain Ridge property, and her car had made it over the smoothed-out rocks and dirt, no problem. If she'd gotten stuck again, she'd never live it down, even if the crew were long gone.

Emma reached into the backseat and undid the buckles of Zoey's car seat. Zoey disliked being strapped down, so the second she was free, she launched herself out of the seat and into Emma's arms. Emma kissed her cheek, carried her up the porch steps, and knocked on the door.

Cam answered, wearing jeans and a T-shirt that stretched across his chest and showed off his tattooed arms.

Emma's heart skipped a couple of beats, and she told herself to focus. This night was about him and Zoey getting to know each other better, not for ogling and lusting after all those muscles. Then again, she'd always been a good multitasker. "Hey."

"Come on in." Cam stepped aside, and she walked into the living room. She'd expected it to look different from the last time she'd been inside, but he hadn't added any personal touches. The place was also extremely clean, to the point of looking unlived in. She wondered if he made his bed so tightly you could bounce a quarter off it, if that was something they really made soldiers do anymore.

How do you even climb into a bed made so tightly?

Okay, no thinking about Cam climbing in bed, or how he probably sleeps shirtless.

Zoey wiggled down and went right for the fireplace.

"No, Zoey! Dangerous!" Emma scooped her back up, scanning the place for other safety concerns. "If Zoey's going to be spending time here, the fire will need a grate. The outlets need to be covered, and if you've got any chemicals or cleansers under the kitchen sink, it'll need to be childproofed, too."

Cam glanced around the room. "I never thought about any of that."

"Yeah, it takes some getting used to."

"I'll get right on it tomorrow."

Despite the other night and the blips of polite conversation they'd had at work the past couple of days, awkwardness still crowded the air, and she wondered if she'd ever get used to this new development.

Speaking of, she supposed it was time to break the news to her daughter—it was part of the plan of attack they'd come up with, after all. "Zoey, you know how I'm your mommy?"

She nodded, her curls bouncing with the motion, and tapped Emma's chest as she repeated, "Mommy."

"Cam is your daddy."

"Why?" she asked.

"You want to take that one?" Emma asked Cam, laughing when his eyes went comically wide. "I'm only teasing," she said, then she turned her attention back to her daughter. "Because everyone has a mommy and a daddy. Sometimes mommies and daddies live separately, but everyone still has one.

"So, I'm your mommy..." Emma took Zoey's hand, tapped it to her chest, and then guided it to Cam's chest, tapping it there. "Daddy."

"Why?"

"And you can call him Daddy."

"Why?"

"Because that's who he is." Emma smiled at Cam, who had an expression between bewilderment and wonder on his face. "Two-year-olds really like asking why."

"I'm starting to see that," he said. Then he picked up the nightstand next to the couch, hoisting it like it weighed nothing, and placed it in front of the fireplace, blocking that hazard area.

"So how was that, soldier?" Emma asked as she bumped the hip not supporting Zoey into his, unable to resist teasing him a bit, slight awkwardness notwithstanding. He'd laid out the plan earlier today at lunch: *Come over at 1900 hours. Tell Zoey I'm her father together. We'll see how that goes and then take it from there.*

She could tell he was used to giving orders and not having anyone ask questions. Since she was still trying to atone for not telling him the truth before, she'd meekly nodded and said okay. But she refused to go back to the quiet, submissive person she used to be in high school, so from here on out, she'd insist on a two-way type of discussion.

Zoey demanded to be put down before Emma could get a good read on Cam's reaction to her teasing, but as soon as she straightened, he leaned in and whispered, "Just fine, smart-ass."

She bit back a laugh, but she wasn't able to suppress the

shiver that traveled down her spine at the feel of his warm breath on her neck.

No surprise, the first thing Zoey decided to investigate was how to undo being cut off from the one place she needed to stay away from—why was it kids were drawn to the most dangerous thing in the room? Emma really hoped the self-preservation instinct kicked in soon, preferably before she had an aneurysm worrying about the many ways her daughter could be injured.

The nightstand in front of the fireplace rocked a little, and Cam steadied it with a hand on top and pulled a Barbie, still in her plastic case, off the mantel. When he handed it to Zoey and said he'd bought it for her, she, of course, asked, "Why?"

"Because I'm your dad, and I wanted you to have something from me."

"Why?"

Cam laughed, squatted lower, and then helped her tear it out of the package—when the doll didn't break free of the cardboard after a minute or so of tugging, he swore.

Zoey copied, the way toddlers instinctively do whenever anyone anywhere swears, and Cam glanced up. "I'm so, so sorry. It just slipped out."

"Don't make a deal about it or she'll say it a hundred times," Emma calmly said, then she pointed at the doll and forced extra enthusiasm into her voice. "Is that Barbie doll wearing a ballerina dress? Just like you?" At least today she'd managed to get Zoey to wear a T-shirt and pants under the tutu instead of pajamas.

"Ball-in-a!" Zoey said, sufficiently distracted, although her frustration at not getting the Barbie into her hot little hands was mounting.

Cam held out his hand for the doll, promising he'd give it right back, and then he pulled out a pocketknife. He sliced the plastic ties and then carefully closed the knife and put it away before handing the doll over, despite Zoey's bouncing up and down, arms waving wildly in the air.

He needs a bit of training, but he understands the safety basics at least.

Emma lowered herself onto the stuffed chair in the corner, watching on. Here and there Cam would glance up at her and rub his neck, clearly unsure how to proceed, but she held herself back, explaining what Zoey was asking instead of stepping in and taking over. Control wasn't easy for her to give up, but she knew he needed to get more comfortable with Zoey to really bond with her, and she wanted nothing more than to figure out a way to do this coparenting thing. If that was what he decided he wanted after he saw everything it entailed.

Emma's phone rang, and she glanced at the display, worry rising when she saw it was the Hope Springs hospital. "I should take this. Are you okay?"

"Yeah," Cam said, so she stepped outside where she could talk.

"This is Nurse Welch, and there's no need to worry," the voice on the phone said, which sent another surge of worry coursing through Emma, because she wouldn't call without a reason.

"Is my grandma okay?" Nurse Welch had called her the last time Grandma Bev ended up in the hospital, and they occasionally had discussions about Grandma's health and the treatments she was supposed to be following, much to her dismay.

"She fainted at bingo."

"Because I *actually got a bingo*," Grandma Bev yelled into the phone. "No other reason."

Emma tightened her hold on the phone. "And because she mixed her pills with Vera Mae's famous punch?"

"That might've had something to do with it," Nurse Welch

said with a laugh. "She did hit her head pretty hard, though, and she lost consciousness for a minute, so—"

"That's just what Judith said, because she wanted to break my winning streak. I'm fine. I told you not to call Emma and worry her over nothing."

"We're going to err on the side of caution and do a CT scan. From the sounds of it, we might have to hold her down..." Nurse Welch was mostly false threats, but she followed through with a look that made most people too scared to push their luck—even headstrong Grandma Bev, which was why Emma requested she be the one to treat her. "I just thought you should know."

The words "just thought you should know" struck her as slightly ironic. She'd used them on Cam, and she saw now how ineffective they were at soothing frayed nerves.

"Can I talk to my grandmother for a minute?" Emma wanted to lecture her, but that'd never done any good, and more than anything she wanted to hear for herself that she was okay, so she figured she'd see how she sounded and then take it from there.

Apparently phrases were striking her right and left today, because now she was thinking about Cam again, and the way he'd told her, "We'll take it from there," all demanding, in a way that should bug her but seemed more like second nature to him.

She glanced toward the window of his cabin, thinking that maybe it was more that the guy was simply hard not to think about.

• • •

Zoey started dancing around, a dance that looked suspiciously like—

"Go potty," Zoey said.

Cam looked to the front door, praying for Emma to come through it, but he could see her pacing outside the window, still on the phone. He didn't want her to think he couldn't handle a few minutes alone, even though he wasn't sure he could.

I have no idea what I'm doing. One thing was sure, he was definitely in over his head.

"Um, bathroom's right there." He pointed at the door.

She grabbed his hand and started toward it. Once they stepped inside the bathroom, she looked up at him like he'd know what to do.

"Need help?" he asked and she nodded, handing him the doll. Tucking it under his arm, he helped Zoey get her pants down and lifted her onto the toilet. She smiled at him, kicking out her legs and looking toward the ceiling for a moment. Then she was done, and he exhaled a relieved breath.

But as soon as he got everything back into place and her hands washed, she demanded candy.

"I don't have any candy," he said.

She pointed at the toilet. "Go potty. Candy." When he simply continued to stare, she wrinkled her face up, and he could tell she was about to cry, the way she'd done after he'd stopped her from climbing on the nightstand earlier. But that was when Emma was still inside, and she wasn't now.

"All right. I'll find…something."

Zoey followed him into the kitchen, and he opened the pantry and eyed the sparse contents. He had several leftover MREs from his army days, but he figured she'd be as unimpressed with the ready-to-eat meal contents as he was after a week straight of choking them down in the field.

The bag of marshmallows he'd bought for hot chocolate caught his eye. He glanced at the door again, feeling like he was about to get into trouble for reasons he wasn't even sure of. So he quickly opened the bag and handed Zoey a marshmallow. She shoved the entire thing in her mouth and smiled at him, one cheek popping out.

Emma walked inside, and he could immediately tell something was wrong.

"What happened?"

"Vera Mae's punch," she grumbled, then she pinched the bridge of her nose and let out a long exhale. "My grandma mixed it with her meds, and she passed out at bingo. She was adamant that she was fine, but she sounded a bit loopy, and long story short, she's going in for a CT scan and I need to head over to the hospital. So Zoey and I have to go."

Cam glanced at the time—they'd only been here for a little over a half hour, but it was getting late, nearing the cutoff of usual hospital visiting hours. In the past few minutes, he'd also witnessed how busy Zoey was. The girl never. Stopped. Moving. He couldn't imagine she'd be still in a hospital, with all its climbable items and machines to check out, and he had a vision of her yanking out cords that definitely shouldn't be yanked out. "Wouldn't it be easier if you didn't have to bring Zoey with you?"

"It would," Emma said, picking Zoey's discarded jacket off the floor, "especially since I'll probably have my hands full with my grandma. But I don't have anyone to take her."

He glanced from Emma to Zoey, who was happy with her marshmallow at the moment, then back to Emma. "I could…I could keep her for a bit." He tried to put conviction behind his voice so it didn't come out as a question, even as he was questioning himself.

Emma's movements slowed. "You're offering to watch her? Alone? She's going to get tired, and I don't have her pajamas—for once she's not already wearing them, and everything else she needs for her bedtime routine is at my house."

He'd survived boot camp and had been on missions in

endless stretches of desert in 110-degree weather. And if bedtime was around the corner, then he could definitely handle a toddler for an hour or so. *Buck up, Brantley.*

"So I'll take her to your place. Or I'll keep her here until you can get back. Whatever you need. I…want to help."

Okay, maybe "want" was a strong word, but he could hardly leave Emma to deal with it all herself when he could practically feel the stress radiating off her.

He could tell she didn't know whether to disagree or to thank him, and he got the feeling that not many people offered to help her. Or maybe she never let anyone help. If that were the case, he'd have to take the option away. He could outstubborn anyone.

"She's potty training, too," Emma said. "I've got her in pull-ups, but she's done so well, and I don't want her to get out of the hab—"

"She already had to go, just a few minutes ago. I took care of it."

"You did?"

He tried not to be offended by her incredulous tone. He supposed he shouldn't be, considering how out of his league he'd felt during the potty incident. "She demanded candy, but I didn't have any, so I gave her a marshmallow. I hope that's okay—I figured since she eats Lucky Charms she could have one."

"Lucky Charms!" Zoey yelled, clapping her hands.

"Rookie mistake," Emma said, but she said it lightly, a hint of teasing. Then she put her hand on his arm, and while he knew she needed to go, he wanted her to keep standing this close, close enough he could smell her vanilla perfume and see the various shades of brown that twisted through her wavy hair. "If you go to my place, all you have to do is put on *F-R-O-Z-E-N.* She'll fall asleep and you can carry her to bed. As far as pajamas go, if it causes a fight, she can just sleep in what she's got on—even the skirt."

"Okay," he said with one sharp nod. "Got it."

She dropped her hand and took one step away, then spun on her heel. "Oh, but her car seat." She sighed. "There's just too much to deal with. It'd need to be moved, and you'd have to strap her in, and—"

Cam put his hands on her shoulders, and she snapped her mouth closed. "Take my truck. I'll take your car. I know how to work seat belts, and I've been driving for a long time. Believe it or not, I even know my way around this massive town."

When she hesitated, not even smiling at his attempted joke, he nudged her gently toward the door. "Go."

"If you need anything, or have any questions, call."

"I will." He'd stored his number in her phone earlier today, and she had his, too.

It took another nudge toward the door before she finally gave in, her tensed muscles becoming pliant under his fingertips. She stopped to hug Zoey, told her that Daddy was going to take her home—which admittedly still sounded weird to his ears, yet sent a swirl of pride through him—and then she rushed out the door.

The engine revved, and he expected a slight grinding, as his truck occasionally needed to be convinced to shift, but she didn't seem to have trouble.

Then she pulled away and he was left with a two-year-old little princess and the pressure to not swear, not screw this up, and keep her safe, suddenly overwhelming now that he had to shoulder it alone.

What the hell was I thinking?

Chapter Eight

Cam zipped up Zoey's jacket and exhaled every ounce of oxygen from his lungs before sucking in a deep breath, the way he used to before he was about to charge into somewhere dangerous. Which was silly. This was just a few hours alone with his daughter, not enemy territory.

"Mommy," Zoey whimpered again and pointed toward the door.

"I'm going to take you home and then we'll watch *Frozen*. How does that sound?"

Her eyes lit up, but her lower lip remained out, refusing to totally give up on the pout.

When he moved to pick her up, she shook her head, and the whimpering turned to crying as she backed away. He held up his hands. "Okay, I won't pick you up. But you need to follow me, okay?"

"Why?"

"So I can take you home. We'll watch *Frozen* and eat Lucky Charms and then your mom will come home."

He could see the wheels turning, and when he opened

the door, she slowly walked outside, bracing her hand on the frame as she stepped onto the porch. It wasn't a very big step, but her little legs made it seem as if it were built for a giant.

So bribery works—good to know. He eyed the lights of the former B and B, considering asking Quinn for help to get through the rest of the night, but again, he'd committed, and he didn't want Emma to think he couldn't follow through. Their relationship was strained as it was, although the lighter moments—like when she'd bumped her hip into his and called him soldier—made him forget all of the complications and the many reasons he shouldn't flirt with Emma Walker.

He debated locking up, then decided he should, even if it was a safe area and there wasn't much to steal.

By the time he spun back around, Zoey was no longer on the porch. His pulse skyrocketed, and he rushed down the stairs calling her name. He saw her blond curls and heard her giggle. A large but shallow puddle had formed in the spot where he'd hosed off Heath's motorcycle—he'd borrowed it for a quick trip to the reservoir and it'd ended up coated in mud—and of course Zoey had managed to find it and jump right in the middle of it. The bottom of her pink pants disappeared into the water, and murky brown droplets ran down her bare arms and clung to the pink froofy skirt. Her discarded jacket floated along the surface of the puddle.

"Zoey, you need to get out of that pud—"

She jumped again, squealing as the water splashed up. Even though it'd been a warmer day, with the sun down, it had to be in the low forties. He couldn't believe she wasn't freezing.

She probably is, she just doesn't care because there's mud and water.

When he moved toward her, she jumped again, sending muddy water everywhere, including onto him.

He squatted down, retrieved her jacket, and gestured her

closer. "Okay, you had your fun. Now come here."

She shook her head. He started around the puddle to pick her up, but she just moved to the other side. Outsmarted by a two-year-old, but not for long—looked like he was going to get muddy and wet, too. He charged into the puddle and scooped her up. Her muddy shoes smeared across his shirt, and cold water seeped through the fabric.

Zoey started crying, and when she couldn't be talked out of it, he tossed her in the air—just a few inches—and caught her. They both froze for a second, as if they weren't sure what to make of the move, but then a smile spread across her face. So he did it again, a little higher this time, and she giggled, clapped, and said, "Again!"

She must've gotten the thrill-seeking gene from my side of the family. He and Heath were always challenging each other to perform stunts growing up. The surreal sensation he'd experienced since finding out about Zoey hit him again. Still weird, but he liked that he could find some semicommon ground to make it a little less so.

A few more tosses and he was as coated in mud as she was.

Now that they were sufficiently dirty and happy, he carried her over to the car. The rust bucket didn't look too terribly clean inside, the remnants of crackers spread across the backseat. Not dirty enough that he thought the mud could go completely unnoticed, though. Zoey started to shiver, and tiny goose bumps covered her arms and legs.

Nothing's worse than being cold and wet—another thing he knew from firsthand experience, as the army never seemed to send him to places with pleasant weather.

After a moment of trying to decide the best course of action, Cam raced back into the house, peeled off her wet shoes, socks, and pants, and grabbed one of his T-shirts. He tried to put it over her, but it was ridiculously huge, and when she attempted a few steps, it made her trip.

Finally he wrapped a towel around her, swapped his wet shoes out for dry ones, and then headed back to the car.

As soon as he stuck Zoey in her seat, she started crying and trying to wiggle free. The dang thing had a buckle with several parts, and some of the crackers were cemented to the spot they all fastened into, making it that much harder to push into place. The towel wasn't helping, either, since the buckle was between her legs. One side finally clicked in, and then Zoey arched out of the seat, half on and half off, her arm sliding free.

Twenty minutes into watching his kid by himself, and so far the score went something like Zoey 3, Cam 0.

• • •

While Emma awaited Grandma Bev's results, she was torn between worrying over her injury and worry over Zoey being alone with Cam. Even though he was her father, he didn't know much about two-year-olds, and that line of thinking led to panic over how she'd left her daughter with a guy who barely qualified as more than an acquaintance.

She'd texted him a couple times—okay, maybe three or four times—while filling out paperwork, and he kept claiming everything was fine.

When Grandma Bev and Nurse Welch walked into the waiting room, Emma shot to her feet.

"I told them I was fine," Grandma Bev said, fluffing her chin-length white curls. "All this poking and prodding for nothing, and now I've got to wait another whole week to beat Judith."

Emma turned to Nurse Welch, wanting to hear she was fine from the person who'd tell the truth.

"Everything looks good," Nurse Welch said, and Grandma

Bev harrumphed, the sound heavy on *I told you so.* "If she has any dizzy spells or vomiting, she needs to call us, though."

Grandma Bev hiked her leopard-print purse farther up her shoulder, then looked at Emma. The righteous indignation faded away, and then she patted Emma's cheek. "Sorry to have worried you, dear."

"You know Vera Mae's punch and your meds don't mix."

"What I know is that if I didn't eat all that fried food you're always harping on, my blood pressure would've crashed before I got bingo. Then I'd have to hear Judith go on and on about how she's still the reigning champ."

Emma shared a *what can you do* look with Nurse Welch, both of them already knowing the answer—absolutely nothing but love her—and then Emma hooked her arm around Grandma Bev's. "Let's get you home."

"Where's my little Zoey, anyway?"

"At home. I got someone to watch her, since it was so close to bedtime." Emma was tempted to spill all, but things with Cam were so new, and it'd already been a circus of a night, so she thought she'd save dropping the bomb about him being not only back in town, but also the fact that he was Zoey's dad, for later. If he decided he didn't want to be involved, she'd rather not have the entire town dragging his name through the mud, and Grandma Bev couldn't keep a secret to save her life. Which was actually how, at eight years old, Emma found out that her father had been quite the rebel in his day, that Grandma had done everything she could to warn her daughter away from him, and that Mom was pregnant *before* they got married.

Grandma Bev had then added that despite her worries over the shotgun wedding, she'd forever be glad of the pregnancy, because Emma turned out to be one of her favorite people.

It'd taken a few more years to fully understand what she'd

said and the implications behind it, but it was why Emma had tried to talk herself out of crushing on Cam in the first place.

Right after she dropped off Grandma and checked that her pillbox was filled correctly, Emma received a text from Cam that said Zoey had fallen asleep and he'd carried her to bed.

She made Grandma promise to call if she was dizzy or experienced any symptoms Nurse Welch had warned them about, hugged her good-bye, and then buzzed home.

The porch light beckoned to Emma as she walked up the sidewalk, its warm glow especially welcoming after the harsh fluorescent lights of the hospital.

Emma quietly slid her key in the door, but it was unlocked. Even though most people left their doors unlocked in Hope Springs, she never did. Hazard of living alone, she supposed. Well, alone with kid.

Cam sat in the middle of the couch, the television on, the volume so low she could barely hear "Let It Go" playing. Her front room had completely transformed, too. The toys were put away, some in shelves where they didn't really belong, but off the floor, and judging from the sliver of the kitchen she could see, the dishes that'd been filling the sink and spilling over had been done.

"Wow," she said. "You cleaned."

Cam shrugged, like it was no big deal, and a string tugged in her heart. She was dangerously close to crushing on him all over again, even though she knew that with everything that'd happened—and the fact that he'd probably never, ever fully trust her—it'd be as futile as it'd been in high school.

He stood and tossed the remote back on the couch cushions. "Is your grandma okay?"

"Yeah. Until the next bingo night, anyway. I might have to pay a visit to Vera Mae and threaten her to tone down her punch."

"Isn't she, like…seventy or eighty by now?" Cam asked, his mouth kicking up on one side.

She pointed a finger at him. "Hey, don't judge. The senior citizens in this town are all headstrong and trouble."

He laughed, and her heart might've fluttered at the sound. "I leave town as the notorious troublemaking rebel, only to come back and find I've been replaced by the senior citizens." He took a step closer, and there was no might've about the fluttering now. "That seems like a pretty low blow to all the street cred I earned through the years."

"Yeah, sorry. You're not as hard-core as you thought you were. I mean, you did offer to babysit." She ran her palms down her jeans. "You were right about it being easier without Zoey. Trying to take care of her while dealing with hospital paperwork and my grandma would've been a nightmare. So? Everything went okay?"

"We managed. There was a"—he rubbed the back of his neck and trepidation seized her gut—"puddle incident. I only took my eyes off her for long enough to lock up my place, I swear, and the next thing I knew, she'd found a puddle and was in the middle of it. I'm so sorry."

She smiled, her concern turning to amusement—she wished she could've been there to witness it, actually. "No need to be sorry at all. The water calls to her, and she loves splashing. You should see me after bath time. I'm soaking wet, more water on me than in the tub, and my shirt ends up totally plastered to my bod—"

She cut herself off short, but the words better suited for a wet T-shirt contest had already spilled out. Cam appeared to be working very hard to not glance down at her chest, and his hard swallow sent a flush of heat through her. She couldn't believe she'd gone from talking about bath time to being so very aware of Cam and how close his body was to hers, but there it was anyway.

She licked her suddenly dry lips. "So, uh, the puddle."

"I cleaned her up the best I could, wrapped her in a towel, and blasted the heater in the car as high as it could go. I brought in her muddy shoes and clothes and put them on top of your washer."

Emma glanced toward it, even though the closed door leading to the laundry room and garage meant she couldn't see anything.

"Oh, and what's up with that car seat? She didn't want to go in it, and it had all of those overlapping snaps and buckles, and her legs were wrapped in the huge towel—it was like defusing a bomb, I swear, and I wasn't sure whether to cut the green or the red wire."

Emma laughed. Then it hit her that the guy might honestly know how to defuse a bomb, which should probably be disturbing but made desire dance along her nerve endings. Apparently she was attracted to weird special skills.

"Oh, and speaking of your car," he said, his tone ominous. "When it idles, it feels like the engine's about to die, probably because you need new spark plugs. The brakes also need replaced and so do the tires, and I wouldn't be surprised if there was a long list of other problems."

Her shoulders sagged. "I know it's got a few issues, and I've been meaning to take it in…" *But repairs cost money and all that sounds expensive.*

"Emma, you can't drive that. It's a death trap, and it needs to be fixed. I don't want you driving it, and I don't want Zoey riding in there."

All the happy attraction vibes were definitely gone now that she felt like she was getting a safety lecture. No wonder Grandma Bev hated them so much. "Okay, I hear you. I'll take it to the repair shop in Green River."

Two creases formed between Cam's eyebrows. "Green River? Why would you drive all the way there? Not that I'm the biggest fan of my dad, but Rod's Auto Repair does good work, and he won't rip you off—at least I can say that much about him."

Money was the biggest reason she'd let her car get so run-down, but his dad was one of the other reasons. She'd heard through the town grapevine that he was trying to get his life together, but she'd seen him start a fight in the middle of the street a few years back—not to mention the way he'd lost his temper the day she'd gone in to try to get Cam's contact information. Plus, she'd known it'd be impossible to go to the shop without unearthing all the guilt she'd smothered down.

"Fine. *I'll* take it in to Rod's," Cam said.

"No, that's okay. I know you and your dad have a complicated relationship, and like I've told you before, I can take care of myself."

He tilted his head and stared, challenging her to challenge him. *Mission accepted.*

"Cam, it's my car. You can't just order me to do something with it. I'm not one of your soldiers, and just because we have a daughter together, and you're kinda, sorta my client right now, doesn't mean you get to control every aspect of my life."

"Well, I have the keys, and I'm not giving them back." One eyebrow arched, and he spread his arms wide. "If you think you can wrestle them from me, feel free."

Irritation rose up, but as she took in his cocky posture, so did that darn thread of attraction. Part of her wanted to dive on top of him and dig around in his pockets, but possession of her keys wouldn't exactly be her top priority if she were bold enough to make that kind of move.

With a smug grin, he lifted his chin. "Keep my truck until I'm done. At least if the car breaks down on me, I'll know how to fix it."

Emma stuck a finger in the air and made an *O* in the space between them. "We'll circle back around to this, so don't go thinking you've won. But before I forget, I wanted to ask one more question about Zoey. Any problems getting her to go to bed?"

"Nope, it went just like you said. I put in the movie, listened to a whole bunch of singing, and she crashed out halfway through."

Emma glanced at the television screen, which had finished scrolling through the credits and was now on the DVD menu, the same obnoxious notes playing over and over. "But you finished the movie anyway?"

He hooked his thumbs in his pockets as a crooked grin curved his lips, the boyish gesture from such a burly guy sending another surge of attraction through her. "I figured I might as well see how it turned out. In case Zoey needed to discuss it later."

"Of course," she said, grinning at him. He grinned back, and butterflies erupted in her stomach.

Okay. I'm going to need to cut myself off before I lose my mind and fling myself into his arms—or before I decide to actually go digging through his pockets. Right now the focus was Zoey. If she and Cam crossed lines—if he even wanted to, which was unlikely—it'd only make a mess of an already messy situation.

Time to employ my self-control. "Well, thanks again. Now, my keys, please, so I can take in my car to get it repaired." She extended her palm.

He smacked it like she'd asked for five, not her keys. "I'll see you tomorrow morning at Mountain Ridge." He hesitated as he started past, and she thought he'd tell her he was kidding about the car and hand her the keys.

But then he ran his hand down her arm and gave her hand a quick squeeze that made her temporarily forget not only her car, but also that she'd decided against lusting after the father of her child. "I'm totally exhausted after a few hours with Zoey. Not sure how you do it all the time, but I swear, I'm going to try to figure out this whole dad thing."

"So that's still the plan? Tonight didn't scare you away?" She was mostly kidding, but part of her expected him to back out. Things would never go back to the same, but she and Zoey could deal better if they found out now, as opposed to dragging it out and getting attached, only to have him change his mind.

"Oh, it scared me a little," he said with a laugh. "And it might take me some time to adjust, but I'm still on board with the plan to get to know my daughter."

With the attraction vibes rising, she needed that reminder. He was here because of Zoey. This talk was good, because it put it all in perspective again.

But it didn't stop her from checking out his butt or thinking about how nicely he filled out his jeans as she watched him walk out the door.

Chapter Nine

Emma sat across from Sadie and Quinn on Friday night and sagged against the back of the wooden bench, sitting down for the first time today, with the exception of driving, which was never as relaxing as it should be.

"Yay, you made it!" Sadie signaled for the waitress passing by and asked her to add one more to their order. Emma didn't even care what the one more was, she'd take it.

"Yeah, Zoey loves Madison so much now that I can hardly get a kiss good-bye, because she's too excited to play." The fourteen-year-old babysitter and Zoey had quickly bonded, which made it so much easier to relax and enjoy her worry-free girls' night out.

"How's your week been?" Quinn asked, leaning in.

"Like the craziest week ever. I have a feeling that you knew that, though."

Quinn shrugged. "Yeah, but I want to hear it from you. Remember how Sadie and I decided that we missed out in high school because we were too busy blathering on and on to each other to stop and get to know you? I'm trying to learn from my mistakes."

Having girlfriends was still new for Emma. She'd had a few decent friends in high school, but none that she'd ever felt super close to, and while girls' night out was new, she was starting to get used to it. She was also finding it made her entire week better.

"Does the rest of the town know?" Emma lowered her voice even more. "About Cam being Zoey's daddy?" She glanced around The Triple S, eyeing the faces for traces of knowing the secret she'd kept for so long. "Who won the pool?"

The waitress brought their drinks before Sadie or Quinn could answer. Coors—that worked—and relief went through her at the sight of the amber-colored bottle. Sometimes Quinn ordered tequila, and history had proved that shots made Emma temporarily lose her mind. Then she went and did things like recklessly sleep with the deploying military guy she'd had a crush on since forever. Ever since that night, she'd stuck with only an occasional drink here and there. Maybe that made her boring, but she was a responsible person who usually followed the rules. No getting around it, and now that she was a mom, it was a necessity.

As soon as they were alone again, Quinn said, "I think the town eventually rewarded the pool money to Lori Branson—she had 'sperm donor' down as Zoey's father, and everyone finally agreed she was probably right."

Emma smiled at the joke the entire town no doubt loved, but inside she cracked a little. Of course they thought she would need a sperm donor. It'd been years since she'd given the town's gossip a second thought—getting pregnant while unwed meant she'd had to grow a thick skin. Several of the quilting ladies had attempted to get information about the daddy out of her, and she knew a pool had been started, everyone throwing in five bucks to make their guesses. She'd thought her ex-boyfriend Ricky would be the popular choice, even though she'd forever be glad Zoey wasn't his.

"Ignore them all," Sadie said, swiping a hand through the air. "As far as I know, the only people who know the truth are Quinn and me. And Royce and Heath, of course. But none of us will say a word. People will probably start to make assumptions about you and Cam spending time together, though, whether it's guessing Zoey's paternity or just gossip about you two possibly being an item."

"He's only spending time with me so he can get to know Zoey," she said, a hint of the dejection she felt over that fact accidentally coming out, and Sadie's raised eyebrow made it clear she'd noticed.

Emma dropped her elbow on the table and tucked her cheek against her chin. "I know the truth will come out eventually. I need to talk to Cam about how and what we want to say. I'm sure once word spreads, everyone in town is going to want to play twenty questions."

The top one would probably be *how*—more like how Emma had landed Cam for a night rather than asking for the exact details of how their daughter was conceived. Although with the nosy bunch of people who lived here, they might get a few of those, too.

Which was an unkind thought most of the townsfolk didn't deserve, especially after they'd showed up with onesies, diapers, and homemade baby blankets, not to mention provided dinners for the first few weeks after Zoey was born. Without their help, as well as Grandma Bev's constant check-ins, she didn't know how she would've made it that first month.

Quinn patted her hand. "Aww, hon. You'll be lucky if it's under a hundred questions. Especially if Patsy Higgins is in charge of the inquisition."

The three of them snorted at that.

"Quinn and I think she's had CIA training," Sadie said

with a laugh. "How else would she know everything that happens in town before anyone else? The grandmotherly exterior is a genius front. No one expects it."

They giggled again, and the ridiculous image of Patsy Higgins with a black ski mask covering her curly gray hair and her glasses perched outside the mask popped into Emma's mind. As silly as that image was, the girls were right. The second the woman heard the news, everyone in town would know.

I better tell Grandma Bev, because if Patsy Higgins scoops her, my name will be mud.

"As soon as Rod finds out he has a granddaughter, he's going to want to meet her," Quinn said, bringing the sober mood back, despite the fact that they were getting more unsober by the second. "Oliver will want to meet her, too. When you're ready, I'm happy to go with you and help support you. Rod's a bit prickly at first, but he's working on it. My advice is to be firm, and instead of letting him intimidate you, stand your ground. Throw the sassy back."

Easy for Quinn to say. She had sassy to spare. Emma usually shut down in those situations and got walked over—again, it was the confrontation thing. Maybe it was because she'd heard too much yelling at home, or maybe it was just her personality, but either way, the thought of that meeting, of the townspeople and their never-ending questions…

All of it overwhelmed her and she took a generous sip of her beer. This was why ducking her head and focusing on her life with Zoey and getting her career up and running was easier, and also why she'd disengaged from town events and distanced herself from most of the people in the town in general. But it'd left her a bit lonely. Honestly, when your grandmother had a better social life than you, it forced you to examine your life choices.

"Dude," Quinn said, her eyes on Emma, "once Sadie and

Heath leave to go tour, I'm going to need more than one girls' night a week, or I might seriously go crazy."

"It'll just be for a month or so," Sadie said. She was Dixie Rush's lead singer, and Heath played the guitar. They'd recorded an album, and it was coming out soon, so they were going on a short tour, playing at venues across the country to promote the release.

Emma rolled her bottle between her fingers. "Unfortunately, I don't think I can manage more than one girls' night a week. Madison can't watch Zoey on a school night. Maybe now that Cam's back, he can watch her once in a while. But I'm afraid I'll still be parked at home most nights."

Quinn took the last swig of her beer and then set down the empty bottle. "I'll just come over, then."

"You're always welcome, but I'm not sure Zoey and I will be very exciting."

"Oh, knock that off. I'm looking for friends, not excitement. I have Heath for that," she added with a grin, waggling her eyebrows and making them all laugh.

Sadie had Royce, her strong, silent cowboy. But Emma had a two-year-old princess, and that was enough. For now.

"Oh, by the way," Sadie said. "Quinn says that architect guy you work with likes you."

"Pete? No." Emma shook her head.

"Uh, yeah." Quinn swung her arms around as she talked, and the movements always grew larger when she wanted to make a point. "He checks you out when you walk, and he's constantly making excuses to talk to you. Come on, you know what you're doing and the job's going so smoothly. There's no reason for him to check in *that* much."

Pete was on the scrawny side, and if Emma was serious, he was *dead serious*. But in an admirable, driven way. He was smart and levelheaded, and he listened to her suggestions and gave fair input, always weighing the pros and cons before they made a decision together. She'd never thought about him as more than a business colleague she needed to impress, and thinking about the possibility of more now made a strange, unsettled feeling come over her.

Or maybe the weird sensation was because she'd already finished her beer. *Man, I'm such a lightweight.*

"He also says he loves kids," Quinn said. Emma looked at her, and she shrugged, unabashed. "I did some checking. Sadie and I promised to find you a guy, remember?"

Obviously Cam didn't even register as an option, and Quinn knew him better than Emma did. Which was fine, because she'd decided crossing lines with him was a bad idea, and this was a good wake-up-and-stop-dreaming-about-Cam-Brantley call.

But still.

"I don't know if I'm even in a dating type place right now," Emma said. "I feel like I should just focus on integrating Cam into Zoey's life and finishing up the Mountain Ridge job."

Quinn folded her forearms across the top of the table. "I'd love to see Cam with Zoey. I can hardly imagine it. Does he just grunt at her? He's so stoic."

Stoic? He might not be Mr. Chatty or wear his emotions on his sleeve, but Emma thought about their conversations, his grin, and the way they'd joked around last night, and thought that "stoic" didn't fit. Reserved and a tad intimidating, yes. Even bossy and stubborn—she still couldn't believe he'd taken her car.

The image of him with Zoey popped into her mind, how he'd given her a ballerina Barbie, and the way he squatted to her level to talk to her. The way she'd chatter and he'd nod, even though he clearly couldn't understand half of what she said.

"He's really good with her, actually," Emma said, and both women smiled. "I honestly thought he'd tell me that he didn't want anything to do with her, but I'm pleasantly surprised by how much interest he's taken. He even watched her last night so I could go pick up my grandma from the hospital."

Emma filled Quinn and Sadie in on the excitement at last night's bingo game and how Cam had offered to take Zoey. She even spilled the story about the mud puddle incident, and how worried he'd been that she'd be mad.

"I would've paid money to see him chasing her through the puddle," Quinn said.

"Speaking of…" Sadie gestured toward the door. In Cam came, sucking all the oxygen in the room toward him. Or maybe just Emma's oxygen. He definitely stood out, the height and rugged features drawing her attention the way they had back in high school and obviously still did.

Emma lifted her hand to wave, but then Angie Simmons stepped in front of him. She squealed, "Oh my gosh, it's really you," and hugged him, throwing her entire body into it. Emma quickly turned around and sank lower in the booth, now hoping Cam didn't notice her. She'd had to watch him and Angie make out in the high school hallway far too often. They were one of those off and on couples who broke up and made up a dozen times a day.

"Is Angie single again?" she asked, despite the questions it'd most likely bring.

"I heard she and what's-his-face broke up," Quinn said.

Emma rubbed her thumb across the condensation that'd formed on her beer bottle. "She and Cam used to date in high school, you know." Quinn and Sadie were in the class below Emma, and since Cam was in the grade above her, they probably didn't remember the epic hallway make-out sessions.

The residual jealousy she'd felt in high school rose up. Back then it was more a longing of having a guy look at her like that. Kiss her like that.

Even though she'd figured out how to tame her frizzy hair with a combination of serum and giving in to the wave instead of trying to brush it out, she'd always be the awkward girl with her hand forever raised, all the educational answers but none of the real-life ones.

Guys commented on her brains, not her looks.

Which was fine. Maybe she should consider Pete.

Emma peeked over the booth at Cam and Angie, who were still talking, most likely reminiscing about the good old days. Angie would mention she was single, and Cam would take one look at that sexy midriff top—the one Emma would never wear anyway, but definitely couldn't pull off after having a baby—and that'd be that.

"Emma?"

She jerked her attention back to Quinn and Sadie.

"You should go ask him to dance," Quinn said, and Sadie nodded her approval. "At least say hi."

Emma shook her head. "It's a girls' night. You guys left your men at home. I have a babysitter. I just want simple fun."

"Dancing *is* fun," Quinn said as the next song started up, a faster one that Emma would never attempt to dance to, even if she were the kind of girl who strolled up to a guy and asked him to join her on the floor. "If not with Cam, then with us."

Before she could list all the reasons that was a bad idea, Quinn jumped to her feet, clamped on to Emma's hand, and started toward the floor. For someone who wore ridiculously high heels, she certainly moved fast. Sadie followed after them, and as soon as they got to the floor, Quinn spun Emma.

Despite herself, she laughed, holding on tight to Quinn's hand and focusing on not falling. Sadie swayed her hips as she sang along with the song, her voice strong and powerful, making it clear why she had a recording contract.

Singing. Dancing. She admired how Quinn and Sadie went all out, never caring what anyone else thought. And so, instead of being the lame, boring one, she closed her eyes and let the beat take her away, laughing, dancing, and singing along with her friends.

· · ·

Cam hadn't seen Emma when he'd first come in, but he sure as hell saw her now. Angie hadn't stopped talking since she'd greeted him, but now he was only catching blips of her chatter.

Emma's laugh carried over to him, that same laugh that stirred up memories and made him feel a type of longing that he couldn't quite name. All week he'd had trouble not staring, and the tight jeans and the way she swayed her hips to the music wasn't making it any easier. She had on a simple tank top and her hair was down, hanging in loose waves down her back.

"A Brantley at the Triple S. Everyone, look out. A drunken brawl's sure to break out."

Cam turned to see Trevor, one of his former classmates, behind the bar, a stupid smirk on his face and a couple of empty glasses in his hands.

He gritted his teeth. *Yeah, and if I start throwing punches, I'm going to start with you, jackass.* Back in the day, Cam had a few rowdy nights here—usually because of people like Trevor running their mouths. But that'd been a long time ago, and he knew Heath frequented the place without stirring up trouble. Dad was a different story and was still banned, but that didn't mean Cam was going to sit here and let the cocky twerp the town used to worship because he had a good throwing arm talk crap.

"How's that football career working out for you, Trevor?" Cam asked, giving him a wide grin. "All those NFL contracts you were going to get offered used to be the only thing you and your family ever talked about."

Trevor scowled, the smirk now nowhere in sight. "I chose to stay here. But if I had your white trash family, I probably would've run away, too."

Angry bursts of heat traveled through Cam's veins, awakening every cell in his body, and the stool rocked as he scooted forward on it. He curled his hands into fists, fighting the urge to reach over the bar, yank Trevor across it by his collar, and show him how easily he could still kick his ass.

It's not worth it. No matter how good it'd feel for a couple of seconds. And then his jab would only prove to be right.

Deploying the methods he'd used before, he searched for that serene image of a lake. It flickered into view, but then he heard Emma laugh again, so he held onto the happy sound and glanced back toward the dance floor, where she, Quinn, and Sadie were still dancing.

"Yeah, obviously he's still a jerk," he heard Angie say, and assuming she was talking about Trevor, he wholeheartedly agreed. Which was why he kept his gaze on Emma.

"Cam?"

He reluctantly dragged his attention away from Emma's dance moves and back to Angie.

"Are you going to buy me a drink, or what?" She batted her blue eyes and twirled a strand of dark hair around her finger, moves that used to hypnotize him into forgetting her mood swings and their many ups and downs. Their high school relationship had been toxic—incapable of expressing feelings or dealing with his pent-up anger, he'd been as much to blame for it as she was, with her constant manipulation and never-ending attempts to make him jealous. While his temper still clearly got the best of him sometimes, he managed it better now, and part of that was staying away from situations that'd trigger it.

That near fight with Trevor proved there were parts of being in Hope Springs that made him almost revert to his high school self, and that was the last thing he wanted to do.

The second to last was starting up something with Angie again, even if she was giving off very strong signals that she was down for temporary fun. "Sure."

She flashed him a triumphant grin, and he signaled Seth Jr. over and said, "Put whatever she wants on my tab." Then he stood and gave her a slight nod. "Nice catching up with you, Angie. Now, if you'll excuse me…"

The song was coming to a close, and he wasn't sure what he was doing, but his feet seemed to have already decided for him. He walked over to Emma, reaching her as the final notes of the song faded away. He sure as hell hoped the next song was slow, because he didn't dance as it was, but he especially didn't do any of that fast spinning country crap.

"Mind if I cut in?" he asked, placing his hand on Emma's back, and he would've loved to snap a picture of the three shocked faces that turned to him.

As luck would have it, the song was slow, the kind that'd give him an excuse to pull Emma close.

"We'll order another round of drinks for after y'all are done," Sadie said. "Coors good for you, Cam?"

"That'd be great, thanks." He watched them go and then turned to Emma, who raised an eyebrow.

"My friendly neighborhood car thief thinks he deserves a dance, does he?"

He laughed and slid his hands around Emma's waist. "Your car's almost done, I promise." She placed her hands on his shoulders and began swaying in time to the beat, and he marveled at how tiny—not to mention perfect—she felt in his arms. "Hope it was okay for me to cut in. You just looked like you were having so much fun, and I thought I'd come see what all the fuss was about."

"I guess I put on a good show, then."

"You do," he said, and that adorable blush crept across

her cheeks.

"I meant…they dragged me out here. Dancing's not usually my thing."

"Could've fooled me." He probably should tone down the blatant flirting, but tonight he didn't really care about shoulds.

Emma linked her hands behind his neck, bringing her tighter against him, and he cared even less about what he should do. He thought of about a dozen questions to ask her, but each one seemed like it'd ruin the mood, so he decided to save them for later.

About halfway through the song, though, Emma bit her lip and her serious-business expression crept into her features. "So, I was talking to the girls, and they made me realize that we have a lot to figure out. Have you told your dad about Zoey yet? I understand that she'll need to meet everyone, but I don't want to overwhelm her, and I wasn't sure if—"

"Emma."

Her gaze lifted to his.

"We don't have to figure it out tonight." He reached up and swept away the section of hair that'd fallen in her eyes, his pulse quickening when she let out a shallow breath. "All those things can wait. Why don't we just enjoy the dance?"

She opened her mouth, ready to contradict him as usual, no doubt, but then she closed it, one corner of her mouth turning up. "Okay," she said, and her fingertips brushed the back of his neck.

An electric zip fired across his skin, and he wrapped his arms even tighter around her. Just dancing with her like this would get people talking, but again, that fell in the to-worry-about-later category. "Okay."

Chapter Ten

Cam spotted Emma on the park bench and headed in her direction. When he'd texted that her car was ready, she'd told him that she was at the park with Zoey, but she'd be home in an hour or two. She'd also said he could just leave it in her driveway if he wanted—that she wasn't worried anyone would steal it, even with the keys dangling from the ignition.

But he couldn't stop thinking about that dance they'd shared two nights ago, and he didn't want to wait till tomorrow at work to see her. So he'd told her he'd bring it by the park.

She spun around as he approached, and his heart caught. The sun played on her features, emphasizing the dark eyebrows and lashes that framed her big brown eyes. A smile spread across her lips, and warmth coursed through his veins. "I thought you'd have on a ski mask. Don't thieves usually try to conceal their identity when they return to the scene of the crime?"

"Technically, this isn't the crime scene, and ever since I heard the senior citizens have taken over the town, I've been trying to up my game. I've just got to find the right time to make my move and take control back." He gestured to where he'd parked the car and then pulled the keys out of his pocket. They jingled as he handed them over, and he couldn't help but hold onto her hand for a second before letting them go.

"Thank you," she said.

For a second he paused, noting all the kids running around on the playground and the other parents seated on benches next to strollers and big diaper bags. Sunday afternoon at the park was apparently a big thing when you had kids, and all of a sudden the whole scene made his internal organs tighten.

It felt fast. He hadn't thought this through. He'd just meant to come see Emma, and he hadn't thought about how…family oriented the entire thing would feel.

Watching Zoey the other night had been eye-opening and completely overwhelming, and while he was working to adjust to having a kid, he wasn't sure he was ready for full-on park time with the whole town watching.

Just as he was about to make an excuse to go, though, Zoey came running over. She eyed him for a second, like she was trying to place him, and then she said something he couldn't make out. He squatted down so he could hear her better.

"What was that?"

She pointed to his chest. "Daddy?"

He nodded, his throat growing tight. The surreal sensation he'd experienced before was still there, but more in the background, and happiness and pride swirled into the mix. "Yep."

He figured he was here now, and he might as well stay. What else was he going to do? His brother was all wrapped up in his fiancée, and besides being the third-wheel at their meals, he just worked while he was at home.

"Up," Zoey said, raising her arms. So he picked her up, standing as he did so.

Emma stood and picked a leaf out of Zoey's hair. She glanced around and then gave him a nervous smile as she fidgeted with the sippy cup in her hand. "If this doesn't get the town talking, nothing will."

Aware that there were, in fact, several pairs of eyes on them, Cam leaned down and kissed Emma's cheek. He'd never cared what people in town thought about him, and he wasn't about to start. "That'll help give them something to talk about."

Emma blushed, and his gaze moved to her lips, where he'd like to plant another kiss. But the little girl in his arms demanded that it was time to swing. He stepped toward the swing set, and Zoey twisted around and said, "Tom on, Mommy."

Emma trailed after them, and once he'd deposited Zoey in the bucket swing and pushed her, she urged Emma to swing, too. She lowered herself onto the flat-seat swing the next set over, and Cam reached over and pushed her.

That awesome laugh of hers filled the air as she wobbled, his push not very good since he was attempting to push her from the front without accidentally feeling her up—even though he wouldn't be opposed to feeling her up in private.

Okay, Brantley, time to tame down the thoughts. We are *at a park.*

Emma slowed to a stop as Zoey demanded going higher. She stood and took a picture with her phone, first of him and Zoey together, and then she moved next to him and took another one, just of Zoey, giggling as she soared through the air.

"Can you send those to me?" he asked, wanting to have a picture of Zoey, as well as a memento of this day. It felt like a tipping point, the one where it finally sank in that all this was happening, and even though it stressed him out, it was also more fun than he expected.

"Of course."

The desire to touch Emma again beat out caution, and he reached over and slung an arm around her shoulders, continuing to push Zoey with the other hand.

Emma looked at him like she wasn't sure what he was doing, and he didn't know, either. Only that he didn't want to let go. The more time he spent with Emma, the more time he wanted to spend with her.

"So all jokes aside," she said, "how much do I owe you for the car?"

Patsy Higgins came out of nowhere, peering at them through thick glasses that magnified her eyes and the curiosity swimming in them. "Well, well. Cameron Brantley. I heard you were back." She arched her eyebrows and gave a pointed gaze to his arm around Emma's shoulders. "And dating our Emma Walker, it seems."

"Oh," Emma said, stepping away. "We're not dating. He's just…we're…"

Maybe there was a right way to do this and a wrong way, but he didn't give a damn. "I'm spending time with Emma. And my daughter."

Once again, he thought he should just keep a camera on him at all times so he could snap pictures of shocked expressions—whatever Patsy Higgins had expected, she definitely hadn't expected *that*, and she looked both thrilled and scandalized by the news. Probably thrilled about spreading it and scandalized that someone like him would think he could be with *their* Emma Walker.

"I didn't realize… You certainly have been gone a long time." The town busybody pursed her lips and crossed her arms. "A little girl needs a father, you know."

"Mrs. Higgins, please don't scold him." Emma took a big breath, like she needed to fortify herself. "It's my f—"

"I know," Cam said. "I should've been here more, but you

know how the military is. I plan to spend lots of time making up for everything I missed, though, don't you worry."

Patsy looked smugly satisfied, as if she'd righted a wrong in the world. "Glad to hear it. You two have a lovely Sunday. In case you've forgotten, the church services are at ten every Sunday morning. Oh, and we'd like to see both of you at the next town meeting—they're the first Wednesday night of *every* month."

He bit back the desire to ask if she had a mouse in her pocket, considering the use of *we* and *our*—basically the woman thought she was the town, her opinion speaking for everyone.

Then Patsy's attention moved to Emma, and she even brought up a finger. "And this doesn't get you out of the picnic auction, just so you know. I expect your basket, and if Cam wants to be your date that afternoon, he'll simply have to bid on it, like everyone else."

As soon as the woman had moved on to guilt the next group of people into doing something they didn't want to, he asked, "What is she talking about? Picnic auction and bidding?"

"Don't you remember the big spring picnic they have every year? Where the women bring the baskets and then guys bid on them, and whoever wins gets to go with the girl on a picnic-type date?"

Cam shook his head. "No. It does ring a bell now that you mention it, but I never went to those hyped-up town events."

"That doesn't surprise me, since you were obviously way too cool for that kind of thing," Emma said. Before he could defend himself and say it had nothing to do with being too cool, she added, "I tried to boycott it, because I think it's sexist, honestly. I get that back in the day they bid on them so they could see how good of a cook the woman they wanted to court was and all, but those days are long gone, and during the one town meeting I attended this year—mostly because I was trying to butter up the town committee so our permits on Mountain Ridge would go through—I suggested they flip it and the guys bring the baskets."

Cam's amusement grew with every sentence, and he could hardly believe they were even having this conversation—he'd forgotten about all the odd town activities, from parades and festivals to auction picnics. "Let me guess. They didn't go for it."

"No! They looked at me like I'd suggested the men start wearing around dresses and doing all the cooking and cleaning—which might be a nice change for a lot of women in town, for the record. Well, the cooking and cleaning. The dresses thing might be weird. I'm not saying they have to do it all the time, but one picnic? It's just sandwiches."

Using one hand to push Zoey, he gave a noncommittal head bob, not wanting to interrupt Emma's rant, because it was rather cute, and he got a kick out of it.

"At least I got the permits pushed through, but then, after the meeting, Patsy cornered me and said she was glad *I'd* brought up the picnic, because she'd noticed I hadn't participated in several years. She went on and on about how the town relies on that money and how it helps fund the town's activities, and then she mentioned that a lot of the single women who usually provided baskets had gotten married this year, and that put them in a tight spot."

Emma huffed and continued to swing her arms around, the movements getting bigger and bigger as she relayed the story. "To add insult to injury, she made sure to add that now that Zoey was older, it really was time for me to get back into the dating world anyway. So, long story short, I'm taking a basket to the stupid picnic, so that it and I can be bid on like some kind of prize."

Cam bit back a laugh, but the grin couldn't be helped. "I'd

be too worried to bid on your basket—from the sounds of it, you'd probably fill it with inedible food or something that'd give a guy food poisoning just to prove a point."

Emma smacked his chest with the back of her hand. "I would no— Actually, that's not a bad idea." She glanced around, guiltily ducking her head when Patsy Higgins looked their way again.

Then they both burst into laughter.

Zoey screeched, barely swinging now and clearly not happy about it.

"You want out?" Cam asked, and she vehemently shook her head, so he pushed her again, swinging her as high as he dared.

When he stepped back next to Emma, she shot him a sidelong glance. "So earlier, when Patsy started her lecture about girls needing their fathers…why'd you take the blame like that? I don't want people shaming you when it's my fault you've missed out on the past few years with Zoey."

He shrugged a shoulder. "I don't care what she thinks. I can take the heat."

"I think I can take some of it, at least." She looked around conspiratorially and then lowered her voice to a whisper. "That woman scares me a little, though."

"Don't worry," he said, putting his arm back over her shoulders. "I've had lots of tactical training. I'll protect you from her."

A smile spread across her face, and he curled her in for a hug, a thrill going through him as she put her hand on his chest and said, with an exaggerated sigh, "My hero."

• • •

"You wouldn't believe the crazy tale I heard regarding you and Cam Brantley," Grandma Bev said by way of greeting when she opened her front door, adding a shake of her head. "Oh, Emma. Of all the guys you could've picked…"

Emma stepped inside, a tired, sun-kissed Zoey on her hip. "Man, I know word travels fast in this town, but I drove over the second I left the park."

"Judith called me. First she beats me at bingo, and now I have to hear about your park outing and the fact that he's Zoey's daddy from *her*."

"I was going to tell you sooner, but…" Well, she'd known the head shaking would start, which was why she'd always kept her crush on him to herself, even though those last two years of high school, when she'd lived here with Grandma Bev, she'd told her almost everything else. "How are you feeling? Any dizzy spells?"

Grandma stuck her fists on her hips. "If you think I'm going to drop the subject that easily, you don't know me at all." She turned her attention to Zoey. "Hey, hon. Come give your grandma a hug."

Zoey went to Grandma Bev, reanimating now that she had a new person to tell about the park and swinging.

Emma took the chance to peek at the pillbox, feeling better when the medications looked to be in order, all the boxes but Monday gone. Tuesday was refill day.

When Zoey went to play, though, Grandma turned her hard stare on Emma. "What about your architecture career? You've used me as an excuse long enough, and next it'll be that Cam fellow. He's just like your dad was, you know."

Emma pinched the bridge of her nose. "He is not." At Grandma's argumentative expression, she raised a hand. "But we're not dating, and I *am* working on my career. I have to finish Mountain Ridge, then I'm going to apply to firms. I swear."

Honestly, she hadn't thought about it much this week, but with dropping the baby bomb on Cam and dealing with the aftereffects and trying to figure out what it all meant, she'd hardly had time.

Emma glanced around for Zoey, and once she saw she was feeding the plant with the pink spray bottle Grandma had bought so she could help water the many plants, she added, "And I don't use you as an excuse. But if I knew you'd take your medications and avoid fried foods and alcohol, I wouldn't feel so guilty about even the thought of leaving."

"Excuse, excuse, excuse." Grandma Bev folded her arms. "Besides, Vera Mae and I have been talking, and she's thinking about selling her place and moving in with me. Then we can keep each other company and help take care of each other."

"And have too much of her punch and end up in the hospital again."

"I've survived seventy-one years taking care of myself, thank-you-very-much. And don't worry, Nurse Welch checked my blood pressure yesterday, and I'm right where I should be. Vera and I already agreed to help each other stay healthier— she makes other things bedsides rum punch, like wheat bread and breakfast smoothies with that hippie kale stuff that's all the rage." Grandma's voice softened, and she put a hand on Emma's shoulder. "I want you to follow your dreams. I think that's why your mama went a little nutso when she and your dad divorced, bless her heart. I know it seems like she ran away from you, but I think she was just running toward all the things she felt like she missed out on."

Emma knew that, she did. Yes, she still experienced the occasional sting of rejection from both of her parents basically running away from her the second they could, and it would've been nice if Mom had come to town for more than a week or two since Zoey was born, but she could tell that Mom was happy living on the West Coast. Whenever she came back to Hope Springs, she went stir-crazy, and she'd once remarked that she wished Emma had learned from her mistake instead of repeated it.

The day she'd said it, Emma renewed her resolve to do things differently than Mom had. To prove that she could follow her dreams, unexpected pregnancy or not, and still make Zoey feel wanted. Which was why she'd worked so hard to finish her degree, and why she'd put her heart and soul into designing the Mountain Ridge cabins.

So that instead of being the girl who *had* so much potential—the girl who took classes with upperclassmen in high school and was first in her college classes—she would surpass what people thought she could achieve.

As much as she hated to admit it, Grandma had a point. She needed to keep her focus so she wouldn't end up with regrets or—as Grandma so nicely put it—going a little nutso. "No more excuses, I promise. Architecture firm or bust."

Which probably meant she needed to push away the visions of her, Cam, and Zoey being the kind of family who spent Sunday afternoons at the park. And she should definitely forget about the ones of putting Zoey to bed and then kissing and cuddling with Cam on the couch.

Or better yet, kissing as they tugged at each other's clothes and headed toward the bedroom.

Chapter Eleven

"You're cheating," Emma said, hammering faster and then reaching for another wooden piece and one of the long nails.

Cam upended the bed frame he was putting together, and she couldn't believe the king-size wooden frame was all but done, especially since she still had a pile of parts to secure into place. "How so? I'm even putting together the bigger bed."

"Yeah, but mine has smaller, more complicated pieces." This cabin was the largest, with the most bedrooms, and after Cam had helped her carry in the boxes, he'd offered to help. They'd decided it'd be easiest to put the bed frames together in the living room, where all the tools already were and there was more space to work, and somewhere along the way, it'd turned into a race to see who could finish faster. "Plus, you have longer legs, which means you can walk around faster."

"Now I'm being punished for long strides?"

She laughed. "Not punished. Just…" A good way to finish the sentence didn't come to her.

He squatted down next to her. "Called a cheater."

"Exactly," she said, shooting him a smile. They'd talked

here and there at work the past few days, but their tasks had usually taken them in opposite directions, and she thought how much more fun work was when she got to do it while talking and laughing with Cam.

He grabbed one of the skinny branch-looking pieces that were going to make up the headboard from her pile and pushed it into place. His arm brushed hers, and his firm chest pressed against her back. "How many of these would I have to do for you to call it an even race?"

His breath skated across her neck, and she attempted to swallow. What she wanted to say was that he'd better do all of them in the name of fairness, especially if he was going to practically wrap his arms around her to do it, but she was trying *not* to flirt with him.

But then she glanced over her shoulder and noticed their lips were lined up, a mere inch or two between them, and every other thought flew out of her head.

Is he leaning in? I think he is… She licked her lips, just in case, and she swore his eyes darkened.

Then Pete walked into the open doorway, his footsteps echoing through the room—she hadn't even realized he was back in town, as he usually alternated about every other week, and he'd spent most of the last one at Mountain Ridge.

Emma quickly reached for another piece, trying to cover up the fact that she'd been about to jump the guy who owned the property they were working on, as that hardly screamed professional.

Well, not the kind of professional she was going for, anyway.

Pete did a double take at Cam, then he wiped his palms on his jeans and turned his focus on her. "Emma, can I talk to you?"

"Of course." She set down her hammer and dusted off her hands, more out of habit than because they were dirty.

Cam had already straightened, and he offered her a hand. Since she figured she could get away with letting him help her to her feet, she took it and stood, telling herself not to keep holding on, even though she wanted to.

After being in a bent position for so long, her knees complained and blood slowly worked its way back through her legs.

With the last few cabins framed, leaving only the small details that Pete usually didn't deal with, she thought his role here was coming to a close. Hopefully he would give her a big shiny referral so she'd have more options when this job ended. "What's up?"

Cam moved back over to the king-size frame, the light tap of the hammer filling the air as he went to work finishing it up. The sunshine coming through the window gave his profile a golden glow, and for a second she got caught up in admiring the rugged handyman look he had going on.

"I…" Pete took a deep breath, and then his eyes met hers, a flicker of…was that nervousness? "I was wondering if I could take you out for dinner sometime."

Emma froze, acutely aware of Cam's presence in the room. Was it her imagination, or did he start hammering with more vigor?

Vigor? Really, brain? But now that she thought about it, "vigor" was a good word for Cam. Everything about him involved more of it, strength radiating from every inch of his large, muscled frame.

Snap out of it. Pete's still waiting for your answer. An answer she had no idea how to give, because giving an answer required knowing what it was. "Oh. I. Oh."

Don't glance back at Cam, don't glance back at Cam. She was an independent woman, after all, one who could make her own decisions. Well, after she took Zoey into consideration, of course.

Which made dating complicated. "Can I get back to you? As you know, I've got to think about Zoey, and—"

"Of course. If you can't find a babysitter, we can take her along. I've been wanting to get to know you better outside of work, and Zoey's such a great kid."

Now she knew she wasn't imagining it—the hammering was harder and louder, echoing across her skin and beating in time to her heart. The boss side of her wanted to turn and tell him not to drive in the nail too deep or it might split the wood, but she instinctively knew not to mention it at the moment.

"I...need to check my schedule." Okay, so she could make her own decisions by deciding not to make one yet.

Pete surprised her by reaching out and squeezing her shoulder. "Just let me know when you find a night that works. My other property is all but finished, so I've got to spend the rest of the week there, but then I'll be back by the weekend, and I'm planning on being here more often than not until Mountain Ridge is open for business."

Unsure what else to do, she nodded. Pete left, and she was scared to turn and look at Cam. She wasn't sure if she was more scared to see if he was mad that Pete had asked her out or if he didn't care at all.

Telling herself not to be a wimp, she turned to face him. His gaze was on the bed frame, and it looked like he was about to secure the final piece. She licked her lips, trying to decide what to say.

Maybe she should simply step up next to him and help finish the project. Or did she pick up her own hammer and resume the race so they could get back to joking?

"Emma?" Quinn stepped inside and blinked, probably experiencing that shift of going from the bright light outside to the dimmer interior. "Can I steal you for a minute?"

Emma glanced at Cam one last time, but he'd picked up another nail, and then he was hammering away again, his jaw tight, his muscles flexing with the movement.

Vigor, vigor, vigor. Shaking away those thoughts, she followed Quinn outside the door and down the porch steps, their feet thumping against the raw, unfinished wood. The warm sun baked it, sending the scent of pine through the air.

Once they got to the next cabin over, Quinn held up a fan of paint swatches, several blue shades to choose from. "This is going to be the more family-centric cabin, so I want it to have a calm vacation ambience, but also maintain that mountain, nature feel. Which pops out to you?"

"Did you tell Pete to ask me out?" Emma blurted, her brain unable to play fifty shades of blue right now.

Quinn slowly lowered the swatches. "When I saw that he liked you, I hinted and encouraged, yes, but last week. *Before* I saw the chemistry between you and Cam on the dance floor."

"We were just dancing," Emma said.

"I was there, Emma. Sadie and I both noticed—in fact, we joked that it looked like we didn't need to find you anyone anymore. Plus, everyone's been talking about how cozy you two looked at the park together on Sunday."

"Even if there is some…interest, he just got back, and having a kid together makes it more complicated, and my analytical side says it's a bad idea. We need to get used to being parents together before we think about crossing any other boundaries." It was so much easier to be logical without Cam in the same room. At the same time, she wanted Quinn to contradict her, and usually she hated when people did that, because she was right and they should just believe her.

"So, you're what? Going to go out with Pete?" Quinn asked.

"I told him I'd have to check my schedule, like some kind of super-organized weirdo."

"Well, you are a super-organized…let's go with person instead of weirdo. But Pete is, too, so he probably thought it was hot." Quinn shrugged and laughed, and Emma couldn't help laughing, too.

But then the reality set in. Pete probably was a better match. She'd tried to be bold and not care about the rules once, and while she wouldn't take it back because that night had given her Zoey, she'd also decided never to try to be someone else again.

The thought of choosing him over Cam, though? A heaviness entered her chest, not exactly what you wanted when considering a guy. Her heart fluttered over Cam, but she knew she needed her brain to weigh in, too, or she'd end up hurt. "Ugh, I don't know what to do. Having Cam witness it all made it weird, too—"

"He was there when Pete asked you out?" Quinn asked, her eyebrows shooting sky-high. "Weird." She opened her mouth then closed it, a contemplative crinkle wrinkling her forehead—she so rarely thought out what she was going to say before she spoke, and that made Emma nervous about what she was going to say. "You've got to admire Pete for having the guts to put it out there anyway."

"Yeah. That was ballsy. Of course, I don't think he knows that Cam is Zoey's dad, either. If he'd heard the chatter you obviously have, I doubt he would've asked me out." Emma sighed. "I have a feeling there's going to be enough gossip swirling around without me dating the out-of-town architect. Without me dating either of them—not that Cam's asked, just to be clear."

And if he thought she was dating Pete, he probably wouldn't. He'd already assumed it from the beginning, which was another sign that she and Pete matched up. Serious girl and serious boy.

But that pairing didn't seem to go with her extremely girlie, energetic daughter. In some ways, having Zoey had made Emma more serious, because talk about heaping on responsibilities. But her daughter had also taught her to laugh when things turned out opposite of how you thought they would, and she'd also learned to relax her perfectionist tendencies, especially when it came to things like cleaning the house and cooking, which she was actually pretty good at when she took the time to do it. Why bother spending time on a gourmet dinner, though, when mac and cheese made your dining partner so much happier?

"Hold up the swatches again," Emma said, not wanting to think about her dating life any more right now. It'd been so long since she'd had one that she didn't know how to go about it, and it wasn't like she'd ever been good at it in the first place. Besides, she'd just promised her grandma that she was focused on her career, and she didn't want to do anything that'd compromise future jobs.

Quinn looked like she wanted to argue, but when Emma crossed her arms, she fanned them out against the wall. They debated a couple of swatches, throwing out the darkest and the lightest.

In the end they went with Ghost Ship Blue, because apparently that was a color. It wasn't too dark, matched the pale wood, and wouldn't overwhelm the rustic touches.

By the time they finished picking the rest of the decorations for the cabin, the crew was packing up. She headed back toward the cabin where she and Cam had been racing, hoping to catch him still there.

When she stepped inside, though, he was gone. The bed frames were, too, but a quick check of the rooms revealed he'd already moved them inside. She'd thought they'd each take an end and carry them in.

And now she was getting sad about work already being done when she had a to-do list a mile long.

So she grabbed her toolbox, which had been neatly packed up, and headed toward the beast. She hoped maybe she'd run into Cam on the way out…

He was nowhere to be seen, though, and she could only walk so slowly without being crazy obvious.

And as she fired up the loud engine of the work truck and started down the road, Emma told herself it was for the best.

But for some reason it didn't work as well as it usually did.

Chapter Twelve

Cam listened to the voicemail Dad had left him and groaned—sure enough, news about Zoey had reached him. After his last parting shot at Dad, Cam had been hesitant to tell him about his newfound daughter, but he didn't want Zoey to be a secret, like he was ashamed of her.

She was a great kid, not to mention so dang cute that he'd looked at her picture on his phone several times. But he was still worried about not screwing it all up, and throwing in more drama—which was inevitable where Dad was concerned—meant things would get messier before they got easier, and they were already tricky.

He thought about how close he'd been to kissing Emma earlier today. And how he'd wanted to charge over, grab that Pete guy by the collar, and tell him to stay the hell away from her.

He'd been damn close, too, despite trying to get his aggression out by finishing the bed frame, and it only reminded him that he sometimes struggled to control his temper.

What would Emma think if he lost control? She wouldn't

want to be around him, and she definitely wouldn't want him around Zoey, and considering his temper, maybe they'd be better off.

Frustration rose, and he raked his hands through his hair. The official Mountain Ridge meeting with Quinn and Heath hadn't exactly helped him calm down. They discovered that while Quinn had the personable side of the business down, as well as the food and housekeeping areas covered, and he and Heath had plans for the tours, everything from hiking to camping, snowmobiles, and horse rides, no one was very well equipped for the bookkeeping portion of the business. There were dozens of minor details—and then the major one involving figuring out the budget—and they were going to attempt to split them up, but it'd overwhelmed them all, he could tell, their first bump on the road to becoming entrepreneurs.

Cam glanced at his phone, telling himself he should call Dad back, but then he saw he had a new email, and checking that was easier. He grinned when he saw it was from Torres, his best army buddy, and the guy who'd been by his side through every mission, the good, the bad, and the ugly.

Torres had been the one to absolve Cam for losing his cool the last time it'd happened, telling him they'd all wanted the information, and if he hadn't been the one to snap and push the interrogation so far, Torres would've beaten the information out of the man they'd caught setting the roadside bomb himself.

While Cam had finally gleaned the information on where the group planned on attacking U.S. soldiers next, his yelling had been why his squad hadn't heard the enemy approaching until they were right on them, which was why he'd never forgive himself. The rest of the guys insisted that Jones would've put knowing the location before more of their brothers in arms were killed above anything else, but it was hard for Cam to swallow, because Jones wasn't here to say what he wanted anymore.

Trying to focus on all the good that'd been done with the

information his squad had extracted, he opened the email and quickly read through it.

Torres had gotten hung up in transfers and said he was emailing while awaiting his flight home to Colorado. He asked about Mountain Ridge and when the tours would start, because he wanted to come visit and head to the mountains that Cam had talked so fondly about.

Then he ended with, "I'll give you a call in a couple of weeks. I'm going to be busy with my girl for at least that long."

They'd all given Torres crap for talking about his girl nonstop, and there'd been a lot of jokes about how whipped he was. The last time they'd been together, Torres had been telling them they were just jealous because his girl was so hot and constantly sending him care packages and then followed that up with the news that once he arrived back home, he was going to propose.

Cam had told him good luck with that—he'd sworn off relationships and said a big no thanks to marriage, ever—and Torres had ribbed him, saying he'd meet the right girl and end up eating his words. Cam couldn't say that he'd completely changed his mind, but he knew Torres would get a kick out of his current situation, so he typed up the email about Emma and Zoey, and how even though he'd always thought a kid was the last thing he'd wanted, he found himself looking forward to the next time he'd get to spend time with her. He even confessed that after he got over his anger, he could kind of see Emma's side, and told him that there was something different about her, and that honestly he couldn't stop thinking about her—but not to get any ideas.

He was currently trying to smother the ones he was having.

As soon as he sent that off, the phone call to Dad couldn't be avoided any longer. So he steeled himself and dialed the number, hoping that he'd get lucky and go to voicemail.

But Dad answered, and he knew his luck was just about

the same as it always was. Pretty much nonexistent.

• • •

Cam had gone to the diner for dinner and ended up parked in front of Emma's. For the past few hours, he'd told himself that she was probably better off with that scrawny Pete dude—he probably never freaking lost his temper.

A few people in town had eyed him as he'd eaten his meal, and he could tell they'd wanted to ask questions, but apparently he still had enough of a reputation for people to leave him alone. Everyone but Patsy Higgins, that was, but she hadn't been around tonight.

He hadn't meant to stop in front of Emma's, only to slow down and give the place a quick glance. To check up on the house and verify that everything was secure. Then he thought that he should check her car's oil since it was sitting out in the driveway, and make sure it wasn't using too much. She'd told him it was driving so smoothly she could hardly believe it was the same machine, and he wanted to keep it that way.

He should probably talk to her about his dad, too. He'd put him off when he asked when he could meet Zoey, saying he needed to talk to Emma before making any plans, and they were trying not to overwhelm her. But it'd come up eventually…

He opened the door of his truck and started up the sidewalk. This visit was preventative maintenance, really.

He knocked on the door and was almost ready to give up when the door swung open. The first thing he noticed was the wet T-shirt and how he could see a hint of her lacy bra. So much for what he'd planned to say, because he forgot how to even speak for a second.

"Daddy! Daddy!" Zoey streaked across the room and ran over to Cam. He squatted and held open his arms, lifting her up when she made contact. His heart expanded as she wrapped her little arms around his neck. Her curls were wet, and she had her pajamas on, leading him to believe he must've just missed bath time.

"Throw me, Daddy." Every time she called him Daddy, she wrapped him that much more around her finger.

He tossed her a few inches in the air—with Emma looking on, much more conservatively than after the mud puddle incident—and she giggled.

"Don't get her all wound up," Emma said. "I'm trying to calm her down for bed."

"No bed!" Zoey shrieked.

Admittedly, for a minute, he was tempted to just give Emma the news that his dad had found out about Zoey and wanted to meet her and then hand Zoey over to Emma and leave her with the struggle of bedtime. But he figured that'd be a double jerk move. So he found himself once again in over his head, but diving deeper anyway. "How can I help?"

"I usually put on a video, but I'm trying to get her on a schedule in hopes the mornings will go smoother. I was about to read her a story and tuck her in."

Story. That seemed easy enough. "I'll do it."

Emma glanced at the laptop on the coffee table and the stack of envelopes next to it. "That'd be awesome. Then I can take care of some of this paperwork. As long as you're sure?"

"I got it."

"Holler if you need me."

Cam took Zoey back to her bedroom, where he got suckered into reading three stories, all tales with princesses, but her eyes finally drifted closed.

He crept out of her bedroom and closed the door, holding the knob and then slowly letting it go. The laptop and envelopes had been cleared, and Emma was digging something out from under the couch, her butt wiggling back and forth, and he took a moment to admire the view before announcing his arrival.

"Hey," he said, and she drew up to her knees, a sippy cup in her hand. "She's out."

Emma glanced at the clock on the wall. "Thirty minutes earlier than usual, too. Maybe this schedule thing will actually work." She stuck the sippy cup on the coffee table and flopped onto the couch with a sigh. "I always wait for this moment where I can finally unwind from the hectic day, but I'm usually so tired I can hardly enjoy TV. But having you here to help… I'm plenty tired, but not at the brink of exhaustion."

Cam moved over to the couch and sat next to her. "So I'm doing an okay job?"

She tucked her leg under her, spinning to face him. "You're doing an amazing job—especially for how short of a time you've been doing it. You must've had some experience somewhere? Maybe Oliver?"

A pang of guilt went through him. "No. Since he came into the picture after I'd already left home, I barely know the kid. I should really make more of an effort. Growing up, I helped Heath as much as I could, but since there's only a year and a half between us, I couldn't do as much as I wanted to. Then I left as soon as possible, when I probably should've stuck around until after he graduated."

"It wasn't your job to raise him—and I can tell you two are close."

"Yeah, it did make us close, I guess." He reached up and ran his fingers over his jaw. "I missed out on Oliver, though. Missed out on two years of Zoey's life, too."

Emma flinched. "Again, that's my fault."

He put his hand on her knee. "I didn't mean it that way."

"I know. But still." A lightbulb seemed to go off, and she reached toward the end table, stretching far enough that a stripe of her creamy skin showed between her shirt and pants.

His fingers twitched, wanting to reach out and glide his hands across it—more and more, the urge to touch her overwhelmed him.

The problem was, they couldn't casually cross lines, not since they had a kid together. Anything they started would automatically be that much more serious, and that thought made him hesitate.

Emma spun back around, a large book in her hands. "I can't change the past, but I can show you some of it."

The booties on the front cover clued him in to the fact that it was a baby book. The first picture showed Emma in the hospital holding a tiny, pink, and sort of wrinkly baby Zoey.

"Who was with you?" he asked.

Emma ran her fingertips over the edge of the picture. "My grandma, and a really nice nurse who cheered me on."

"What about after?"

"My mom visited briefly, and my grandma came over when she could, but she was dealing with some health issues at the time. The two-year-old stage is busy, but I'd take it over those first months of her crying all day and night, when I was here by myself, no idea how to take care of her. Those were some of the longest days and nights of my life—I thought they'd ever end."

Even in the field, during the most hectic missions, he always had a team. He couldn't imagine how alone Emma had felt. "I can't believe you'd choose to do that alone."

"At the time, I didn't feel like I had a choice." She glanced up at him. "Honestly, what would you have done if I'd emailed and told you I was going to have your baby? Would you have come home?"

He exhaled and ran a hand through his hair. "I don't know. I'd be shocked at first. I'd probably also want proof she was mine—I know that makes me sound like a jerk, but it's the first reaction."

"I get that. As I've said before, you and I didn't know each other that well. Or at all, really."

"I remember you from school, though. You always had your hand up. Always had the right answer."

A small groan escaped her lips as she brought her hands to her face and shook her head. Then she slowly dragged her hands down her cheeks before letting them drop in her lap. "Yeah. I was a *huge* nerd and super eager about it. I was so awkward. And pretty much all the things that make you unpopular in high school. I'm not surprised that you and I never hung in the same circles."

"I'm sure you remember me as the town bad boy. My brother and I were blamed for every bad thing that ever happened."

"That's not how I remember you," she said. Then she quickly turned the page, her attention going to the pictures. "This one's from Zoey's first day home."

He grabbed her hand. "Uh-uh. You can't just say that's not how you remember me and then change the subject. Spill."

"No way. I was awkward, and you were Mr. Cool, and all the girls wanted to date you. Let's leave it at that."

How was he supposed to leave it at that? "Did *you* want to date me?"

She dropped her gaze and tucked her hair behind her ear. He took that to mean yes, and it amused him to no end. Of course, back then he'd been stupidly wrapped up in Angie—not to mention overwhelmed with his crappy home life—and dealing with all the drama both of those things brought along with them. How different would his life be if he'd paid more attention to Emma? Maybe he wouldn't have felt the need to flee.

Okay, now you're getting carried away. Besides, the army was good for him. He'd channeled his rage and learned skills to protect his country and the people in it. It helped him kick the rebellious streak that had pushed him toward slightly illegal activities, too, like underage drinking and hanging around guys who shoplifted and started using harder drugs that gave them even stupider than usual ideas.

He'd never regret his time in the army.

What he regretted was the one time he'd gone too far, focusing so much on the mission and extracting information that he'd let his anger free and his guard down, and then the enemy had found them, and all hell broke loose.

Then he'd had to drag two of his injured guys out, and one of them hadn't made it.

"Cam? Are you okay?"

He shoved the bad memories away and looked up into her pretty face. "Yeah. Just thinking about how all of our decisions lead to places, some good and some bad, and how it doesn't do any good to wonder *what if.*"

She ran her fingers over the top of his hand, and it managed to calm the storm inside that he hadn't been able to shake away—he knew it'd never be gone, and that despite what he'd just said, a part of him would always wonder what would've happened if he'd gone by the book that day, even if he'd saved countless lives by occasionally pushing hard.

He focused on Emma, on her soft touch and the way she was looking at him, and something tugged in his gut. He thought about her earlier words, about how she apparently thought she'd seen something more in him, even back in high school.

Maybe this pull he felt whenever he was with her wasn't totally one-sided. Hope, fragile and dangerous, rose up, and he wasn't sure whether to embrace it or tell it to take a hike.

"If I'm being honest," he said, returning to Emma's original question, "if you'd sent me an email that said you were pregnant with my baby, it'd be easier to deny. Meeting Zoey and seeing so much of myself in her was proof enough.

But without that…?"

He hated to face the harsh truth about himself, but she'd asked for honesty, and he resolved to give it to her. If they were doing this—whatever this was—she deserved to know the type of guy he really was. "I probably would've told you I was too busy to deal with it. Eventually I would've come back for a short visit and a paternity test during my leave—most likely I would've been an asshole about it, too. Back then, I wasn't in a very good place. And the truth is, even after I found out she was mine, I wouldn't have been there for either of you much. My job in the army…I don't think I could've done what I needed to do while thinking about having a daughter out there. So I don't want you to keep punishing yourself for not telling me."

"Are you saying…you forgive me?" Her voice cracked as her eyes locked onto his.

This time he didn't stifle the urge to touch her—he reached out and cupped her cheek. "I forgive you. I can't even count on two hands the mistakes I've made. I'm just sorry you had to go through so much alone. But for the record, you've done an amazing job."

She threw her arms around his waist, hugging him tightly and whispering, "Thank you."

Before he could get a good grip in return, she sat back, looking embarrassed again. In school, he would've pegged her as shy; that night at the bar, she'd been anything but. He wanted to know what had flipped the switch, and he hoped that they'd get to know each other well enough that she'd be comfortable with him again, regardless of everything that'd happened. Their lives were connected forever now, after all, whether they crossed into more or not.

But you're not going to cross that line, remember… He couldn't help but wonder for one quick second if she'd be open to it, though.

She hadn't turned down Pete, which meant she might

already have her eye on someone else to fill that position.

Jealousy rose, fast and furious, and he curled his hand around his knee and squeezed, working very hard to redirect his thoughts so he didn't lose his mind and demand Emma stay away from the guy, as well as any others who dared to ask her out.

He cleared his throat. "Okay, show me more pictures. I want to know everything about the time I missed."

Emma explained each picture and told little anecdotes about Zoey as she flipped through the pages. He grinned at the expressive faces his daughter made, seeing himself and Emma in so many of them—the scowling ones definitely looked more like him. When he pointed that out to Emma, she laughed.

"It is kind of true," she said through her laughter, then she whipped her hand up over her mouth to cover it.

"Sure, mock me now, but when she's a little brainiac in school, I'll be pointing out that it's all your fault." He nudged her with his elbow. "Proudly pointing it out."

"Let's just hope some of your coolness gets in there somewhere. Because if any little twerps make fun of her, they're going to have to deal with me."

"Me, too," he added, frowning and clenching his fist. No one better ever mess with his princess.

With the book open to a picture of Zoey scowling at the camera, Emma lifted it, holding it next to his face and nodding. "That's it, all right."

"Very funny," he said, poking her in the side. A swirl of warmth went through him at her squeal. It made him want to do it again, but she caught his hand, holding it back and giving him a stern look that only made him want to kiss her.

By the time they got to the end of the book, he'd heard so many cute stories about his daughter, and he couldn't help admiring Emma for keeping it all together while taking care of Zoey and working to bring in money for her family.

They'd already covered a lot of emotional ground, too, so he decided the talk about his dad could wait. When it came down to it, he knew he'd just needed an excuse to stop by, but now he felt like he didn't need an excuse. He simply wanted to be here with her, and his bad day had faded away the second he'd walked in the door.

She offered him some ice cream, and he said, "Yes, please," then pulled the book into his lap, looking at his favorite pictures again. He paused at one of Zoey and Emma, two pretty girls smiling at the camera.

Again, he felt the pressure to make the lodge work so he could take care of his daughter. *And Emma, too*, he thought before another voice told him he needed to be careful or he was going to get carried away.

When things turned difficult in relationships, women walked away from him. Starting with his mom and ending with his last girlfriend, who had gotten sick of his job, how closed off he was, and all the times he couldn't be there for her. She'd told him he couldn't give her what she wanted, and since she'd been talking marriage and a house in the city, he'd agreed. He supposed she was better than the girlfriend before, though, who'd cheated on him while he'd been deployed.

He got that he wasn't the greener pasture guy and never would be. His goal when he'd come back to Hope Springs was a literal green pasture — or mountainside — to get lost in. Now that he had a daughter, his goals had shifted. Everything in his life had shifted, actually, and he needed to reassess, before hope and the magnetic pull between them got the best of him and he jumped in without thinking.

But as soon as Emma came back into the room, handed him a bowl of ice cream, and took a seat next to him, her vanilla scent filling the air, he thought it might be too late to avoid getting carried away.

Chapter Thirteen

Cam watched Emma grab her lunch box and take a seat at the picnic table. Pete sat right next to her, way too close, and with a big love-struck grin on his face. Despite telling himself that the guy might be better for Emma than he was, he couldn't take it anymore.

Not after having such a great time with her the past few days, and not when the thought of her with another guy sent a toxic burning through his gut. Not to mention the overwhelming urge to knock the guy out.

I swear, if he lays a hand on her...

Keep your cool. Remember that saying "I just snapped" doesn't take away the damage. That was something he'd learned from life with Dad, and so he clenched his fists, took a few deep breaths, and slowly exhaled the anger.

Now back in control of his temper, he walked over and held his hand out to Emma. "Come eat with me." He jerked his head toward the tree line. "Up the trail a bit."

More than a few pairs of eyes were on them, and the disgruntled look on Pete's face practically called him rude for interrupting, but he didn't care. Emma let him pull her to her feet, and then he grabbed her lunch box, keeping her other hand in his as he started toward the greening pines. A few still had brown splotches left over from winter, but each day more color spread, and within a few weeks it'd be green as far as the eye could see.

Once he and Emma reached the top of a small hill, he guided her off to the side, where the perfect picnic rock sat, flat on top and warm from the sun. They pulled out their lunches, and he noticed Emma's *Frozen* thermos.

"Like mother, like daughter."

She shot him a smile. "I couldn't find mine today, so I stole Zoey's and gave her a juice box, figuring the sugar would keep her from noticing."

Cam bit into his ham and cheese sandwich and looked out over the valley. "I used to practically live in these hills. Every chance I could escape, I'd come out here and hike or fish or hunt. Ever since I got back, I have these moments where I look out my window and think, 'I didn't dream it. The mountains are now my backyard.'"

"It is a beautiful backyard. I'm happy for you. And Heath."

"We dreamed up this idea when we were kids. Then I enlisted, and honestly, I thought that'd be my life. Even when Heath and I were exchanging emails about buying the property and everything we could do with it, it didn't seem real."

"It's real, and you deserve it," she whispered, putting her hand on his, and the dreamlike feeling washed over him. He often woke up expecting desert. Three other guys and makeshift bunk beds crammed in a ten-by-ten room. To get new orders and snap into motion to complete them.

The past few days he hadn't felt antsy, and he'd managed to keep the bad memories away better than he'd ever done before.

Even in his wildest dreams, he'd never imagined a daughter or a woman like Emma, but he found that being around them helped cut out the noise, and he didn't want to lose that.

"Don't go out with him." It burst from him, too bossy sounding, he knew, but how strongly he felt about her not dating Pete made it hard to be neutral. He cupped her cheek and worked to soften it. "Please. Give me a chance."

"A chance like…?"

Did she really not see it? Could she not tell by his constant checking her out? Or how he'd intentionally danced, no threat of death or dismemberment required? The way he made excuses to work with her instead of the other guys, and how he'd stopped by her house last night just because? He peered down at her, those lips he'd been having a hard time keeping out of his thoughts calling to him.

Then he lowered his head and kissed her.

Without the fuel of drunken lust, this kiss was much different than their first. It started slow, a tentative brush of lips. But when she reached up and curled her hand around his arm, holding tight, he increased the pressure, parting her lips with his and deepening the kiss.

It was the sweetest kiss he'd ever taken part in by far, but it still made his blood fire hotter.

Then she pulled away, and he immediately missed her lips, her touch. He held his breath, waiting for her to tell him he wasn't the type of guy she wanted. He knew he fell short on the stability scale, and he was too harsh for her, no doubt, but he wanted her anyway. At least a chance at having her, regardless of telling himself that the last thing he should do was start a relationship. A couple weeks ago he'd been so sure that he didn't want one, but now…well, everything else had been thrown out the window. What was one more thing?

"This is all happening really fast," Emma said. "And I'm worried that rushing into something is a bad idea. Think about Zoey. I don't want to confuse her—she's getting used to you being her daddy, but you and me together... Then the entire town will probably get involved, adding more pressure. You remember how nosy they all are, right? And if it doesn't work, it'll be that much messier."

It was perfectly logical, which was something he didn't want to be right now. He wanted to kiss her again. To forget the other crap in his life and focus on the bright spots, one of which was definitely Emma and Zoey. "Do you always worry about hypothetical future problems before they even have a chance to happen?"

"Yes."

He nodded, letting that sink in for a second and trying to figure out how to respond. Do the smart thing? Or forget about rules—which was definitely the more tempting of the options. "I've had almost every day of my life planned out for me since I was eighteen, so to be honest, I don't want plans. But what I do want is to feel like I'm starting to live again."

Cam reached up and brushed a strand of hair behind her ear, dragging his thumb across the top of her cheek as he did so. She closed her eyes, like she was soaking in the moment, then opened them and locked them onto his.

"I like you, Emma," he whispered. "I can't stop thinking about you."

"I...I like you, too."

"So we'll go slow. Take it a day at a time. We don't even have to let anyone else know we're trying it. If anything, we owe it to Zoey to see if we can work it out."

She tipped her head one way and then the other, like she was mentally weighing her options. "I suppose that's a good point. And I do have fun with you—honestly, I can't stop thinking about you, either."

A smile tugged at his lips, and he let it break free. Then he leaned down and kissed her again. This time, she didn't hesitate. She responded quickly, bracing her hand against his chest as she leaned into the kiss, both actions making his heart thump faster and harder under her palm.

His life was all dreams right now, and he hoped he never woke up.

Chapter Fourteen

Emma pulled her hair up, frowned at her reflection, and shook it out. Then she put on makeup, lining her eyes in brown, and after she'd swiped on mascara, she pulled half her hair up, teasing it at the crown before securing the hairdo with a couple of bobby pins.

Excitement had zipped through her in bursts every time she thought about a night out with just her and Cam, but her nerves had also punished her all day long, to the point she'd had trouble concentrating on even the smallest task. She'd boiled dry a pot of macaroni and had to start Zoey's dinner over, and a smoky smell still hung in the air, even after opening every window and running the fan.

The other reason for her absentmindedness and nerves was because her brain had decided to focus on one of her biggest fears: *What if we get out alone and he realizes that I'm not just boring because we've had to spend most of our time with a toddler in tow, but because I'm just boring?*

Scolding herself for letting the downer thought poke its way in, despite her resolve to shut it out, she slicked on shimmery lip gloss, pressed her lips together, and let out an exhale. This was her, take it or leave it. In fact, when she had the time to do hair and makeup and wear clothes that weren't for work and covered with whatever food Zoey had eaten, she actually liked what she saw in the mirror.

Zoey paused in the doorway and peered up at her. "Mommy looks pretty," she said, and Emma bent down and rewarded her with a kiss on the cheek.

"Thank you. Mommy needed to hear that."

The doorbell rang, and butterflies swarmed her gut. She tossed her lip gloss into the drawer, shut it with her hip, and went to answer the door. She'd asked Cam if she should see if Madison could babysit again, even though she'd done it last night for girls' night, but Cam said he'd already taken care of it.

Before Emma could greet Cam, Heath, and Quinn, Zoey shot past her and flung herself at Cam. "Daddy!"

He tossed her into the air, her ever-present tutu flaring out—high enough that Emma flinched, sure her daughter would hit the ceiling. But of course she didn't, and Zoey released a happy squeal. Cam caught her and kissed her cheek, right over the spot where some of Emma's shimmery kiss mark remained.

Emma quickly showed Quinn and Heath around, went over everything she thought they'd need to know and then some, and then hugged Zoey good-bye.

Cam hugged her next, and she protested at his leaving, tugging on his hand and whining for him to play dolls with her. He bribed her like a champ, with the promise of *Frozen* and Lucky Charms—and once she was distracted by Quinn and the big red box with the leprechaun on the front—they made their getaway.

As soon as they stepped onto the porch, Emma sucked in what felt like her first full breath of the night. Cam put his hand on the small of her back. "You look nice."

"Thanks," she said. Then she let herself check him out, the jeans, button-down shirt, and scruff. "You look nice, too. You're taking advantage of the no-shaving thing, I see."

He grinned and shook his hair, which was also getting longer. "No regulation haircuts or rules about shaving *is* pretty sweet. Besides, I've got to pull off the mountain man look for when people show up for the lodge. Who's going to trust some clean-shaven guy who looks like he works at a desk?"

"Not me," she said with a laugh, and she wanted to reach up and run her hand down his whiskered cheek, but she wasn't quite bold enough.

So far they'd stuck with flirting and a couple of sweet kisses when they could get away with it at work, staying in relatively conservative territory. Vastly different from their first night together, when they'd fast-forwarded past the little gestures and getting-to-know-each-other chats and slid right into home plate. Which was perfect, because she certainly wasn't ready for that step anyway—even though her body often forgot the memo, like now, when heat was radiating out from Cam's touch and sending her pulse racing.

He helped her into the truck then climbed in behind the steering wheel. "I've got a plan, but the place I want to take you is in the next town over. Hope you don't mind a bit of a drive."

Cam frowned at the distance between them, grabbed her hand, and tugged her until she was right next to him on the bench seat. Then he curled his fingers around her knee.

A drive sitting next to him, inhaling his musky cologne and feeling her skin hum under his touch? She didn't mind if the drive took all night.

• • •

Cam pulled up to the large park, glancing toward the area where people were taking blankets and chairs, and noting they'd arrived with thirty minutes to spare until the first band went onstage. "Is this lame? I searched for something going on this weekend, but there weren't a whole lot of options, and Heath suggested this place. But we can go somewhere else if you think it's lame."

"Are you kidding me?" Emma scooted closer to the windshield, twisting her neck so that she was looking over at the carnival area, where the Ferris wheel rose up over the rest of the spinning rides. "I *love* carnivals! I'm usually overly cautious, but carnival rides are, like, contained risk. I can let my thrill-seeking side loose in a contained, safe environment."

"I don't know that I'd call carnival rides safe. If you think about how many times they've been unassembled and reassembled, and the little training that goes into—"

She smacked his arm. "Don't ruin this for me! It's my only thrill-seeking activity, and I don't want to think about consequences or safety."

Another thrill-seeking activity popped into his head, desire going through him now that the heat of her thigh was seeping into his and that tempting mouth of hers was so close. He reached up and brushed his thumb across her lower lip, the desire surging at her sharp inhale.

"Okay. I won't ruin this." He decided not to tell her that he'd planned on listening to a couple of bands while they sat in the grass and had had no idea there'd be a carnival set up right next to it. Honestly, the *last* thing he wanted to do was go toward the flashing lights and inevitable screams from the riders, but she was so happy that he couldn't bring himself to say he'd only brought her here to listen to music in the park.

He peered into her big brown eyes, the makeup she'd put on emphasizing one of his favorite features of hers even more, and he couldn't help leaning down and giving her a quick kiss—one of many he planned on giving her tonight. Then he grabbed her hand and scooted out of the truck, pulling her with him.

As they neared the ticket booth, he laced his fingers with hers. Warmth flooded his chest when she squeezed his hand and flashed him a smile.

The scent of fried food grew stronger, and he noticed the food trailer nearby, which was the only part of the carnival he could totally get down with. He bought a book of tickets, slid them in his front pocket, and glanced down at Emma. "Did you want to grab some food first?"

"What are you, a carnival rookie? Rides, then food." Tightening her grip on his hand, she pulled him toward the zipper. Even though he disliked confined spaces, he'd ridden plenty of rides before, and even used to brag that none of them scared him. But now he was thinking too much about the shoddy workmanship, wondering how long they'd taken to put together the contraption, and if they'd tightened every bolt, and suddenly he wished for the invincible feeling from his youth.

This might be the stupidest idea I've ever had.

But as they stood in line, Emma bounced on the balls of her feet, excitement radiating off her. When it came their turn to load, she practically sprinted onto the ride. Then they were both belted in, together in a metal death trap, and she gave a squeal and kissed his cheek.

And he decided he'd ride every stupid ride if it made her this happy.

As soon as the ride jolted into motion, though, he immediately regretted everything. Emma obviously didn't feel the same, considering the way she laughed and rocked the cage they were in, making it spin even more. When the metal bar shifted—only a few inches, but still—he threw out his arm and held Emma in place.

"Oh my gosh, you're totally soccer momming me," she said with a laugh.

The ride threw them forward, and the shift was enough to push her breasts against his arm. He tried not to think about that, but it was kind of hard not to notice the way her curves pressed into him as they slid and spun, their bodies bumping together. He refused to let her go, despite her mocking him, too. Just in case the bar didn't work well enough.

The cage turned upside down, all the blood rushing to his head, and he couldn't believe that at one point in his life he'd thought this was fun. His heart pounded too hard, the metal bar dug into his hip with each flip—and because it was set for him, Emma was sliding around way more than he liked. And he hated to admit this, but his back was probably going to hurt tomorrow morning from all the jerking around.

Finally the ride slowed to a stop, and he tapped his fingers on the metal bar, waiting to escape. Over the past few years, he'd been crammed into a lot of confined spaces, but he never got used to it. The itchy, lung-tightening sensation hit him, and he wanted to bolt. How stupid that he couldn't do something so normal without reliving too many close missions.

"You okay?" Emma asked.

He tapped his fingers faster. "Of course."

She brushed her hand across the top of his, and the tightness in his chest eased. Instead of clinging to the bar, he turned his palm and clung to her. The door swung open with another screech of metal—the entire thing should be bathed in WD-40—and sweet, open air greeted them.

He stepped outside then offered Emma a hand. When the cage rocked and she stumbled forward, her body bumped into his. He wrapped his arms around her, glad for the excuse to hold onto her for a moment—her nearness was much more enjoyable with nothing but sky surrounding them, too.

She tipped up her head and dragged her thumb over his biceps, making his pulse race after her touch. "We don't have to go on any more."

"Oh, we're riding every single ride." Yes, he'd probably experience a bit of claustrophobia, but he could get through it, especially with Emma by his side.

He noticed she picked out more open, less jarring rides after that, though, and he didn't think it was for her benefit. After several rides, the ground seemed unsteady under his feet, and they wandered into the area with more of the booths.

Emma glanced at the rows of stuffed animals hanging behind the shooting game. "You know, it's funny, because so many nights I wish for a small break from mommy duty, then when I get away, I spend so much time thinking about Zoey and missing her. She'd love this place."

"I guess we'd better take her back a stuffed animal, then."

"Yes, these ones are extra awesome, because they've usually got an eye going the wrong way. They're like the stuffed animals who've lived near the nuclear power plant for too long and aren't quite right."

Cam laughed. He looked at the rows of stuffed animals, noticing how true that was. He paid the guy and picked up the BB gun. Then he took aim and pulled the trigger. He frowned when it didn't hit the center, lined up the shot, and hit the same spot again. He repeated, adjusting as he pulled the trigger again and again, but it wasn't until the last one that he neared the bull's-eye.

"Close," the guy working the booth said. "You hit enough for one of these." He pointed to the tiny mutant fish. At least there was a pink one.

As they walked away, Cam muttered, "That game was totally rigged. I've had training. I earned top marks. I can hit a—" He stopped. That was a little too much information, and not something he wanted Emma to ever think about him doing. "I'm an expert marksman," he quickly said to cover, and now he wanted to move on.

Emma tucked her hand in the crook of his elbow. "Don't

worry, after you protected me in the big bad cage of the zipper, I have no worries about your tactical skills. Not to mention the Patsy Higgins thing. And Zoey will love her fish—I don't have space for one of those obnoxiously big teddy bears that will split apart and shed fluff everywhere, anyway."

He wrapped his arm around her, loving how she always saw the bright side of things.

"I hear music," she said, turning toward the park where he'd originally planned on taking her.

"Confession time?"

She whipped her head toward him, worry etched in her features.

"It's much less of a confession than you're thinking. I was just going to tell you that I meant to bring you here for the music. Not the rides."

"Why didn't you tell me?"

"You were so excited about the carnival." He tipped his head toward the park. "But I do have a blanket in my truck. Want to grab some food and then we can go listen for a while?"

She nodded and said she'd get the food while he retrieved the blanket. They met up at the entrance of the park a few minutes later. Once they found an open spot, he spread out the blanket and she carefully balanced the food, nearly losing her grip as she lowered herself to the ground.

After eating her hot dog, Emma dug into the cotton candy, her lips turning blue from the spun sugar. "Thanks for tonight," she said. "It's been a long, long time since I went on a date."

"Me, too." Even back in high school, he didn't really do official dates.

"Yeah, that's just because you were away serving the country. Mine was more because no one was asking."

"If I recall, you had another offer just this week." He twisted the bottom of her shirt in his hand and tugged her closer, dropping a quick kiss on her blue lips. "Thanks for not taking him up on it, by the way. It'd be bad for business if I had to take out the scrawny architect."

"As if it was even a competition…" She shook her head and muttered, "Mr. Caveman." She pinched off a piece of cotton candy and extended it to him.

Cam leaned over and ate it out of her fingers, adding a grunt that made her laugh.

Once the food was gone, he propped himself up on his palm and pulled her back against his chest. The bands were pretty good, although maybe he was just seeing everything through Emma-tinted lenses now. When she shivered, he pulled her closer and ran his hands up and down her arms.

"I need to talk to you about something…" The thought of where he needed to steer the conversation was enough to put a dent in the happy vibe, and he hated to ruin the easy mood. So he decided to put it off a little while longer and change the path of the conversation to another subject he'd wanted to bring up. "Now that the weather's turning warmer, I was thinking maybe we could take Zoey up to the lake and spend a day fishing. As soon as the lodge opens, I know things are going to get busy fast, but I thought a sort of practice run would be fun. What do you say?"

Emma twisted in his arms so that she was facing him. "You'll help me carry the billion bags that taking Zoey anywhere requires?"

"What else would I do with all these muscles?" He flexed to add to the joke, and she giggled.

She leaned in, her lips mere inches away. "Sounds like a perfect way to spend a day."

He closed the gap and kissed her again, and all of his past mistakes and bad memories pushed that much farther into the background.

Chapter Fifteen

The entire night seemed like one big dream, similar to the whimsical dates Emma had always envisioned back in high school. Carnival rides and music under the stars with a guy she was crazy about keeping her warm. This date had made up for all the ones she'd missed in her life, to the point that even the fact that she hadn't gone on a single one in the past three years no longer felt like a big deal.

But as they exited the carnival grounds, she couldn't help noticing the way women looked at Cam, their gazes lingering. One was so bold as to wink, even though Emma's hand was in his, a clear sign they were together. At least she thought it was pretty clear.

She could read their expressions, too, looks that said, *Why is* he *with* her?

The question echoed through her head, unwelcome and stirring up the self-esteem issues she thought she'd conquered years ago. If Zoey wasn't in the picture, would he be with her?

Probably not. A sinking sensation went through her gut. In fact, he'd even brought Zoey up when he'd asked her to give him a chance, saying they owed it to their daughter. She understood, because she wanted the best for Zoey, too, but just once, she wanted to be wanted for her.

She thought of her parents, of all the fights where her father made it clear he would walk away if they didn't have a daughter together. She'd sat in her room and promised herself that she'd never settle for such a conditional excuse for love. In the end, it hadn't kept them together, either. It'd only driven a wedge between them, one filled with mean words that'd left all of them miserable, along with the issues that came with feeling unwanted and unloved.

Why am I thinking about this? It's way too soon. Like Cam had pointed out, she worried about hypothetical future problems before they even had a chance to happen.

At the same time, the beginning was when all that passion and having trouble keeping their hands off each other was supposed to happen.

She wanted intense kissing, and to run her hands down his whiskered face, down his body, but she wasn't going to be the one to push the boundaries and make a fool of herself, even if just the thought of it sent a spike of desire through her.

Emma was fairly confident Cam enjoyed her company, but she couldn't help but worry a little. Their kisses were sweet, with none of that passion from the night they'd first hooked up, when she'd been pretending to be someone else.

He did say I looked nice.

Yeah, nice, not hot. Not pretty.

Don't start overanalyzing it, or you'll ruin everything.

When Cam pulled open the passenger door of his truck for her, she forced a smile onto her face and climbed into the cab.

For most of the ride back, it was quiet. Not uncomfortably so, but clearly there was still a lot that she didn't know about Cam. She knew he had a complicated relationship with his dad, and as intimidated as she was by Rod Brantley, she thought it was better to get it out in the open instead of having an awkward run-in in the middle of town.

She reached up and twisted a strand of hair around her finger. "I assume your dad's probably heard about Zoey by now…?"

Cam's hands tightened on the wheel. "It's come up, yes. In fact, I need to talk to you about something, but I didn't want to ruin the night."

Maybe she should've kept her mouth closed on the subject. Why hadn't she started with something simpler? Like favorite color? Or favorite food?

"Earlier this week, my dad did call and ask me when he could meet her. And today he called again and told me he understood you and I were still figuring things out, but he would love for the two of you to have Sunday dinner with us all tomorrow night. I realize it's late notice, and I should've brought it up earlier. I've just been going back and forth on the whole thing, because I'm not sure I want to pull you and Zoey into the mess that is my screwed-up family."

Emma swallowed. "I understand. And it's not like I have a busy schedule."

"You don't have to check your calendar?" he asked, a hint of teasing in his voice.

"Well, of course I have to consult that. I'm just saying I *might* be able to pencil you in." Which reminded her that she still needed to have a talk with Pete. He'd left soon after asking her out, so she hadn't had the chance, and it was another awkward conversation she wasn't looking forward to.

Let's just focus on one awkward situation at a time… "If you want Zoey and me to come, we can." She was proud of how firm her voice had come out, considering everything inside her suddenly felt shaky.

Cam reached over and grabbed her hand. "Quinn offered

to host at Mountain Ridge, so there'd be more room, as well as it being more neutral territory. The truth is, while I'm still figuring out my relationship with my dad, he was actually pretty cool about the whole Zoey thing. I thought he'd throw things I'd said to him back in my face, but all he said was he wanted to meet her."

Emma wasn't sure exactly what his version of "pretty cool" was, but she hoped Rod would save some of it for her. She supposed she'd never declare herself truly ready to meet Rod Brantley, not after keeping Zoey a secret for so long. But ready or not, it was a step they needed to cross eventually to avoid that whole awkward encounter situation that had led her to bring it up in the first place. "We'll come to dinner and meet everyone, then."

Cam lifted her hand and kissed the back of it. "Thanks. It'll be fun for Ollie to meet her, too. I think he's going to be thrilled about being an uncle." He huffed a laugh. "As long as it doesn't interfere with baseball."

Emma nodded, her mind already formulating a game plan for the meeting. It was hardly the way she'd wanted to end the date, but again, she supposed her complicated life made it impossible to have normal dating rules.

At least with Cam by her side, she felt like she could take on anything, be it family dinner or heading into the mountains with a two-year-old who didn't like to stay put.

· · ·

Cam waited outside the lodge for Emma and Zoey while the buzz of conversation continued inside. The more space he and Dad gave each other, the more likely they'd still be getting along when Emma and Zoey arrived. The way Heath had forgiven Dad for everything was admirable, but Cam wasn't so sure he could do the same.

He'd warned him to be nice to Emma, though, and as long as Dad did that, he'd at least suffer through the evening.

Dust kicked up on the road, and pretty soon the little gray car he'd repaired with enough new parts to practically make a new one pulled up in front of him. One look at Emma and he could see the apprehension written across her face. He took the porch steps a couple at a time and reached out for her as she climbed out of the car. He helped her to her feet and gave her hand a squeeze in an attempt to take away some of her worry.

When she smiled at him, though, he was the soothed one. Then his fears rose to the surface. Would she meet Dad and worry that he'd end up like him, the way he sometimes did? Would she look at him the same way if she knew all the things he'd done? Could a sweet, smart girl like her really want to take a chance on a guy like him?

Cam reached into the back of the car and unfastened Zoey, who'd fallen asleep in her seat—his daughter was probably one of the few things he had going for him with Emma, and he hoped to take that wiggle room and earn enough to deserve both of their affection.

His daughter was a little furnace, and he boosted her a few inches higher in one arm before wrapping the other around Emma's waist. "Ready?"

"No," she said, but then she started toward the entrance of the former B and B—they really needed to figure out if they should stick to calling it a lodge, or if they should call it a B and B still, or if…well, now he was stalling so he didn't have to think of his two worlds colliding.

Thank goodness Quinn and Heath would be here to help dispel some of the tension.

Right before they got to the door, he spun around. Bracing one hand on the still-sleeping Zoey, he leaned down and kissed Emma, putting everything he could into it with the use of only one hand. She gasped, and he took advantage, sweeping his tongue in to meet hers.

She stared at him through half-lidded eyes, and he wished he'd taken the time to give her a proper kiss good-bye last night. He felt like Emma was constantly holding back, probably because of the way they'd first gotten together, and he didn't want her to think he expected more. Not until she was ready.

"What was that for?" she asked.

"So you'll remember how much you like being around me."

"My, someone thinks highly of his kisses," she said, but then she tipped onto her toes and gave him another. Then she turned toward the door, her chin notched higher, and she actually looked ready to go in now.

As soon as they stepped into the main room, the conversation died down. Dad's gaze bounced from Cam to Emma to Zoey.

Dad stood, wiped his hands on his jeans, and then extended one to Emma. "Rod Brantley."

"Emma Walker. Nice to meet you."

Zoey stirred as the rest of the introductions were made— Emma already knew Quinn and Heath, of course, but she hadn't officially met Oliver or Sheena.

"And this is Zoey," Cam said, rubbing her back as she blinked at everyone.

When Dad moved closer and said hi, she dropped her head back on Cam's shoulder.

"She fell asleep on the drive over," Emma said. "She might need a few minutes to wake up."

As if to prove her mom wrong, though, Zoey's head popped up. "Puppy!"

Trigger, Heath's little blue heeler, came bounding over, and Zoey wiggled to get down. She squatted, her bum all but hitting the floor, and wrapped her arms around the puppy, who went to licking her face. Both of them were way too happy about the situation, and it warmed Cam from the inside out.

Pretty soon, six adults and one eight-year-old boy were crouched around a puppy and a little girl with blond curly hair. Dad's hand came down on Cam's shoulder and he looked over at his father, waiting for some kind of criticism.

"I can't believe I'm a grandpa," he said. Most people probably wouldn't have heard the catch in his voice or seen the awe in his eyes. Cam had thought Dad might be a bit brusque with Emma about not telling any of them about Zoey, or that he'd say something highly inappropriate to her. He'd also expected a jab about the lodge and his boys leaving him to run the shop alone, until they inevitably failed, and couldn't she at least talk some sense into him if she was going to be around?

Never in a million years had he expected Dad to get emotional about having a granddaughter, and it made his own heart knot. One by one, they stood—they'd never outlast Zoey, who could squat for hours in that position. It was the kind of stance they used to break grown men in boot camp, but it seemed to be her home base.

Dad turned to Emma, and despite the recent warm fuzzies, Cam still took her hand, wanting her to have his if she needed something to hold on to.

"So, she's two?"

Emma let out a shallow exhale and nodded. "Yes, sir."

"Oh, no need for this 'sir' business," Dad said, swiping a hand through the air. "Please call me Rod. After all, we're family now—even if you and my son don't work out."

Well, there was the bluntness, but at least he hadn't edged it with animosity. As far as Rod Brantley went, that was a warm welcome.

Cam slipped his fingers between Emma's, feeling the

need to tighten his hold on her, and gave her hand another squeeze. She squeezed back, her touch bringing the same calm it did last night, and making him think that despite the odds and their unconventional start, maybe they actually had a shot at making this work.

Chapter Sixteen

Two weeks went by, in which the last cabins took shape, even their interiors all but finished.

During that time, Cam often came over to have dinner with her and Zoey and to help with bedtime. The three of them had even gone to eat at the diner one night, which had stirred up plenty of talk.

Since then, people had stopped Emma on the sidewalk, or in the grocery store, or even when she was pumping gas and stressing about how late she was running, to ask what was going on with her and Cam Brantley. Mrs. Branson had gone so far as to warn her that from what she'd heard, "that Brantley boy" had been quite the hoodlum in high school, and she was pretty sure her stolen garden gnomes were his doing. She'd added that if Emma found out where they were, could she let her know, because she hadn't been able to find any just like them since.

As if Cam actually had some secret place where he stashed stolen garden gnomes.

Cam mentioned that he'd been told how sweet Emma

was on more than one occasion, and a couple of women wanted clarification on if he was truly Zoey's father, like they suspected he and Emma were playing some big prank on everyone. Then, after he'd confirmed that he was, they'd asked him why he'd taken so long to make things right.

So basically, the town was trying to get involved, just like she'd worried they would. She'd learned to simply smile and change the subject when the prying started. Mostly because it was none of their business, but the truth was, she wasn't sure exactly what was going on. This past month had been a lot of fun, and during last weekend's fishing excursion with Zoey, she'd laughed more than she ever had before.

Every time Cam cast his line, Zoey would walk over next to him and throw rocks in the water, which kept the fish far, far away—he'd been using salmon eggs, anyway, and in her experience, the fish in the reservoir always turned their noses up at them. Despite both of their attempts to keep Zoey from venturing past the shoreline, their daughter was wet and muddy about an hour after they reached the reservoir.

More than anything, it felt like playing family, but Emma supposed they weren't playing. They *were* a family, even if a little unconventional and still trying to figure it out.

But there was a difference between working side by side and raising a child together, and having the kind of relationship she wanted, one with fireworks and passion.

To be fair, nothing got in the way of intimacy like a two-year-old—the last couple of times Cam had been over, Zoey had started crying right as they'd settled onto the couch to catch their breath from the day, obliterating the chance to see if kissing would turn into a little more.

But Emma's worries from the night of their first and only date sans Zoey hadn't completely gone away. More than once, after Cam had left with nothing more than a kiss good night, she'd heard Ricky's voice in her head: *It's one thing to have a boring job that you talk about nonstop, but it's another when the thought of having sex with you makes me yawn. I just can't make it work anymore.*

He'd said it like the entire relationship had been a chore. With bedtime rituals, toddler tantrums, and having to pack two extra bags for a simple fishing trip, how could being with her not feel a little bit like a chore?

The knock on the door jerked Emma back into the present. She set aside her laptop, which had an application to an architecture firm in Casper on the screen, and answered the door.

"Everything okay?" she asked when Grandma Bev stood on the porch, the light illuminating her bright red coat and matching lipstick.

Grandma stepped inside. "For the record, I prefer more of a conventional greeting. Like, 'Hello, dear Grandma. It's so nice to see you.'"

"How about, 'Hello, Grandma who's hell-bent on giving me a heart attack. I'm so glad you took time out of your busy social life to stop by'?"

Grandma rolled her eyes, but a smile tugged on the corners of her mouth. "That'll do." She looked around, doing a wide sweep of the living room and kitchen. "That fella isn't here?"

"Not tonight."

"How do I always manage to miss him?"

Because apparently I'm luckier than I thought. Eventually they'd have to meet, of course, but since Grandma Bev would most likely go into interrogator mode the second after names were exchanged, Emma wanted to put it off a little longer. Until she felt sure enough about the relationship that she could confidently answer that she did know exactly where it was going.

The worries that'd occupied her mind a minute ago tried

to rise up and make her wonder if they'd actually get to that place before the nosy townsfolk and family obligations got too much for Cam.

But then she reminded herself how good he'd been about everything. The image of him attempting to fix Zoey's ponytail after it'd fallen out the other night popped into her head. In typical Zoey fashion, something as little as an undone hairdo could be treated like the end of the world, and when Emma's hands were occupied with making dinner, Cam had jumped in to help.

When she'd seen that, she'd told herself she was stupid for caring about anything else when he was such a good father.

Thinking about the way that ponytail had stuck straight up, giving their daughter more of an antenna than a hairstyle, made her bite back a laugh.

Grandma perched on the edge of the couch. "I just wanted to let you know that Vera Mae officially put her house up for sale today. A moving truck is coming at the end of the month, and then she'll be living with me. So to reiterate, there's no reason to use me as an excuse anymore, and I hope you've been moving forward with your plans instead of waiting around and twiddling your thumbs."

"Gee, I really miss those thumb-twiddling days," Emma joked. "They were so much fun, but they're definitely hard to find after having a kid."

Grandma Bev shot her a look that made it clear she didn't consider this a joking matter.

Truthfully, Emma had put off filling out applications, but the Mountain Ridge job would be done soon, and she'd promised herself—and Grandma Bev—that she was going to move forward with her career.

That was before things happened with Cam, though, which was why she'd started daydreaming about him after she'd reached the end of the application instead of actually sending it.

But she didn't dare say that, or she'd be accused of turning into her mother, and neither one of them wanted that. So she picked up her laptop and swiveled the screen to face Grandma. "I was just applying to this firm in Casper, actually. The city's currently experiencing an influx in their population, which means they have a need for more housing, and I figured it'd be the best place to start."

A mix of apprehension and guilt rose up at the thought of taking a job in Casper, because now there was more to it than leaving Grandma behind.

There's no harm in filling it out. And it's only a little over an hour's drive from here, which isn't bad.

Before she could change her mind, she hit send and promised herself she'd fill out another one tomorrow night.

Chapter Seventeen

With the weatherman promising lots of blue skies this weekend, Cam's thoughts turned to the mountains. The last trip with Emma and Zoey had been the opposite of the experience he'd envisioned, but even though he hadn't returned with a single fish to show for his efforts—thanks to Zoey's love of throwing rocks—he'd had a blast.

Now he had another kind of trip in mind, more along the lines of a major hike to a lake farther up with an overnight stay, and he was wondering how likely it'd be to convince Emma to leave Zoey with Quinn and Heath so she could go with him.

Admittedly, the thought of it made him a bit nervous, but he also knew that Heath would be touring with his band soon—not to mention how busy they'd all be once Mountain Ridge officially opened—and if Cam didn't take a chance on some alone time with Emma while he could, he'd regret it.

Quinn approached, waving a flyer in the air. "There's this big sale, and they have a used four-wheeler. You and Heath mentioned it'd be nice to have one, but I'm starting to stress about how much money we've already sunk into the place. Then again, if we can get it cheaper now…"

Cam took the flyer. "Did you show it to Heath?"

"He left last night—Dixie Rush has that show in Casper, remember?"

Crap. He hadn't remembered. "When will he be back?"

"Tomorrow night," Quinn said. "The big tour's not for another month."

Cam glanced at the details of the four-wheeler, but it wasn't sinking in. His thoughts were still too busy turning over his plan. "Hey, if I asked you and Heath to watch Zoey on Saturday, all the way through Sunday afternoon, how scared would you be?"

"Not scared at all," Quinn said with a laugh. "I'm guessing you and Emma need a little alone time." She nudged him with her elbow.

Cam shook his head. "I have a feeling you already know way too much about me and Emma."

"Girls talk."

"So, do you think she'd be interested in an overnight trip? And I'm not saying that anything has to happen. I'm just saying…" He rubbed the back of his neck. "Never mind. Let's pretend this conversation never happened." He lifted the flyer and studied the many vehicles. "I think that we can wait. Did you balance that ledger thing?"

"No. Just because I'm the Asian one doesn't mean that I'm going to do all the math." She crossed her arms.

"I wasn't saying—"

Quinn laughed and shoved his arm. "You're too easy! I'm just busting your balls." She took the flyer from him. "I'm working on it, but I got caught up organizing the kitchen and trying out recipes. Emma and I are about to have a meeting about rates and that kind of thing, though."

She took a few steps away and then spun around. "And

Cam?"

He braced himself for whatever his future sister-in-law was going to say, although with her, bracing did little good when it came to what popped out of her mouth.

"Yes, we'll watch Zoey, and yes, I think Emma will be happy to take an overnight trip with you. In fact, I think you both could use a break from everything."

Cam expelled a deep breath, excitement that the trip he'd envisioned with Emma might actually happen rising up and taking hold. "Thanks."

"Yep. Can't wait to hear *all* the sordid details," Quinn said, then she laughed, and Cam shook his head, the little bit of relief he'd felt flying right out the window.

• • •

"How's it working with Pete now?" Quinn asked Emma as they sat at the large table in the main room of the lodge for coffee and their meeting.

He'd had a work emergency in Salt Lake City, and then he'd called Mr. Strickland to say he had to deal with meetings and couldn't make it back to Mountain Ridge for a few weeks. At first Emma had worried that he'd been avoiding her after she'd politely declined his date offer, regardless of his claim that he understood about her and Cam.

"Fine. He came in this morning and we just went on as usual. I'm the queen of awkward, too, so I'm pleasantly surprised that it hasn't changed anything. Actually, he showed me pictures of a property his company had just acquired. They're planning on renovating a ski resort in Park City, Utah, and he wanted to get my input on a few of the ideas he had for the place."

She couldn't help but beam at the compliment, but she knew Quinn would get it—after all, Quinn's determination to change her career had landed her Mountain Ridge. And Heath, actually.

"Well, if I were him, I'd want your input, too," Quinn said. "I never could've made it through this construction phase without you. And I can't thank you enough for taking a look at our books."

Quinn turned the laptop toward Emma. "I'm trying to see where I can cut down some overhead, but I also want us to have a reputation as the perfect place to escape. Not the place where there aren't any amenities and we price gouge people."

Emma pulled up a search window and typed in "Wyoming Resorts" so she could get a feel for what other places were doing before she gave her opinion.

An hour later, she and Quinn were still sorting through figures and debating the finer points of what all Mountain Ridge would offer guests.

"I really think you should cut lunch," Emma said. "At least until you see how profitable breakfast and dinner are. Lunch is usually the meal where people will be out and about anyway, either in the mountains or checking out the town, and the cabins have the stoves and all the dishes and pans—people can make their own lunches. And look how much it'll save you…"

Emma plugged the numbers into the Excel worksheet she had open, since Quinn didn't have an adding machine—or QuickBooks for that matter, although Emma told her she would need both, no question. Then she hit enter and watched the cell for the grand total.

"Whoa," Quinn said, pointing at the figure. "Seriously? We'll cut that much?"

Emma nodded.

"Lunch is getting the ax, then." Quinn leaned over and hugged her. "Thank you, thank you, thank you."

A quick glance at the time and Emma realized why she

was so hungry. "Speaking of lunch, I need food."

"Oh, hold up one sec." Quinn turned to her, but then her phone rang. "Sorry. It's Patsy Higgins. So hold up a few more secs—I don't dare let her go to voicemail."

"I get it," Emma said. But when the conversation looked like it'd take a while, Emma slipped outside to grab her lunch. The rest of the crew had obviously already eaten, and she didn't see Cam, so she headed back inside.

The second Quinn hung up, she let loose a squeal. "Oh my gosh! I just got the best news! A pipe burst and it flooded the park!"

Emma drew her eyebrows together. "I never took you for someone who'd take joy in damaged parks."

Quinn grimaced. "Yeah, that came out wrong. It's super bad news in some ways—the town's going to need to dig up the pipe and replace it, and despite Patsy Higgins's best attempts to"—she made air quotes—"'hasten the process,' they won't have it done in time for the picnic auction."

Now Emma understood the excitement, because although she loved the park and the entertainment it provided for Zoey, she experienced a major thrill over the thought of not having to deal with making a basket. "Thank goodness. I was totally dreading that stupid auction."

Quinn frowned. "No, that's not the good part—the auction is still happening. But instead of the park, it's happening here!" A grin spread across her face. "It'll be a great opportunity to show off what we've done and get buzz going. It's perfect."

Emma's happiness faded, and she groaned. Then she sat up straighter. "Wait. You'll probably need my help making sure things run smoothly behind the scenes, which will make me way too busy to deal with bringing a basket, right?"

"Wrong. Do you honestly think I'd risk Patsy Higgins's anger? I'm making a damn basket, you're making one— hell, even Sadie's taking one. Haven't you heard? Until we officially tie the knot, like so many other people have done this past year, it's up to us to shoulder this fund-raiser."

"Oh, I heard." Emma ran a hand through her hair and then slowly pushed away from the table. "I guess I'd better go get to work so that the property is perfect before the picnic."

"Before you go, though, I do have some good news."

Emma narrowed her eyes. "After your last declaration about good news, I no longer trust your definition of it."

Quinn laughed. "Okay, I might deserve that. But you and Cam deserve a long weekend away. This morning he asked me if Heath and I would watch Zoey so you two could go on an overnight camping trip." She waggled her eyebrows.

"That's so nice, but having Zoey overnight is a lot different from a few hours. I've never left her overnight before, either."

"I realize that. But we're loving being Uncle Heath and Aunt Quinn, and getting to know Zoey better. Plus, if I really need it, Sadie and Caroline are down the road. Caroline, who not only raised Royce, but takes care of troubled teens at Second Chance Ranch. I have your grandma's number, too. Between all of us, we can definitely handle watching her for a couple days. And more than that, I owe you for today, and for the picnic, not to mention you're my friend. We can do it, I swear." Quinn stood and grabbed Emma's hand. "Just let us do this for you."

The thought of leaving her daughter wasn't easy, but alone time with Cam? The fact that he'd gone to the effort to make arrangements for an overnight camping trip sent hope tumbling through her. So she nodded. "Okay. Thank you."

"Don't thank me," Quinn said. "Thank the guy who wants to take you camping."

"Oh, I plan to," Emma said, and then she felt heat settle into her cheeks. A hint of nervousness crept in as she thought about all that time with Cam. And a night alone in a tent. But she was tired of being scared, and she didn't want to hold back anymore.

She wanted to explore this thing between them so she'd know if she could take it into account as she started making plans for the future.

Chapter Eighteen

Emma welcomed the burn in her legs and lungs, even though it made her feel completely out of shape. When they'd taken Zoey fishing, they'd driven most of the way and then made the short mile and a half hike to the reservoir. But Cam said he wanted to take her to Blue Lake, which she'd never been to before. It was higher and deeper into the mountain range, and you could only get there by foot. She'd always felt like she knew the hills fairly well, so adventuring to a spot she'd never been made a swirl of excitement go through her, and she used that anticipation to help her push past the tired muscles.

Well, that and Cam, because watching his powerful legs eat up the distance with ease was quite the sight, one she could fully get behind. He glanced back at her. "Sorry. Am I going too fast?"

"No. I'm…" Her lack of oxygen chose that moment to show itself, and a stitch lanced her side. She bent over, hands braced on her knees. "Okay, maybe a little too fast. I'm not in as good shape as I used to be."

"Your shape looks just fine to me," he said, flashing her a

smile that was fairly perky for so early in the morning.

She studied his face, looking to see if he was simply being nice or if there was more. She worried that she wanted there to be more so badly that she might see it even if it wasn't there.

After Quinn had convinced her to let them take care of Zoey overnight, her friend worried aloud that maybe Cam had wanted to surprise her and she'd gone and opened her big mouth and blown it. Honestly, Emma had needed the advance warning to calm her concerns over the idea of leaving her daughter overnight. But she promised she'd let Cam bring it up.

When he did ask her, though, he didn't call it a getaway, or even a date. He'd said he needed to test out the harder trail for tours.

Still, he could've gone with his brother, and instead, he'd asked her. That had to mean something.

Cam extended a water bottle to her, and she unscrewed the lid and took a large drink. A couple more breaths and the cramp in her side eased up enough that she could straighten. "Okay. I'm good."

"Let's just sit for a while."

"Really, I'm fi—"

"I know. But I need a break." Cam grabbed her hand and tugged her over to a large log. They sat down on it, the sounds of birds and rustling leaves in the breeze the only thing filling the air. This was why she used to crave heading to the hills. Peace and quiet—something she didn't experience much with a two-year-old.

Of course now she missed her two-year-old's constant chatter, even as she was excited to have a minibreak. Worry rose up, too. She pulled out her phone, looking at the weak signal.

"I've got the satellite phone in case of emergency," Cam said, patting his backpack. "But Heath and Quinn will take good care of Zoey. I bet she's chasing Trigger around and getting into mud puddles as we speak."

Emma laughed. "I'm sure she is. I can't help but worry, though."

"I know. I do, too. But I'm glad you're doing this with me." He patted her leg, and she tried to let the *with me* part reassure her. "It's been a long time since I went this far into the hills, and I swear, the air, the water…everything's different up here."

Emma took a deep breath of the air. That she could agree with. She wished, just once, he'd let her see a bit more inside his head and what he was thinking, especially when it came to their relationship.

What if he still doesn't completely trust me? There was a difference between forgiveness and forgetting, after all. And if that were the case…you couldn't have a relationship without trust. Not a solid one.

He'd also made it clear that he didn't want to make plans, and she didn't want to come across as pushy—she was sure that was about as desirable as boring.

But she told herself that it'd been a month and a half, and while he might not want to make plans, she couldn't not make some—not with her current project wrapping up, and pressing decisions about the future getting closer by the day.

So once they'd had a rejuvenating day and had settled into camp for the night, she'd take some initiative and ask him where they stood. Maybe she'd even be so bold as to tell him that she cared about him, and she was glad they'd had this time to get to know each other—she could do that much, at least.

Maybe that made her serious and a planner type, but look where she was, and what she was doing. Did boring girls traipse into the woods looking for adventure?

No, they did not.

Cam stood and extended his hand. "Ready?"

She slapped her hand in his, and he pulled her to her feet. "Ready."

Instead of turning to head up the trail like she thought he would do, he lowered his lips to hers. She wrapped her arms around him, getting blocked by his massive backpack for a moment before settling for holding onto the sides of his waist.

He still kissed her a little too carefully, so she decided to see what'd happen if she pushed it further, even as nervous butterflies swarmed her stomach, mixing in with the happy, twitterpated ones. She slid her tongue inside and rolled it over his, releasing the moan that she'd held back.

Apparently it set *something* off inside him, because he drove his fingers through her hair, cupped the back of her head, and deepened the kiss. His other arm came around her waist, and he molded her tightly to him as he stroked her tongue with his, kissing her long enough to make the world around them spin.

When they broke the kiss, she gripped his arms, needing a moment to steady herself. *Whoa. There were the fireworks I was hoping for.*

Cam rested his forehead against hers. "You keep kissing me like that, woman, and I'll be tempted to pitch the tent right here and forget the lake."

She bit back a smile. "But how would you demonstrate your fishing skills? After last weekend, I'm still not sure you have any."

His mouth dropped. "I had a two-year-old sabotaging my attempts."

"Sure," she said, laughing. "Blame it on the two-year-old, not the fact that you were using the wrong bait."

"You think your bait is better than mine?"

She nodded.

"That's it." He kissed her hard on the mouth, then took her hand and started up the trail. "Once we get there, it's on.

Whoever catches more fish owes the other…" He glanced at her, his eyebrows ticking together. Then mischief flickered in his eyes, and she wondered if she'd bitten off more than she could chew. "A striptease."

Emma could feel the heat rising to her face. "Trust me, you don't want a striptease from me."

"That's where you're wrong," he said, his husky voice echoing through her and putting her hormones on high alert. "But if you're too scared…"

This is the passion I wanted—now it's time to grab it by the horns and own it. "When *I* win, I expect dance moves with the stripping. Just so you know."

He laughed, and they took off at a quick pace again, with her having to take two steps for every one of his strides. But now she had a new goal: she was going to catch as many fish as possible, because there was no way she was going to have to stand in front of Cam Brantley and do a striptease. Watching him strip, on the other hand…

She nearly tripped on the gnarled roots of a tree when she thought of all the muscles hiding under his clothes.

But once she recovered her balance, her goal remained the same: win at all costs and receive a show she was sure she'd never forget.

. . .

Cam was so used to long treks that he kept forgetting that Emma hadn't spent the last several years marching here to march there to march somewhere else.

Besides, he needed to save his energy for fishing. Not that it took a lot of energy, but suddenly he had a whole lot of extra motivation to catch as many fish as he could. He'd been trying to honor Emma's request to take things slow, but that kiss had made it hard to think about anything besides having her tight little body under his again.

His mind started replaying blips from their night all those years ago—Emma running her fingers across his torso until he'd been about to explode, her short skirt and dragging his hands up her thighs, crawling over her as he laid her down on the bench seat of his truck and kissed her neck. She'd made such sexy noises, too, and she'd been the one that'd reached for the button of his jeans.

Tree branches scraped his shoulders and cheek, and he wondered when he'd strayed toward the thick group of pine trees—his thoughts were making it hard to keep his concentration on the trail. He shook his head a bit, trying to clear it, because it wouldn't do for them to end up lost. So he forced his gaze ahead, guiding Emma back to the barely there trail.

Blue Lake was one of his favorite places, one that seemed completely untouched by man, and while he missed his little girl, he was glad to finally have some alone time with Emma, without interruption and split attention.

All of his attention was definitely on her now, from the way she kept licking her lips to the color in her cheeks and the determined way she took on the steep trail. Truth was, he probably wouldn't take many people up to this point. There were plenty of other lakes and valleys that'd work for the tours, and some places were sacred.

They took one more break and then made the final climb. When they crested the ridge, where you could look across the bowl-shaped indention with the lake at the bottom, Emma's jaw literally dropped—he'd been studying her, wanting to see her reaction, and it didn't disappoint. Her gaze moved to the waterfall on the other side of the ridge, white water spilling down into the crystal-blue basin that reflected the sky.

"It's…I can't believe I didn't know about this spot." A few strands had spilled out of her ponytail, and the wind toyed with them, swirling them around her face where the sunlight caught them and adding a glowing effect. "It's beautiful."

Cam almost let something horribly cheesy slip and said, "It is," while staring straight at her. He could see she loved it up here, the way he did. She'd surprised him at every turn, and day in and day out, he found his thoughts constantly drifting to her. She was beautiful, too, an effortless kind of beautiful.

She turned the smile on him, and his heart caught—he experienced that familiar tug he often felt around her, only it went deeper this time, down to his very core. "Race you down?" she asked.

"Are you sure you want to lose twice today?"

Two creases formed between her eyebrows.

"The race, and then our bet about who can catch more fish."

Her confusion morphed into a feisty expression that heated his veins. "Oh, it's on, soldier."

Before he could come up with a clever comeback, she was moving down the hill, so fast he worried she'd fall and injure herself, especially with the extra weight of her backpack.

He took off after her, and when it came to balance, she had the advantage. Finally they reached the bottom—he let her win by a couple of steps, because he already felt bad that she was going to lose the fishing bet. Not bad enough to take away the terms—because thoughts of naked Emma were rolling around his head on repeat, and he couldn't wait for the real-life version—but enough he'd decided he would give her the race.

She reached into her pack, retrieved the pieces of her fishing pole, and started to assemble it. "In a few hours, we're going to be hungry, and let's face it, if we wait until nightfall, it'll be a bit chilly for stripteases, so I say we go till noon." She glanced at her watch, and he did the same. That gave them about four hours.

After eating breakfast at six thirty and then their ninety-minute hike, they'd probably be more than ready for lunch by then. Not to mention, fish usually bit better earlier anyway. "Deal. I guess you know this means you're agreeing to strip in daylight."

"Turn that guessing and what you know right back at yourself, buddy."

Of all the things he'd expected for this trip, her competitive streak wasn't one of them. Honestly, he'd hoped there might be more kissing and even a bit of nudity, but he'd planned on playing it by ear and seeing how the rest of their day together went. He knew Emma was more of a nature buff than the other girls he'd dated, but there was still a difference between a leisurely hike and backpacking into a remote location.

There was also a difference between casting a fishing pole and actually catching fish.

As she went to bait her hook, she glanced at him, then turned away, blocking him from seeing what she was using.

Like he was going to copy her—night crawlers were where it was at when it came to this lake, he knew that much. He didn't bother hiding as he baited his hook, pushing the worm into place so that it covered every inch of silver.

They both cast, giving each other a couple of yards' space, and then set their poles.

After a few minutes, Emma said, "So, tell me more about the tours. What all are they going to include?"

"There'll be a few different options. Like a simple fishing trip to the Hope Springs Reservoir, or other lakes with trails that take about thirty minutes to an hour to hike to, like Rock Lake or No Name Lake—"

"Ah, No Name's pretty. I used to go there a lot, especially during times I knew the reservoir would be crowded."

He loved that she knew these hills so well and that he could talk to her about it without her zoning out. "Yeah, and for those who want to avoid crowds and are willing to take more intensive hikes and pack in their supplies so they can stay a night, or even a week, I'll bring them places like here. Once hunting season starts, Heath and I will do some tours that are more tailored to the areas and the type of game."

Talking it all out was actually helping him not feel so overwhelmed—there were a lot of things he, Heath, and Quinn still needed to iron out, but at least the tours were solidly planned. "But if you've got any suggestions, I'm definitely open to them."

"That all sounds good. When it comes to families or people wanting shorter, easier hikes, I'd say give them a lot of time to just be at the destination. Remember, a lot of them won't be used to hiking or the higher altitude…"

"I didn't even think about the altitude difference."

"That's why I make the big bucks," she joked. "Back when I could hike all the time, it was about escaping for a while, without plans or the hectic pace of life getting to me. The only time it didn't work was after I'd found out I was pregnant. Partly because I couldn't stop puking," she added with a laugh.

"That'd put a dent in the fun."

She nodded, and her gaze drifted to a faraway place. "I kept thinking that I'd only ever done one bad thing in all my life, and I was being punished for it." She turned to fully face him. "Not that you were a bad thing—that came out wrong."

"No, I get it. I'm far from the smart choice."

"I wouldn't say that, either. You were the impulsive choice that day, although as you now know, I'd kind of had a…thing for you for a while."

"You never said you had a thing for me. Just that you wanted to date me." He scooted closer and bumped his shoulder into hers. "You had a *thing* for me?"

She wrinkled her nose and brought one hand up to cover

her face. "Yes, okay? I had a huge crush, which was why I was rather...forward that night."

"Hey, I'm not complaining. I'm sorry that you felt like you had to pay for it afterward, though."

"At first I did feel that way—getting pregnant interrupted the plan I had for myself, the one that involved a fancy job in the city. I'd already put off moving in favor of going to the local college and living at home to save money, and I was a little mad that all that cautious living hadn't guaranteed me the future I'd worked so hard for. Once I accepted I needed a new plan—one that involved being a single mom—I had to find a new way to deal with life. The little victories and future possibilities got me through the hardest days."

"Yeah, thinking of doing this adventure tour business with my brother really got me through the last few months I was deployed."

Emma kicked at the grass. "Was it awful over there?"

"Depends on which 'there.' Yeah, a lot of the places I was stationed were pretty awful. But I felt like I was making a difference. It was the times when missions didn't go as planned, or when we'd lose people that made it awful." *Damn it.* He didn't want to get into that.

Emma scooted closer and grabbed his hand.

He charged on before she could ask more. "It made me realize how many things I took for granted, even growing up the way I did."

"With your dad, you mean."

Cam sighed—apparently every subject held a land mine. At least this one was easier to deal with, because he didn't feel like it was his fault, so much as it ended up making him who he was. "I'm glad he seems better, but like I said before, he was hard to live with. He got angry, and he took it out on me a lot. I almost feel guilty telling you about it, because now your life is sort of tied to his, too, and apparently he's worked hard to change. I can tell he's really happy about being a grandpa."

"I get that. But you can talk to me about it. I know all too well how hard it is when you don't have anyone to talk to." She glanced at the end of her pole, then released his hand to reel in the line just a bit before moving next to him again. "What about your mom? I've heard different versions, of course, but I'd rather know the real one."

"It's not like my parents ever got along very well—"

"That's something I can relate to," she said with a mirthless laugh. Then she bit her lip. "Sorry. Didn't mean to interrupt. Just saying I understand what that's like. If that helps."

"It does, actually," he said, lacing his fingers with hers. "Basically, after my dad was in an accident and couldn't work, all he did was drink. They fought even more, and one day she simply yelled that she couldn't take it anymore. She packed her bags and left. She used to call and check in from time to time. I remember this one especially bad night, about two years after she'd left, she called and I begged her to come home. Like, I fully broke down…"

He stopped, inwardly flinching at the admission.

"There's no shame in a little breakdown," Emma said, wrapping her arms around him in a side hug. She tucked her chin on his shoulder, facing him. "Especially when you were just a teenager who was taking on way too much responsibility."

He didn't ask how she knew, because she'd clearly read between the lines. Despite wanting her to see him as the guy who could protect her and Zoey from everything, it was a relief that she knew. That she obviously understood.

"I told her how bad it was with Dad—told her how he'd gotten more violent, too—and she told me that she'd try to come home and talk to him, but until then, I needed to be strong. Then she just never called again."

Emma clenched her jaw. "Wow. I want to say really horrible things about her, but then that feels mean, and she's your mom, but…no mom should put that on her child."

Cam shrugged. "I got over it eventually. Got through life with Dad, then I joined the army. I feel like I did a lot of good there, but it wore on me, and I felt…lost." There. That was a good word for it without having to tell her why. "Once the property came into play, I felt like I had a purpose again."

He looked into Emma's eyes and realized his purpose had grown to include her and Zoey. But instead of adding stress, it made him feel like he was found again.

"I'm glad you have that. And I'm glad that you came back to Hope Springs." She tightened her hold on him, and his heart swelled. "I feel like I've missed out on not knowing you better all these years."

He was about to kiss her, but then she shot forward, yanked back her pole, and started reeling for all she was worth. The fish on her line splashed the surface of the water, sending silver droplets that matched its scales through the air.

Once Emma had reeled it in, she held it up proudly and looked at his deadly still pole. "One to zip. If you wanna go ahead and admit defeat now, I'll accept your surrender."

Cam pulled Emma to him and kissed her, drawing it out the way he had earlier. He dropped his fingertips to her collarbone and swept them across her skin, grinning when she practically melted against him. "The only one who's going to be surrendering at noon is you—you'll have to surrender your clothes, and I'll be the one to say when you get them back, so you'd better be nice. Now, if you'll excuse me…"

He reluctantly let her go and reached for his fishing pole. "I've got to go to my secret spot and amp up my game." He turned and gave her his best gentlemanly nod. "Until noon."

"Until noon," she echoed, and then she whistled at him as he walked away, making it hard to not turn around, scoop her into his arms, and kiss her until she forgot that they were in the middle of a competition.

Chapter Nineteen

Emma glanced from the end of her pole, to her watch, to the water, to Cam on the other side of the lake, back to her watch.

In eight minutes, the clock would strike twelve noon, and she wasn't sure how many fish Cam had caught. She'd seen at least two, but he'd disappeared into a heavily wooded area and she'd switched spots so that he couldn't spy on her, either. She'd caught one more since the first, and she really wanted to snag another. They'd made the bet in good fun, and she'd happily played along, but with the time ticking down and a measly two fish, her stomach decided to betray her and tie itself in knots.

Striptease? In front of Cam? She'd seen those arms, felt the firm muscles of his torso pressed against her not-so-firm muscles. He was the last guy who'd seen her naked, and since she'd had a baby since then, she couldn't help thinking it was better for the past naked version of herself to remain frozen in his memory.

Of course, that'd mean he'd never see her naked again, and that option was a bit depressing, too, as she hoped they'd get to that part in the relationship—sooner than later, to be honest. But there was a difference between dimmed lighting and strategically placed lingerie or covers, and the sun freaking shining down like a spotlight.

Ugh, why did I agree to this stupid bet?

Six minutes and counting…

Emma slowly reeled in her line, hoping that the movement would catch a fish's eye. Couldn't one of them hook a sister up? Even if she was sort of setting them up for a night in the frying pan? Hadn't they heard of taking one for the team? Sacrificing for the greater good?

At least I wore my nice underwear, just in case… She'd felt stupid putting them on, because they were hardly good for hiking—the lacy panties had drifted up the entire way, giving her a perma-wedgie. A sports bra would've been nice for the jolting race down the hill, too, but if the evening turned romantic, she didn't want to risk unflattering uniboob.

Four minutes…

Now she was glad for the silly extravagance, even if she was also wishing she'd taken one of those strip aerobics classes that the quilting ladies swore by. When she'd balked, they'd looked at her like *she* was the ridiculous one for not learning how to strip, and now she was thinking they were right.

Her ex was right.

Everyone but her was right.

The end of her pole dipped toward the water, the jerk nearly pulling it out of her hands. She let out a squeal and fought with the fish, her heart hammering against her rib cage at three times its normal speed.

Emma attempted a calming breath, one in, and then right back out. Cam would be the one stripping, just as soon as she snagged this stubborn fish.

The line slackened, and for a couple of panicked seconds she thought she'd lost the battle. Finally she sucked it up and jerked her pole back, even though she was scared it'd only confirm her suspicions.

Instead, the fish picked up its fight.

The muscles in her arms strained as she reeled as fast as she could, keeping the line tight, and then the fish broke the surface and she swung it onto the bank. Out of the corner of her eye, she noticed Cam making his way over. She unhooked her prize, set it next to the other two fish, and then quickly covered them and straightened in an attempt to look all calm and collected.

Cam rounded a huge sagebrush, and calm and collected flew right out the window as she took him in. There was something about the mountain background that brought out his rugged features even more, from the strong square jaw to the scruff covering it to just…him. She'd never thought she'd be so turned on by muddy pant legs and a baseball cap that looked like it'd been to hell and back.

And before their bet got pulled into it and things became more awesome or super awkward, she decided to at least complete a semibold move. She took a large step forward, ran her palm down the side of his face, and planted a kiss on his lips.

A grin spread across the rugged features she'd been admiring, and he wrapped one arm around her waist. "Just so you know, you touch the beard, I touch your butt."

Flashing him a saucy smile, she reached up and ran her hand down it again, dragging out the gesture before brushing her fingertips across his jaw.

He kept his promise, one hand lowering to the curve of her butt. Using the solid grip, he hauled her against him and kissed her again. Then he whispered, "If this is your attempt at getting out of stripping for me, it's a good try and all, but a bet's a bet."

With a laugh, she backed up and put her hands on her

hips. "Well, then. Let's see 'em."

"One fish," he said, lifting it out of his cooler bag, and then he slowly brought out another one.

"Two fish, red fish, blue fish," she finished, even though he was only holding two rainbow trout so far. When he cocked an eyebrow—Cam, not the fish—she shrugged. "Hazards of reading Dr. Seuss over and over. *And over.* Before Zoey's *Frozen* phase, she made me read that and *Ten Little Monkeys* until I had every word memorized. So if you pull out any monkeys, I'll start quoting that book, too—you've been warned."

Cam chuckled. "Monkeys in Wyoming. That'd be quite a trick."

"Yes, and I'm sure Zoey would beg us to let her keep it as a pet, and let's face it, neither one of us could probably hold up to those big blue eyes."

"Too true. Then we'd all get monkey pox."

"Wow, that went dark quickly," Emma said with a laugh. "Apparently you haven't been reading enough Dr. Seuss."

Cam shook his head, then he shot her a look. "I think someone's delaying the inevitable."

She innocently batted her eyes. Let him think he'd won. Just when she was about to reach for her fish to show him she'd upped him by one, he pulled out another, also a rainbow trout, but big enough that the other two could fit inside it.

"Whoa! That's huge!"

A proud grin stretched Cam's lips. "Ready to admit defeat?"

"Pretty cocky for a guy who only caught three fish," she said, working to put every ounce of confidence she had into her voice. "But unfortunately for you, it's not good enough to beat me."

His grin slid off his face. "Well, this one is so big, it should count as two."

Emma crossed her arms. "Size doesn't matter."

Cam clucked his tongue. "Oh, I think we both know that's not true."

Biting back the urge to smile or to gasp and act scandalized at that, she lifted her chin and kept hold of her poker face. "A bet's a bet. Let's see your dance, soldier. I can't wait to see your moves."

He set down his fish, and two different kinds of flutters went through her stomach. The first because she'd pulled off the implication that she'd beat him, followed quickly by the second one, because she was about to get a show.

Cam reached for the hem of his shirt, but then his eyes narrowed on her. She swallowed and worked to keep her features in the calm mask. "Wait," he said. "Let's see 'em."

Don't crack now, she told herself, even as her blood pressure started to steadily rise. "See what?"

He strode toward her, and she automatically backed up, nearly stepping on her covered fish. Her *three* fish.

Cam reached down to uncover them, and she tried to block him, but he wrapped an arm around her and held her out of reach. "Emma Walker, you liar!"

"I never actually said that I had caught more than you. Just that you hadn't beaten me and that I wanted to see you dance."

He shook his head and curled her to him. "For that, I definitely win."

"No, it's a tie. I guess neither of us has to strip."

"Wrong." The deep timbre of his voice sent a swirl of desire through her, even as she fought the urge to run. He glanced toward the lake. "It's a nice day for a swim, don't you think?"

She was afraid to commit either way.

He let her go, backed up a few steps, and then grabbed his shirt by the back of the collar and stripped it off, right over the top of his head in one smooth motion. Rendered speechless, as well as motionless, all she could do was stare at the muscles. They'd had the same effect on her years ago—that night, the sight of them had caused her to be completely reckless, and she felt that same pull now.

Only she wasn't going to be the kind of reckless that left her pregnant—she'd learned that lesson.

"What are you doing just standing there?" he asked. "Tie means we both lose…and we both win. If you strip and jump in the lake with me, I'll settle for swimming instead of dancing."

She stared some more, like that'd change anything. Well, and because it was hard to look away. But again, he had all *that* going on, and she'd given up gym time for running after a toddler. It didn't burn nearly as many calories as it should, and add the countless boxes of mac and cheese…

"Need help?"

Digging deep, she tried to find the fearlessness she wished she had—tried to find the forward girl he'd slept with all those years ago. Faking confidence she hoped would come along for the ride once she made the first move, she slowly peeled her shirt off, two-handed, because only guys could pull off the overhead drag.

Cam's gaze ran down her, and his Adam's apple slowly bobbed up and down. "Damn," he whispered, and the way he looked at her shoved her insecurities to the background.

And with real, genuine confidence rising up, it suddenly wasn't so hard to undo the button on her jeans. Or slide them off her hips as seductively as she could, keeping her gaze locked on Cam's the entire time.

• • •

Now down to only his boxers, Cam was the one staring. His

mouth had gone dry some time ago, his thirst for Emma growing stronger by the second. She was quite the sight standing there in nothing but her sexy underwear, the sunlight dancing across her tempting curves and all that soft skin, the beautiful scenery surrounding them paling in comparison.

He extended a hand toward her, grinning at her when she took it.

They walked over to a large rock he decided would provide a perfect platform for diving, and then he helped her up the grooved, warm surface. Maybe he didn't need to steady her quite as much as he did as they climbed, but the excuse to touch her soft skin was more temptation than he could handle.

A bit of her boldness seemed to be wearing off as she glanced into the blue depths of the lake.

"I got you," he said, squeezing her hand tighter.

She sucked in a breath, her chest rising and falling, and he lifted her hand to his lips and kissed the back of it. *How'd I get so lucky?*

This trip was turning into everything he'd wanted it to be and more, and he found himself doing the one thing he'd sworn he didn't want to do: he started making plans. Plans that involved Emma by his side, hiking, camping, and challenging each other in the best possible way.

Because he'd also wanted to feel like he'd started living again, and standing up on this rock, her hand in his, he'd never felt more alive.

He worried he was getting carried away again, but for the first time in a long time—strike that. For the first time *ever*, he wanted to get carried away. Simply jump, no holding back.

She glanced at him, and judging from her anxious expression, she was going to bolt. But then she blinked, resolve set in, and she said, "On three?"

He gave one sharp nod. "On three."

As he counted down, she gripped his hand tighter, and he gripped it right back. Then they were soaring through the air, the water coming fast, and she yelled, but it was more of an excited squeal than a shout of fear.

The icy water shocked his system even more awake, and he kicked toward the surface. Emma bobbed up seconds later with a gasp, and then she broke into laughter.

"Oh my gosh, it's cold." She slapped the water, sending a spray right at his face. "This is all your fault."

He swam closer. "I think this was generous of me. My giant fish beat your puny three any day."

She shook her head, but a smile broke free. When he circled his arms around her, she reached up and ran her hand down his face again, and he took that as a sign that her butt was fair game.

He moved his hands lower and pressed her closer. "I warned you."

"Do I look scared?" she asked.

He studied her face for a moment, taking in every feature and the droplets of water clinging to her eyelashes. Then he lowered his lips to hers. Keeping them both afloat became more challenging, so he kept the kiss short, despite how amazing her body felt against his.

They swam around for a while, eventually becoming numb to the cold, but then hunger replaced all other emotions. So they swam to shore, where they dried off the best they could and, shame that it was, put on their clothes.

Cam quickly went to work building a fire, and by the time he was done, Emma had cleaned the fish, seasoned them, and wrapped them in foil. Only proving again that she made the perfect person to bring with him on these kinds of trips.

He thought about how the past six weeks had been some of the best of his life. Once he'd gotten over the shock and started to embrace being a dad, he was surprised at how much he enjoyed it. They had a great kid, they had fun together…

He'd always thought that "other half" stuff was crap, but he could almost see it. In a way, he was a fuller person when Emma was by his side. Thinking about that and what it might mean sent a thread of panic through him, because he wasn't sure he was ready for everything that'd come along with it, and there was a big difference between making plans and taking giant leaps.

So he shoved those serious thoughts aside and told himself to live in the moment and just enjoy being here with her.

After their late lunch, Emma asked to use the satellite phone to check in on Zoey. After Quinn reported that she was happy and well—she'd jumped on every bed in the B and B, and Trigger apparently provided her with endless hours of entertainment—they set up camp, then kicked back in their canvas chairs. They talked and laughed, and basically pretended that they didn't have a single worry or care in the world.

Before long, Emma's nose was in a book, her legs draped over his. He busied himself tracing lines across her thighs as he halfway dozed, every muscle in his body completely relaxed.

"Cam?"

He lifted his head and peered into her big brown eyes. "Yeah?"

"Thank you for bringing me."

"I'd rather be here with you than anyone else," he said. And more than that, he meant it.

· · ·

Today had been a series of bold moves, and Emma figured it was time to make one more. She unzipped the tent and stepped inside, fully aware that she smelled like lake water and smoke.

Fortunately for her, she kind of loved both of those scents.

She also loved the way the guy who came in right after her kept brushing his hand across her shoulder, her waist, her back… They'd touched more than not this afternoon, and she was quickly becoming addicted to his caresses, his smiles, and his laugh. Man, she loved his laugh. And the way he always checked on her. And basically everything about him.

After a firelight dinner, followed by enough s'mores to feed a small army, they'd snuffed out the fire and stumbled toward the tent with only the light of the moon to guide them, even though they had flashlights, just in case.

As she thought about the new territory she hoped they were headed toward, drunken butterflies swirled through her gut.

Well, the territory wasn't exactly new, but last time they'd been under the influence, and tonight the only influence they were under was chocolate and a starlit sky. While her nerves could use a drink or two, she wanted to remember every detail of this night with perfect clarity.

Since standing wasn't possible for her—and definitely not for Cam—she dropped to her knees on the sleeping bag, and Cam lowered himself next to her.

"Hey," he said, even though they'd been talking for hours.

"Hey," she whispered.

For a moment, they stared at each other, then she threw her arms around him and kissed him, putting everything she had into it.

He gripped her hips and pulled her onto his lap so that she was straddling him, and then he swept his tongue inside to meet hers, taking control of the kiss. Today's kisses had been far from sweet, and this one bordered on downright indecent…in the best possible way.

It gave her the boost she needed to reach for the bottom

of his shirt. As soon as she stripped him of it, his lips moved to her neck and a pleasant shiver traveled down her spine.

Between kisses, he peeled off her shirt, and then they lost clothes a layer at a time. When they were down to just their underwear, Cam laid her back on her sleeping bag.

"You're beautiful, you know that?"

His words warmed her from the inside out, even as she fought the urge to deny it.

"You are," he said, and his fingertips drifted down the center of her body, over her belly button, right to the waistline of her panties, where he dragged his finger back and forth, causing an intoxicating mix of anticipation and desire. "And if you want to stop here for tonight, we can. Just tell me what you want."

"I don't want to stop," she whispered, pushing up onto her elbows. "But it's, uh, been a while. Like, since you and I…"

He cupped her cheek. "I promise it'll be better than that time."

"From what I remember, that time was pretty dang good."

He chuckled and traced her lower lip with his thumb, sending her desire into need-right-now territory. "Yes, yes, it was. But still, this is going to be better. Because we're going to remember everything."

She couldn't help laughing at that.

But then he crawled over her, his weight pressing into her, and the passion in his eyes made her breath catch in her throat. Several times in the past few years, she'd daydreamed that one day a guy would come into her life and sweep her off her feet. She never expected this guy, and she certainly hadn't thought she'd land a guy who looked like Cam.

Then again, she wasn't sure she'd landed him—she pushed that thought aside, not wanting to question this night. Maybe her one reckless night had ended with her pregnant and alone, but she liked the middle ground she'd found with

Cam. He brought out her adventurous side, and he was an adventure she wanted to enjoy for as long as she could.

She raised her mouth to his, and he kissed her, thrusting his tongue into her mouth, leaving sweet far behind. She arched her body, wanting more, needing more. He'd said to tell him what she wanted, so she opened her mouth and did just that.

"I want this," she whispered. "I want you."

Cam covered her body with his, his weight, his kiss making it feel like the ground had fallen out from under her. And in the very moment she thought that this night couldn't get any better, he moved his lips right next to her ear and said, "I want you, too."

Chapter Twenty

Emma snuggled in deeper as the early morning air tried to penetrate the cozy warmth of the tent and her and Cam's shared sleeping bag. Every place her body touched his was nice and toasty. The back half of her, kept warm only by the sleeping bag, was jealous of the front half. As it should be.

Emma's eyelids fluttered open, and she couldn't help taking a moment to study Cam's peaceful face. The second she moved, though, he shot up and looked around, his eyes frantic and his hands searching for something.

Then he seemed to notice he wasn't…her guess was in a military camp, and his muscles relaxed.

"Sorry," she said. "I didn't mean to wake you."

He glanced down at her, and a slow smile spread across his face. He leaned over her, kissed her squarely on the mouth, and then rolled, pulling her on top of him. "If one has to wake up, this is definitely the way to do it."

She giggled and nestled closer. The mountains came alive, though, little creatures making noises, the rising sun making the east side of their tent glow. Even the rush of the waterfall

seemed to grow louder, telling them it was time to wake up
and start the day.

"Breakfast?" Cam asked.

Emma nodded. "And coffee."

They scrambled to find their clothes, dressing quickly to
fight the chill of the cool morning air. Cam tossed her his thick
flannel jacket.

"Don't you need this?" she asked.

He pulled a flannel button-down over his white T-shirt.
"I've got this. It's all I'll need—I brought the coat just in case
an unexpected storm rolled in."

"Double flannel might be too much for me to take in on
you anyway. You already look like a lumberjack right now,
and I've gotta say, I kind of want to watch you chop down a
tree."

He let out a soft laugh and then pulled her close and
kissed her. "You'll have to settle for gathering wood this trip,
since I left my ax at home, but I'll make a note to wear flannel
more often."

She slipped his jacket over her hoodie, the warmth
immediately soaking into her—the tingly flashes of heat
brought on by being with Cam first thing in the morning
helped quite a bit, too. He unzipped the tent, extended his
hand, and they stepped into the cool morning air together.

The beauty of the mountains hit her all over again. From
the sea of green trees to the blue-gray rock the rushing white
water of the waterfall cut across like a ribbon to the orange
rays of the sun shooting out over the ridge they'd climbed
down yesterday.

Smoke filled the air as Cam lit the fire, mixing with the
dewy-and-pine-fresh scent. While they waited for the pot of
water to boil, he pulled her in front of him, wrapped his arms
around her, and tucked his chin on the top of her head.

She gripped his wrist, wanting to hold on to him, to this

perfect moment. They stood and enjoyed the view as birds chirped overhead. It was one of those scenes that almost seemed like a picture, because it was too amazing to be real.

But it *was* real, and that made it better than any daydream she'd ever had. She relaxed further into his embrace, twisting her head so that she could plant a kiss on Cam's sexy lips. Then she returned her gaze to the view, smiling when he nuzzled her neck.

"I didn't realize just how much I missed the chance to truly get away," she said. "Worries, cares…they all seem so far away. It makes me feel a little guilty, but I'm not in a big hurry to rush back to reality."

"You deserve a break. Especially after all you've had on your plate the past few years."

She also knew that going back meant complications. It meant the town watching and adding their unsolicited opinions, the inevitable meeting she'd put off between Cam and her overly opinionated grandma, being interrupted by their little blond angel, and dealing with bills and all those things that made being an adult less fun than you imagined it'd be when you were a kid. "Let's just move up here. Live in a tent the rest of our lives. We'll need a fence to keep Zoey out of the water, of course."

Cam laughed. "You think that'll contain her?"

"For a day or two, at least. Then she'll learn how to climb it, and we'll never get a moment's rest again." She shook her head and sighed. "Okay, so maybe I didn't totally think this through."

Cam tightened his arms around her, and his whiskered cheek brushed the side of her face as he nipped at her ear. "We'll escape as often as we can between tours and crazy schedules."

She knew they were talking in dream scenarios, but she hoped that meant he was growing as attached to her as she was to him. "Deal."

They sealed it with a kiss and then attended to the coffeepot and breakfast, shedding layers as the sun rose higher in the sky.

Once they finished eating, Cam stood and stretched, a few inches of his toned abdomen showing and giving her flashes of last night. His smile said he'd caught her looking.

"Want to hike out by the waterfall?" he asked. "It's a bit steeper, but the view's amazing, and then we could circle around until we meet up with the trail. It'll take about an extra thirty, maybe forty minutes."

"Sounds like an adventure." See? Totally down with steep trails by waterfalls, skinny-dipping, and sex in a tent. All things that weren't anywhere close to boring. Even better than that, something had definitely changed between her and Cam last night. It had been as amazing as their first night together, but the connection was deeper, more emotion behind every kiss, every touch.

Add in this morning, waking up together and the way he'd held her in his arms, and she was dangerously close to falling head over heels in love.

Together they packed up the camp, everything a little more challenging to shove into backpacks after being allowed to spread out and fill with air. Her sleeping bag wouldn't quite go into the small bag it'd arrived in, even after she'd forced out all the air and rolled it as tightly as she could, kneeling on it as she did so.

Cam approached and motioned for her to hand it over. "Let me show you a little trick I learned in the army." He pulled out the sleeping bag, undoing her tight roll, and then he started shoving it in the bag.

"Your trick is shoving?"

"You have to shove and expel the air at the same time. It's practically an art form." He shot her a sidelong glance, and one corner of his mouth kicked up. "Okay, it's just shoving. With a lot of muscle behind it."

She crossed her arms. "What are you saying about my muscles?"

"Have I mentioned how pretty you look this morning?"

Her mouth dropped open, and he laughed. Then he handed her the sleeping bag, all put away in the tiny case it came in, no longer bulging half out.

"You don't talk about the army much," she said, testing the waters, because she felt like he purposely avoided it. Everything he'd told her so far was mostly surface. He'd hinted that his job was intense, but he hadn't come out and said it, and his expression always changed, a shadow of something—sorrow? Regret?—crossing it each time. She didn't want to push or ruin the mood, but she wanted to better know this guy she was falling for.

Cam put on his backpack, and she thought he was going to ignore her attempt at getting him to open up about it, but as they started toward the side of the lake with the waterfall, he said, "I learned a lot of good life skills in the army, and it gave me the stability I'd never had in my life. It gave me a sense of purpose, too, and the men I served with became family…"

He held back a branch so she could pass through a narrow gap without ending up with a face full of pine needles. "Torres, one of the guys I served with the longest, might even come for a visit sometime in the near future. He and I met and were instant friends, so he's heard me talk about Mountain Ridge for years. He emailed and said he wants to go on one of the tours once we open. I'm not sure he will, because it's one of those things you talk about, then life happens, but if he ends up coming, you'll have to meet him."

"Torres?"

"Corporal Jay Torres," Cam clarified. "He went home to

Colorado to propose to his girlfriend. I told him about you, though."

A tangle of tree roots spread out in a web across the trail, and she chose her footing carefully through the maze they made. "You did? How much did you tell him?" In two seconds flat, she'd gone from flattered Cam wanted to introduce her to scared the guy would hate her on principle.

"At first, just that I found out I had a little girl." He glanced at her. "Actually, I also told him that I was having a hard time not thinking about you. A few days ago, he wrote and asked how it was going, and I told him that you and I were dating now. Since a couple of months ago I'd assured him that the *last* thing I wanted was a relationship, he made sure to add a lot of 'I told you so' in his return email."

"That's better than him saying, 'that girl's obviously the worst and you should dump her,' which is what I'd expect after everything I put you through." She didn't love hearing him say the last thing he wanted was a relationship, either, but everything had changed—that's what this trip proved, right?

"We've been over this already," Cam said with a shake of his head. "You had your reasons. Besides, Torres wouldn't say anything like that—he sees the good in everybody. Even me."

Emma slowed her pace and placed her hand on Cam's arm. "That's because you're a good guy. Of course he sees good in you."

All the air seemed to deflate from him, his shoulders and head dropping. "I…I've made mistakes—I told you that before—but I made a really big mistake last mission, and…if it weren't for me, one of my men would be on his way home, too. Instead he's buried in a cemetery. That's why I don't talk much about the army."

The pain in his voice sent a twinge through her chest.

"I lost my temper, and I wasn't on guard like I should've been." He started hiking faster, taking huge strides, his gaze never straying from the trail. "Gunfire erupted, and Jones— one of the soldiers in my squad—didn't make it. For the most part, I've come to terms with it, but sometimes…sometimes I go down the what-if hole, and that's when I feel lost. When I start wondering if I ran away instead of choosing my path, even though Heath and I had the lodge plan for years."

He ducked under the branches of a tree, and she wished she could catch up and see the expression on his face instead of only having a view of his back as he moved farther out of her reach. "Maybe I should've signed on for another two years. But then I'd only doubt my judgment, and that's a good way to get more people killed."

Despite the burning in her legs, she pushed harder and faster. "I can't pretend that I know what it's like to go on the kind of missions you went on, or to lose a guy you obviously cared about…" Her heavy breathing made it hard to put the kind of emphasis behind her words that she wanted to. "But I think you're being too hard on yourself."

He stopped and turned to her. His eyes caught hers, and she wasn't sure what he was looking for, but she hoped he found it. "I lost my temper, Emma. I let the anger blind me for just a few minutes and… I have a short fuse—you should know that about me."

He said it as if she should be scared, almost like a warning. She closed the gap between them, ignoring her tired muscles and lack of oxygen, and gripped the sides of his waist, never breaking eye contact. "Everyone makes mistakes, and a lot of us do it in less hectic situations. We get angry; we lose our cool—it makes us human. What I know about you is that you're a kind, patient person and a good dad. That you make me feel safe and happy, and I trust you completely."

She'd almost added that she was also falling hard for him, but she worried it'd scare more than assure him, and it didn't feel like the right moment. It felt like making it about her, and she didn't want to do that after he'd confessed something that'd obviously been difficult for him to talk about.

A smile seemed worth the risk, though, and she hoped it'd help lighten the mood. "And not to brag, but I'm pretty smart, so you should listen to me."

He cracked a smile, barely there at first, but then it caught fully and spread. She wanted him to have some kind of breakthrough where he agreed with her, but she supposed that was overly optimistic. He hugged her, though, and she hugged him back, wishing she could squeeze him tight enough to put together any broken pieces inside of him that might remain.

After lacing his fingers with hers, he started up the trail again, this time slower so she could keep pace. By the time they reached the waterfall, she was definitely ready for a break.

She snapped a few pictures of the waterfall with her phone, and then she moved the screen so that Cam was in the frame, the spraying droplets catching the sunlight behind him and creating a backdrop that was just as breathtaking as the subject.

"Hey, no pictures," Cam teased, and she stuck her tongue out at him. He grabbed her hand and tugged her to him. Then, like the twitterpated fool she was, she took a picture of their kiss.

When he grunted and batted at the phone, she scolded him, then forced him to pose for a picture where they were both looking at the camera.

Emma swiped her phone screen with the bottom of her shirt, clearing off the water droplets. When she looked up, she caught Cam checking her out, the way she'd done to him this morning. Happiness filled every inch of her, and she felt like she could float—which would be convenient, considering the hike home.

"It's a bit slippery right here," Cam said, extending his

hand and helping her across the wet rocks. Her backpack was bulky and weighed plenty, but Cam had the tent in his, as well as the cast-iron skillet—not that the weight seemed to slow *him* down. If they were going to do this more often, she needed to get in better shape. A couple more trips, though, and she should be a pro.

As soon as they were across the rocks, they stared down at the lake they'd left, and she said a silent good-bye to the spot, hoping they would return, maybe even with Zoey.

It'd make sneaking time in the tent so she and Cam could have a repeat of last night a bit harder, but she was sure they'd find a way to work it out.

Cam draped his arm around her shoulders. "Shall we get back to our little girl?"

Our little girl. She saw days and nights with her, Cam, and Zoey, endless weeks and months of fun with the family she'd always wanted.

Just like that, she surpassed starting to fall for Cam Brantley and headed into free-falling territory.

Yep, Tom Petty was definitely playing through her head, a sure sign that she was not only falling, but also in that deliriously giddy place that she hadn't been in…well, ever.

"Yes. Let's go home."

Chapter Twenty-One

Cam would never get over how amazing it was to have his little girl run toward him like his existence made her day. The rug in the entryway of the B and B slipped under her feet, but it didn't slow her down. "Daddy!"

He bent and scooped Zoey into his arms, planting a kiss on her chubby cheek. "Hey, sweetheart. I'm so happy to see you."

She'd spotted Emma coming through the door right behind him, though, so instead of answering, Zoey made a dive for her mom. He kept his hold, just in case, as Emma kissed Zoey and ran a hand over her blond curls.

"I missed you so much," Emma said, taking their daughter's full weight and hugging her tightly. "Did you have fun?"

With that, Zoey launched into a big story, and he only caught words here and there—something about the puppy and Uncle Heath and Aunt Quinn and ice cream.

Emma turned to Quinn and Heath, who looked a bit more tired than usual. "Thank you so much. I know she can be a handful."

"It was fun," Quinn said. "I mean, I'm totally exhausted, and I have a whole new respect for parents in general, but we had a great time. How was your trip?"

If Cam wasn't mistaken, his soon-to-be sister-in-law added an eyebrow raise in Emma's direction that implied there was more to her question than simply asking about camping.

Emma's blush pretty much gave them away, so he wrapped his arm around her waist and kissed her cheek. "We had an amazing trip."

Emma's eyes locked on his. "We did."

Zoey chose that moment to demand to be let down, and it was clear that from now on, they'd have to steal what moments they could and make the best of them.

"I think I better get my little girl home and take a shower," Emma said.

Cam dropped his backpack in the entryway—and Quinn gave it a stern look. If she thought there wouldn't be hunting backpacks cluttering the entryway when they opened, she was in for a big surprise, but he decided in the name of goodwill, he'd try to keep his crap out of the way. "I'll get it in a few minutes. I just want to walk Emma and Zoey to the car."

"Of course. I don't mind, I just..." Quinn laughed. "Well, I'm still getting used to how much gear it takes for hiking and fishing, and how it's always covered in three layers of dust and mud."

Zoey gave Quinn, Heath, and Trigger hugs good-bye, and Cam took Emma's backpack and shouldered the bag with Zoey's stuff. Then his daughter insisted she wanted him to carry her, too, and he could hardly refuse. He did refuse Emma's attempt to take some of the bags, because while she wouldn't admit it, he could see how exhausted she was from their long hike. He loved that she didn't complain, though.

Like Quinn with the hiking and fishing gear, Cam was still

getting used to how much baby gear Zoey required, and then there was the damn car seat with all its buckles. He managed to snap it into place in one try, though, which was something he never thought he'd feel quite so victorious about.

With Zoey secure and the camping gear in the trunk, he turned to Emma. He brushed her hair out of her face. "See you tomorrow morning at work?" He wanted to add, "unless you want me to come over tonight," but part of him still worried he was jumping in too fast as it was. He'd gone from sure he didn't want a relationship to a family of three, and when he thought about the responsibilities and all the ways he could screw it up, the panic he'd felt earlier rose up and grew, binding his lungs for a moment.

But then he thought about how instead of letting his confession earlier today drive a wedge between them, like he was sure it would, Emma had assured him, her words and touch taking away his worries. She seemed so sure of who he was that he wanted to be that guy for her.

So he smothered the panic and focused on her as she said, "I'll be here, bright and early."

She's not like other women. This weekend had shown how well they fit together, and he wanted to explore all the ways they could fit together more. He kissed her good-bye, thinking he might as well accept that he'd already jumped, so there was no going back now.

She hadn't even left, and he was already counting down the hours until he'd see her tomorrow.

"So," Quinn said, stepping out onto the porch, a canary-eating grin on her face. "It's pretty obvious that the trip went well. I'm really happy for you guys."

"Thanks," he said. "And thanks again for watching Zoey." Before she could press for more details or ask him to expand on his feelings—which he was sure was coming any second—he grabbed his gear then headed to his cabin, his thoughts on a shower and kicking up his feet.

He dropped his backpack the second he stepped inside and glanced around his one-bedroom cabin. He still hadn't furnished or decorated more than what was already in place, and it didn't feel homey, the way Emma's place did. But he thought that probably had more to do with his girls being there.

His girls. They were why Hope Springs was starting to feel like the perfect simple life he'd always wanted.

He was ready to make a move. To start discussing the future. This separating for the night thing suddenly felt all wrong, and he thought how nice it'd be to have Emma and Zoey living on site.

He envisioned a bigger cabin, with a room for Zoey with a dollhouse, a rocking horse, and all the princess toys a bedroom could hold. Emma sitting in a large bay window that overlooked the mountains, where she could read and watch the sun set over the property.

The more pieces that fell into place, the more he liked the idea. It'd be easier for them to escape to the mountains now and then, and after the trips that she couldn't go along on, nothing would be better than coming back to find his girls here at Mountain Ridge.

Moving in together was a big commitment, though. His blood pressure automatically rose, that panic he hadn't quite dispelled coming along for the ride. *We'd probably do it eventually, and it'll take a few months to build a cabin like that anyway. Worst-case scenario, we'd have another rental if it doesn't work out.*

Now I'm just being a wuss. I can only imagine Emma's reaction to saying I might *want to live with her* someday, *but only if I have a way to back it up financially. What's wrong with me?*

At the same time, he didn't want to make the decision

lightly and end up hurting both of them in the long run—not to mention Zoey. She needed stability, and right now he could see why Emma had hesitated to start a romantic relationship in the first place.

She deserves romance, too. Since that was an area he had absolutely no experience in, he almost tabled the entire idea completely, thinking it was always a decision he could make later.

But that didn't sit right with him, either.

He thought of Torres and how excited he'd been to go home and ask his girl to marry him. If anyone could assure him how wonderful commitment could be, it'd be Jay.

The phone's screen seemed brighter than usual to his tired eyes as he scrolled to Torres's contact info. He'd get some advice so he didn't screw up this relationship stuff before he even started and see about making a loose plan for a trip here.

Torres could bring his fiancée, too, and then they could all get to know each other. He'd never thought group dates and family hangouts would be his idea of a good time, but he pictured him and Torres barbecuing while they tossed back a few beers, the women chatting and laughing while Zoey ran around in the big fenced yard their cabin would definitely need to keep her safer, and he couldn't think of a better way to spend a weekend.

The phone rang and rang, and he expected the voicemail to click on, but then Torres answered. "Brantley. Hey."

Something sounded off. "Are you drunk?"

"Not drunk enough, but I'm working on it."

"Bachelor party?" Cam asked—there'd been talk of a Vegas wedding, so it wouldn't surprise him if they'd fast-tracked everything.

The laugh that came over the line wasn't filled with joy, though. It had a biting edge, and Cam wished he wasn't a state away, because it sounded like his buddy needed him.

"What's up, man? Are you okay?"

"She cheated on me," Torres said. "With some guy at her work. She said she didn't mean for it to happen and blah, blah, blah. Dude, you were right. Women, you can't trust them, and relationships and all that true love bullshit? You're better off without it."

Well, this wasn't exactly the pep talk he'd been hoping for.

"She said I'm too angry, too. That I scare her sometimes, and that I need to work on my issues. She screws another guy, pretends we're cool every time I call and email, and *I* need to work on my issues?"

A cold lump formed in Cam's gut. "That sucks, man. I'm sorry."

"I'm going to live it up. There's a hot waitress here now, so who needs a relationship. Hey, sweetheart? Bring me another, why don't you?"

Cam thought of all the times Torres had talked about his girlfriend, from jokes to serious talks late at night where he'd said thinking of her waiting back home got him through the rough times. No matter what the guy claimed, he obviously wasn't handling things very well. "You should head up here, man. The cabins are done, so we've got a place for you to stay. We can hike and fish and you can get away from it all for a while."

"Yeah, maybe." Loud music blared in the background. "Hey, I can't hear you very well. I'll talk to you later, 'kay?"

"Later."

After Torres hung up, Cam stared at his phone.

Emma wasn't like other women, he knew that much. Sure, she'd withheld the fact that their daughter existed, but those had been extenuating circumstances. He knew he could trust her.

He was fairly sure.

He was at least sure that she'd never walk away from Zoey

the way his mom had done to him and Heath. She'd protect that little girl, and she'd raise her to be a strong, independent woman.

Cam knew he had some issues—he was still a bit jumpy when he woke up, and yeah, he struggled with keeping his anger in check. But he didn't have to deal with situations that made him angry here in Hope Springs. And Emma made him calmer, better.

Still, the phone call wouldn't leave him, and now he was questioning everything he'd been so sure about only moments ago.

Chapter Twenty-Two

There was some kind of odd comfort in the usual craziness of Monday morning. In the frantic rush of breakfast and getting Zoey to day care, and even in finding that her good-bye hug had left Emma with a green clover marshmallow smear on her shoulder.

She scratched at it as she climbed out of her car, which of course made her coffee cup slosh over a bit, but she'd missed her shirt and shoes, so win! She armed herself with her trusty clipboard and took an extra moment to enjoy Mountain Ridge's backdrop, her thoughts drifting to the few days she'd spent camped out among its peaks and trees with Cam.

He hadn't come into town for park time with Zoey yesterday, which was fine. She understood he probably needed to catch up on other things after spending the first half of the weekend with her. Thanks to the burst pipe, the park had been a mess, too, a large trench where the old pipe used to be, the mud and soggy grass taking up the area where most town functions took place. But the swing sets were still fully functional, and Zoey had made good use of that fact.

Of course Patsy Higgins had caught Emma and reminded her that the picnic auction was this Saturday, and she needed to have her basket to Mountain Ridge no later than eleven a.m. so the committee could sort them before the auction at noon. Like she would forget now that the auction was taking place where she spent most of her days. The construction job was all but done, but she'd promised Quinn she'd help get the property ready, too, which meant the coming week was going to be a hectic one.

On her way over to brief the guys about this week's to-do list—which now included mowing, tree trimming, and planting flowers, not to mention final decorating touches on the cabins—she saw Cam hammering away on the last cabin.

She lifted her hand in a wave, and he gave her a nod, but then he got back to work.

Which was also fine. The dreamer side of her had envisioned a different type of greeting after their romantic weekend, but they *were* at work, and remaining professional was important.

Even though he hadn't seemed to care ever before, blatantly flirting with her and grabbing her hand and dragging her away from the patio tables so they could have more private lunches. *It's Monday morning, though. No one's perky first thing on Monday mornings.*

"Hey, Emma!" Quinn came racing over and extended a steaming to-go mug toward her, even though she still held the one she'd brought from home. "So I've made a list, and I already did what I could this morning, but I got hung up on what to do for decorations in the bigger cabin."

Okay, so Quinn's *perky on Monday mornings. Even perkier than usual, too.* Since she'd need to keep up, Emma took the mug of coffee and added it to her barely warm quarter of a cup, figuring the more caffeine the better.

Quinn's obvious excitement as she talked about this huge

opportunity for Mountain Ridge was catching, and a swirl went through Emma as well. While the auction might not be on her list of favorite town events—and she hadn't even bought a stupid basket or decided what to put in it yet—she'd been a big part of Mountain Ridge's transformation. She couldn't wait for the whole town to see how it'd turned out.

She quickly briefed the guys, who attempted to tell her mowing and tree trimming weren't really in their job description. Instead of begging or bargaining, she simply smiled and said, "Well, it is now. Thank you for being willing to finish the cabins faster so we can get to it." She turned to the most senior guy, the one everyone else looked up to. "Tom, you'll make sure it gets done?"

There were a few murmurs, but then Tom answered, "Yes, ma'am," and they all took up their tools and headed to the various jobs she'd assigned them.

Go me. At the beginning of this job, I would've let them push me more. That was one of her main goals, and she lifted her head a bit higher, thinking she could finally check it off.

After spending most of the day on decorating touches with Quinn, Emma headed back across the property, hoping to find Cam and at least say a quick hi. Maybe steal a kiss.

"Hey, Emma," Pete said, stopping midstride to lower his clipboard and offer her a wide smile. She noticed he'd made neat lines through most of the items on the top page, although his list wasn't color coded. They were alike in a lot of ways, and while she'd once thought that Pete might be a better fit for her, she couldn't help being glad that things had worked out with Cam instead. The guy definitely didn't get her heart pumping the way Cam did.

Of course, then she immediately felt bad for even having that thought when Pete had helped her so much through her first big job. There'd been a few times he'd even encouraged her to be more firm with the crew, and while it'd been impossible to not take the criticism the tiniest bit personally, she had taken it, and as this morning had shown, the crew were way more responsive to her orders now.

Honestly, for the first time in a long time, she felt in control of her life. *Crap, I really need to pay those bills that I've been putting off.* But she was still in control. Mostly in control—getting there, anyway, and that was what was important.

In fact, she'd even decided that she'd ask Cam if he'd go with her to visit Grandma Bev this evening. It was high time the two of them met, and with everything that'd happened this weekend, she felt ready to have whatever battle transpired from it. Maybe once Grandma met him, she'd see that he was nothing like Dad, and that talk of what a rebel he had been back in high school was greatly exaggerated.

Cam was pretty much impossible not to like, after all, and she knew that more than anything, Grandma Bev wanted her to be happy.

And I'm so, so happy with him.

She noticed that Pete was looking at her expectantly, and she realized he must've had a follow-up statement or question.

"Sorry," Emma said with a self-deprecating laugh. "I was so caught up in what else we need to do to finish the cabins and get the property ready for Saturday that I zoned out for a second." Hopefully the tiny white lie wouldn't end up biting her in the butt.

"I asked if I could talk to you," Pete said. "I'll try to keep it short so you can get on with your list."

"Oh. Sure. Of course."

Pete glanced around and then gestured her toward the nearest cabin. When she stepped on the first step, it wobbled unexpectedly, and she nearly lost her balance. She reached for the rail, and Pete's hand was already on her back, steadying her.

"I'm making a note right now to have that step fixed,"

she said.

Pete wiggled back and forth on it, putting his weight on the front and then the back—he nearly lost his footing and she had to catch him. "I suppose I should've just taken your word for it," he said with a laugh, and Emma laughed, too.

"I'm just glad it's not my horrible coordination."

"No, it's definitely the step."

Emma smiled at him and then swept her arm in a go-ahead motion.

"After you, please," Pete said. "That way if there are any more loose steps, you can find them."

They shared another laugh, and Emma climbed the last few steps, gripping the railing and cautiously testing the wooden planks with part of her weight before fully stepping down. Luckily, the first step was the only one in need of securing—probably just an oversight by the crew who'd been in a hurry to grab lunch or get off work for the day.

As soon as they entered the cabin, Pete's expression turned all business. "I'm pleased to say that this is one of the most well-organized projects I've ever worked on. You were very clear about everything, open to changes, and you've got a good crew."

"I do," Emma said, nodding in agreement.

"But you also deserve a lot of the credit. Your designs are the perfect mix of beauty and function, and you've done an excellent job overseeing the building of them."

The compliment added to the sense of accomplishment she'd felt earlier and left her with a light, happy feeling. "Thank you so much."

After this job finished up, she'd take a few days to pay bills, spend some extra time with Zoey and Cam, and gain that last bit of control.

"Such a good job, actually, that…" Pete reached into his messenger bag, riffling through the papers. "You know that property I showed you? The ski resort in Park City, Utah?"

She nodded. "Of course."

"Well, I'd like you to help me with the building schematics and consult on the project from start to finish. Precision Commercial Design would like to offer you a permanent position in our Salt Lake City office, actually. My business partner and I have been looking for another person to add to our team, and I know you'd be a great asset to our company."

He muttered, "There it is," and then produced a document. "The contract is for one year, and the salary and benefits are all outlined in here."

Emma's hand trembled as she reached for the document. Her eyes scanned down the page, but there were so many words and figures, and the unexpected job offer totally threw her for a loop, making it that much harder to concentrate.

"I... Wow. That's very flattering."

"Look, I know that I...might have crossed a line asking you out before. I want you to know that while I do like you—as a person, you know—this is strictly a professional move. No strings attached. Just a job that you're highly qualified for."

A tinge of awkwardness crept into the air, but she'd had years of experience trying to charge through those kinds of moments. "Again, I'm flattered." She ran her fingers along the top of the contract, where the black letterhead spelled out the company name and address. "Salt Lake City. That's a big move for me."

"It is. But you'll only be a couple of hours away from here, which makes it easy to come back and visit, or for people here to visit you. Part of your benefits include moving expenses, too, as well as a discount rate if you choose to move into one of our properties. It's all outlined..." He flipped the document to the second page and pointed at a chunky paragraph. "Here."

She read about the property, the 25 percent off rent she'd receive if she moved into one of their town houses, and that they'd cover five hundred dollars in moving costs.

Emma thought about her little house in the tiny town she'd lived in all her life, and about packing up and moving Zoey to a city. In another state. She could still remember how, after visits to the city when she was growing up, she'd turn around in the backseat of the car and stare at the tall buildings and lights and think about how someday she'd live in a place like that.

The long-ago dream of her designs being in magazines flashed through her mind, too. She'd never been closer to making that a reality than she was right now, this job opportunity laid out before her.

It'd be so nice to have more breathing room when it came to my finances, too. She was good at running numbers and making do, but she'd scowled at the price of diapers and formula before—and now pull-ups, and toddler clothes and shoes that got too small too quickly—and wondered why everything had to be so expensive. She'd also wondered what it'd be like to buy the name brands, to not have a panic attack over unexpected expenses, and to have enough extra to start a college savings account for Zoey.

While she was working on becoming bolder, Emma still couldn't quite find the actual salary for the job, and she felt rude bluntly asking, which she knew was silly, but there it was anyway.

Then there was her one other thought, the one that shouted louder than the rest, despite it being the newest development: *But what about Cam?*

Other questions came on its heels. Where would that leave them? What about Zoey's relationship with her dad?

How could she tear her daughter away from her father right when they'd connected?

Her gaze snagged on a figure, and when she realized it was the yearly salary, she couldn't stop staring. It was significantly more than she made now. Yes, the price of living would be higher in the city, but Precision Commercial Design was willing to offset that some if she lived in one of their town houses. She'd seen pictures online, too, back when she'd found out Pete would be consulting and looked into his company. The town houses were nice—far nicer than her run-down current home.

The tornado of emotions swirled higher and faster, and then she realized Pete was standing in front of her, and she should say something. Anything. "Wow." Okay, she needed something else, something she hadn't already said. "I'm so flattered by this generous offer. Can I think about it? I'd like some time to look over the contract."

"Of course, of course." Pete flashed her a smile that had a salesman's edge, although she didn't doubt it was also genuine. "I really think you'd love working for us, Emma. As great as your crew here is, the one we use in Utah is a bit more organized, and we get through projects faster than any of our other competitors. You'd have the chance to design more, too, and I know opportunities to do that don't come around often here. I've seen the way you work, and I know you'd fit right in."

"Thank you." Unsure what else to do, she headed toward the door of the cabin—the one thing she *was* sure of was that she needed more air.

She jumped over the last wobbly step to avoid an accidental face-plant, and Pete stepped over it. Then he stopped her with a hand on her shoulder. "Call me if you have any questions," he said. "In fact, if you'd like to discuss it over dinner tonight, I was planning on heading to Seth's Steak and Saloon."

"Oh, I've got Zoey, so…" This was her future career, though. "Let me get back to you on dinner."

"No worries. I'll be there at eight. Come if you can, and if not, we can discuss it tomorrow when you get a chance."

Tomorrow? She was supposed to decide her entire future in one day? With this job coming to a close, she knew she needed to worry about where her next source of income would be. Hope Springs Construction was a great company to work for, and Mr. Strickland had been so good to her, but they had a lot of slow months where her salary dropped to the bare minimum. Plus, most of those jobs were strictly construction.

She'd promised Grandma that she'd take the big leap, too, and escape to the big city like she'd always talked about.

But lately she hadn't felt the need for an escape like she used to. She'd started to finally feel like she belonged in Hope Springs.

And a big part of that was a certain guy who'd spent the weekend in the mountains with her, making her think that a fairy-tale romance might still be in the realm of possibilities for her.

• • •

Cam watched Emma walk out of the cabin she'd just been in with Pete. He wanted to follow her and demand to know what they'd been doing in there. Before they'd disappeared inside, he'd seen the brief touches and shared laughter, and he'd wanted to go throw Emma over his shoulder in some caveman-like display and grunt, "Mine."

The longer they were in there, the stronger that urge grew, and he'd been seconds from storming over, barging in, and asking what the hell was going on.

Honestly, he didn't think he'd be able to keep himself from picking up the little dude by his collar as he yelled at him to stay away from Emma.

So he'd held his ground on the porch the next cabin over, continuing to work with the rest of the guys as he told himself it was nothing. That they worked together.

But that gesture at the end when they'd come out together and Pete had squeezed her shoulder…

Another toxic surge of jealousy flooded his veins. Cam already knew the guy had asked Emma out, too, so there was clearly interest on his part.

Through the rising anger and suspicion, he reminded himself that when he'd brought up how the guy had asked her out, Emma had told him it'd never even been a competition. Reminded himself that they had a daughter and things were good between them, especially after their trip.

If he charged over and showed how ugly his temper could be, he'd ruin everything.

Of course his phone call with Torres chose that moment to resurface, which didn't help matters.

Just like that, his patience wore out, and he wanted information. Assurances.

Right as he was about to charge after Emma and demand both, he saw that she was on her way toward him, her toolbox now in her hand.

Cam gripped his hammer tighter, telling himself to start easy. To avoid yelling.

"Hey, boys," Emma said as she approached, giving him a small smile before turning to the rest of the guys. "Where are we at?"

Tom stepped forward and listed the finishing touches that needed to be done and told Emma that they might just be able to wrap everything up by tomorrow night, even with the mowing and trimming.

Which sent a sense of urgency through Cam he didn't exactly understand. Not having her working on the property daily would suck, but it wasn't like she was going anywhere.

She tipped her head toward the cabin she and Pete had been in together for more than ten minutes. "The bottom stair on cabin three is loose. I'm going to take care of it, but I want every porch checked. Add that to the list of final touches, please."

Tom took his pen from behind his ear and wrote it down.

"I'll come with you," Cam said as she started down the steps, bouncing on each one before moving to the next.

They walked over to the cabin, and he held it in as long as he could, but then it burst out of him. "Something going on with you and Pete?"

Emma looked at him, her eyebrows drawing together. "Just work stuff."

"It looked more friendly than that."

"We're friends. Why are you being so weird?"

"I don't like him." *And if he puts his hands on you again, I'm going to have to break them.*

"He's been really great to me."

"Yeah, because he wants to get in your pants."

Offense pinched her features. "Or maybe it's because he thinks I'm a valuable asset. I've worked my butt off on this job, and it wasn't easy. You've only seen the end product and the finishing touches. Do you know how hard I had to work to get the guys to listen to me in the beginning? I've always wanted to be part of a project like this, and there were times I was sure I was going to screw it up, and it's nice that at least *someone* believes in me."

"Who says I don't believe in you? And why are you changing the subject?"

Emma scowled at him. "You're being so weird today. You didn't even come to say hi first thing this morning—in fact, you haven't talked to me *all damn day*—and now you're getting mad because I talked to my coworker." She knelt down in front of the bottom step. "Just go back to the other cabin. I don't need your help."

He tried to suppress his growl, but it came out anyway.

Emma stuck a nail in place and started hammering away.

"Emma."

She kept on hammering like he'd never said anything. No denying she was pissed—there was the ignoring, missing the nail as often as she hit it but continuing to pound it in as if it had personally offended her, and she didn't usually swear, either.

"I believe in you, okay?" He crouched down next to her, ignored the risk of smashing or impalement and caught her swinging arm, and then used his free hand to brush her hair off her face. "Even if you are putting that nail in crooked."

She gasped, and he couldn't help it—he laughed. Since that didn't seem to be winning her over, he lifted his hands in the air, showing that he gave. "I'm sorry, okay? You're right. I've been a grouchy ass all day."

He thought she was going to hold onto her anger, but then she shrugged a shoulder, and her expression softened.

He slowly took the hammer out of her hands then kissed her cheek, leaving his lips on her soft skin as he spoke. "Hey, baby. How are you today?"

One corner of her mouth lifted. "See? Was that so hard?"

He cupped her chin and gently twisted her face toward his. Then he kissed her—really kissed her, lips and tongue and given and taken breaths, not caring that they were in the middle of the workday. And okay, maybe a little bit hoping Pete would see, as well as the rest of the guys. Let them know she was his.

When he pulled back, though, a hint of worry remained in her features. "You okay?" he asked.

"Yeah, but I…" She licked her lips, and he got a little lost in the movement and the desire to kiss her again—this was what he needed to remember. Emma calmed him. He could trust her. He…well, something more than liked her. "I need to talk to—"

"Cam?" Heath strode over. "Sorry to interrupt, but it's Dad. He was at the shop, working on a car, and he dropped the differential from it on his foot. Sheena's there, but she can't convince him to go to the doctor—even though he's bleeding and it nearly chopped off his big toe—so she called me. I could use some backup, in case we have to carry his stubborn ass into the emergency room."

Emma stood along with him and put her hand on his shoulder. "Do you need me to go with you? I can…well, I'm not sure how effective I'd be at talking sense into him, but I can try. Or provide moral support. Whatever you need."

Who knew what Dad would say or how ugly this would get? "It's okay," Cam said, covering her hand with his. "You stay and keep things going here. Talk later?"

She nodded. "Okay. If you need anything, just call."

He gave her a quick peck on the lips, then he rushed off with his brother, thinking this entire situation felt a little too much like high school and the incident that started everything bad. Well, it made the bad way, way worse—from constant drinking to Mom walking out on them all when she couldn't handle it.

Fingers crossed alcohol wasn't the cause of it in the first place, or he might just lose his cool for the second time today.

Chapter Twenty-Three

Emma thought she felt her phone vibrate against her hip, so she switched the plate of cookies to her left hand and pulled her cell out of her pocket, frowning when she didn't have a message.

"Waiting for a call from a certain someone?" Grandma Bev asked, her hands full with a platter of brownies.

"No." Emma shoved her phone in her pocket, walked up the last few stairs to the church, and pulled open the door. Instead of walking through, Grandma paused in the doorway and gave her a skeptical eyebrow raise, complete with pursed lips.

"Come on, Zoey," Emma called, trying to keep her daughter's attention on climbing the last few steps before a butterfly or bird flew by and distracted her. Then they'd have to play twenty questions, all of them *why?*

Not only was Zoey not rushing, Grandma Bev was clearly still waiting for a different answer than the one Emma had given. "Okay, kind of. Cam's dad had a minor accident this afternoon, and I'm waiting for an update on how he's doing."

Cam wasn't very informative when it came to texts. They were bare minimum, only pertinent information, with the first saying, "He's fine," which she thought meant out of the hospital, but when she pressed he'd added, "They say he needs a cast." That was an hour or so ago.

"I noticed you still haven't brought that boy to meet me yet," Grandma said, crossing the threshold of the church and then leaning against the door to help keep it open.

"I've been meaning to, I swear, but we've been busy."

"And you don't want me to scare him off."

Both confirming and denying involved land mines, so Emma turned and urged her daughter to hurry, for both their sakes.

Finally Zoey managed the last step and strolled through the open doorway, into the bright hallway. The quilting ladies usually met during the day, but they always made quilts for newlyweds and displayed them at the reception, and with Sadie's and Quinn's weddings coming up, they were making two. Which meant the occasional evening session, and those were the only ones Emma could attend. Even then, it was usually by coercion on Grandma Bev's part. But she figured she could put in an hour or so before Zoey would get too crabby. Unless Cam texted or called to tell her he needed her. Either way, it'd be a good way to keep her mind busy, and right now, she desperately needed that.

"Emma! Long time, no see," Doris, who was Sadie's grandma, said. Then she smiled at Zoey and asked how she was.

"Uncle Heath has puppy. I stay with it."

"Do you like puppies, then?" Doris asked, and Zoey nodded emphatically.

Grandma Bev glanced at Emma, questions swimming through her eyes.

"Cam and I went camping over the weekend, and Zoey stayed with Heath and Quinn." Emma set down her plate of cookies on the nearby table and took the platter of brownies from Grandma so she could do the same with them. "Zoey's obsessed with their puppy."

"Sounds like it's getting serious."

"Yeah, Zoey and Trigger have shared Goldfish *and* an ice cream cone, so they'll probably make it official any day now."

A few of the other ladies laughed, but Grandma Bev just let loose a long-suffering sigh. Emma took the coloring book and crayons out of her bag and set them in front of Zoey. Before Grandma could get a chance to grill her further, Emma sat down and picked up a needle and thread, concentrating on the double wedding ring pattern in front of her and searching for the spot where she needed to start.

Grandma sat next to her and picked up her own needle and thread. "What about architecture firms?" Of course she wasn't going to let it go. "You're not thinking of giving up on working for one, are you?"

Emma thought about the contract for the job offer she'd received, now buried in the depths of her bag. Earlier she'd held back the news about the job with Cam—just for a second, because he'd made her mad, ignoring her all day and then accusing her of having something more with Pete. But right as she was about to tell him, they'd been interrupted.

Now she'd had too much time to think about the job offer without anyone to bounce it off. The reality of the situation had sunk in, and she desperately needed to talk about everything, but Grandma Bev was far too biased, and she'd just tell her that she'd be a fool not to take the job.

Having this conversation in front of all the quilting ladies would be a disaster, too, each of them throwing their opinions into the mix and adding to the mess of thoughts already swirling through her head. Not to mention Patsy Higgins would be here any second, and then there'd be no chance of any of it being kept private.

So she was keeping her lips zipped until she had the chance to talk to Cam—she wanted him to hear it from her, not through the town grapevine. She shot Grandma the sternest look she could summon and said, "Later."

"Okay, but I can't help remembering two other people who gave up their dreams for small-town life and how it didn't turn out so well in the long run. I'd hate for you to make the same mistake and stay, only for you two to end up resenting each other like your parents did."

The words stung, and as they sank in, they also dug at the part of her that worried about ending up like that. Would she resent Cam if she stayed? Would he later resent her for pushing him to make such a big decision so quickly, when he was still processing having a daughter as well as all he had on his plate with Mountain Ridge?

Man, where am I even going to start when I do finally get the chance to talk to him?

Their relationship had shifted during their camping adventure, but they still hadn't had a serious talk about where exactly they stood and what they both wanted in the long run. She didn't want him to feel like she was giving him an ultimatum and that he'd have no choice but to be with her or to be without Zoey.

She thought back to growing up in a house where the word "mistake" was thrown around often, and how both of her parents talked about feeling trapped. The last thing she wanted was for Cam to feel trapped, but at the same time, she couldn't give up the amazing opportunity to work at an architecture firm, the way she'd always dreamed of doing, if he wasn't willing to give her more of a commitment.

If Cam committed, she knew he'd stick by it, but she didn't want to be just a commitment. She wanted him to *want* to be with her.

Since she couldn't do anything about that now, she focused on making tiny stiches and tried to enjoy the light conversation. Every once in a while, Grandma would glance at her, and it was clear she still wanted all the answers, but Emma needed some before she could give any to her.

When Zoey tired of her coloring book and tried to climb on Emma's lap, making it harder to sew, one of Vera Mae's granddaughters came over, asked Zoey if she wanted to play with them, and then took her hand and led her over to where she and her sister were playing with dolls. Zoey was in heaven playing with the seven- and nine-year-old girls.

Right as Emma was about to excuse herself and Zoey, Amy Case came in, wearing the colorful scrubs she wore for her job at the hospital. "Sorry I'm late, ladies. Work was crazy today." She grabbed a cookie and an empty chair and sat next to the quilt. "Rod Brantley nearly chopped off his toe. That's the most excitement we've seen in a while."

"Is he still at the hospital?" Emma asked.

"He left a bit ago. I had to stay and finish up my charts that I didn't get to while I was helping out the doctor."

"He's okay, then?"

"Yeah, a few of the bones in the top of his foot are broken. They put him in a cast and discharged him. He'll need a month or so to recover, but then he'll be okay."

"We better get a sign-up going," Doris said. "His family will need meals."

"On it," Patsy Higgins said, pulling a fat, worn notebook from her purse. "Sheena's been staying with him most nights, too, along with Oliver. So meals for three people."

Emma's heart swelled as they all sprang into motion, making plans to help Rod Brantley, regardless of the fact that he'd never had the best reputation and ignored most of the town's events.

Maybe people here gossiped and loved to interfere and force people to participate in picnic basket auctions, town meetings, and quilting night, but there was caring and love behind most of their gestures.

Suddenly the thought of walking down crowded sidewalks where people simply passed each other by seemed sad. Of people breaking limbs or having babies and not immediately receiving casseroles and flowers. She glanced at Zoey and thought about how she didn't think twice about letting her play with other kids or wander around the park, because she knew the people here, and it was a safe place to live.

If she moved away, she'd also miss Grandma Bev like crazy, even if they did occasionally drive each other mad.

An overwhelming wave of sorrow and gratefulness hit her, and she worried if she didn't leave, she'd burst into tears. Then she'd have a lot of explaining to do, and no one in this room would take no for an answer.

Emma quickly tied off her thread and scooted her chair back. "Thank you, ladies, for tonight, but I think that I better get Zoey home before she reaches the hungry-and-tired meltdown phase. I'll see you all later."

Grandma reached out and caught her hand. "You and I need to have a serious conversation sometime."

"I know." Emma leaned down, hugged her grandma, and pressed a kiss to her cheek. Then she gathered Zoey's stuff and headed home.

A box of mac and cheese for Zoey later, Emma paced the kitchen, her mind spinning. She'd read through the contract twice now, and while common sense—and math—said she should take the job, something still held her back.

Namely, someone.

Because she could weigh all the pros and cons she'd thought of since the job offer—including all the lovely things she'd realized she'd miss about Hope Springs during quilting night—and none of them took as much space as Cam.

Earlier I told myself I'd need more commitment from him to even consider turning down the job, but I think I'd even take a slim chance of us working out, which just shows how far gone

I am for the guy.

Zoey came running in and demanded her sippy cup be refilled, and Emma looked at her little girl, wondering which would truly be the best decision for her. Financial stability was definitely a bonus, but they'd made it okay here.

If she pretended her bills would stop stacking up, raising a kid would somehow get cheaper, and that she would have another big job around the corner to keep her income steady, she was sure they could keep making it. The odds of more big jobs weren't great, but maybe the little ones would be enough to keep them afloat.

On autopilot, she poured milk into the pink-and-purple sippy cup.

There was no question Zoey needed her daddy, and Emma was starting to feel like she did, too.

For a second, she entertained the thought of managing a way to keep hold of both the job *and* Cam. *Would a two-hour drive back and forth make or break us?*

Probably. It would definitely suck.

Then again, opportunities that paid so well didn't come along every day. Maybe she could just sign on for the Park City job and see how she liked working for Precision Commercial Design and how hard it was to balance the project while maintaining a long-distance relationship. It was only a year.

Which didn't sound long when she put it like that. But when she thought about breaking it out into months and weeks and two-hour trips—that were really four including the drive back—it seemed like a freaking eternity.

Emma secured the lid on Zoey's cup and handed it back to her daughter, who muttered a polite "tanks" before running into the other room.

Emma glanced at the contract again. Then she looked at her open laptop, the website for the fancy town houses she and Zoey could call home still displayed. She lifted her phone and looked at the screen, hoping Cam would have answered her last text asking for an update.

But there weren't any new texts or missed phone calls.

She thought about how she'd offered to go with Cam earlier and how he'd told her no. How he hadn't answered her last two texts. She wanted to help him however she could, but she worried those were signs he wasn't thinking about her as a permanent fixture in his life, not the same way she was thinking about him.

Which made her question everything all over again.

"I don't know what to do," she said to the stack of dirty dishes. They, of course, were completely unhelpful. She eyed the clock. She wanted to discuss everything with Cam, but there were a few points in the contract with confusing wording, and Pete would be having dinner in twenty minutes.

I owe it to myself to at least make sure I've got all the details before I talk to Cam, much less make a decision.

With that thought in mind, she picked up the phone and called Madison. She hated to leave Zoey with a babysitter again, since she'd just left her over the weekend, but she'd only be gone an hour or two at most. Plus, having more information when she talked to Cam would be better than having to say, "I don't know," to every question he'd ask.

She also knew that once they talked, she was going to have to lay it all out, including exactly how she felt about him, because what he said in return would obviously factor into her decision. Maybe it was faster than she'd planned, but life had a way of throwing wrenches into plans—she knew that better than anyone.

As she made arrangements with the babysitter, she eyed the papers again. There was a certain sense of irony in the fact that the type of job she'd always wanted had suddenly become the one thing that might get in the way of the family she'd dreamed of having.

Chapter Twenty-Four

As Cam walked up the sidewalk to Emma's, he scrubbed a hand over his face and tried to pull himself together. Big surprise, Sheena wasn't very good at the sight of blood and had nearly passed out twice. Cam had seen his fair share, so he'd helped change Dad's soaked bandages and applied fresh ones to the gruesome wound, while Heath tried to keep Sheena and Oliver calm and occupied.

Every time he'd gone to call Emma and give her an update, another person would knock on the door, or Sheena would have another meltdown, and it felt like he and Heath had put out one fire only for two more to pop up. The entire afternoon had gone by in a hectic blur, and now all he wanted was a quiet night with Emma.

He glanced at the time—Zoey would probably still be up for a little while, too. After their little girl was asleep, though, he planned on taking Emma into her bedroom, where he could kiss and hold her the way his body craved, and ask if he could stay the night. Forget all the rules and taking it slow. He didn't want slow anymore. He wanted his family.

Only when he knocked on the door, Emma wasn't the one who answered. A teenage girl with braces had Zoey in her arms.

"Daddy!" Zoey launched herself at him, and he caught her. She put her hands on both of his cheeks and gave him a big, smacking kiss.

He bounced her higher in his arms and stepped farther inside the house. "Is Emma here?"

"Oh, no she's not. I'm watching Zoey so she could go meet someone. At the Triple S, I think."

The skin on Cam's neck prickled, the blood in his veins immediately pumping hotter. Then he told himself it was probably just Quinn and Sadie, and he needed to calm down.

"I'm Madison, by the way," the babysitter said. "Cam Brantley, right? My little brother is in Oliver's class."

Cam extended his hand. "Nice to meet you."

"Need milk," Zoey said, pointing at her sippy cup on the floor.

"I can get it," the babysitter said.

"It's okay. I got it." Cam lowered Zoey so she was upside down and dangling over her cup. She squealed and grabbed the cup, giggling when he swung her back up. Hugging her tight, he kissed her cheek. Already the stress of the day was fading—if Dad didn't have to fight everything so damn hard, it would've been much easier. Finally Cam had asked a nurse to slip him something. She'd looked horrified by it, but whatever pain meds she'd given him had calmed him down enough for the doctor to cast the foot he claimed was "just fine."

As soon as Zoey had her refilled sippy cup, she ran to show it off to Madison. Cam noticed the messy kitchen and thought he'd pay the babysitter and tell her she could go home, then he'd tidy up and watch Zoey until Emma arrived.

But the document next to the pot of mostly eaten mac and cheese caught his eye. When he lifted it, he bumped the open laptop and it came to life. As he started to read down the page, his lungs tightened. Then he glanced at the screen and noticed the town houses Emma had obviously been looking into were in Salt Lake City.

Where she was apparently going to be working.

What the hell? She's moving, and she didn't even think to tell me? Anger rose, quickly taking over his body. How could she do this? She hadn't told him about his daughter for two years, and now, after they'd lived in the same town for six whole weeks, she was going to take her away?

Over his dead body.

He strode into the living room, and in an effort to not scare the babysitter or his daughter, he forced a tight smile onto his lips. "I'm going to go find Emma. You'll be okay with Zoey for a little while longer?"

She nodded. "Yeah, I've got her."

Cam told his daughter good-bye, promised he'd see her soon, and then he got in his truck and headed toward the Triple S.

He charged inside the restaurant, a man on a mission. And when he saw that not only was Emma there, but she was having an intimate dinner with Pete, he released the hold on his anger, not bothering to fight it back anymore.

• • •

Emma glanced up from her untouched fries to see Cam heading toward her, and while her heart first skipped a beat at simply seeing him, the second beat it missed was because of how angry he looked.

"What the hell, Emma?" He slammed his fist down on the table, making the plates and, in turn, her, jump. "You're going to move to Salt Lake City without even telling me? Just like you didn't bother telling me about Zoey in the first place." He shook his head, disgust clear on his features. "And I thought you were different."

It felt like her internal organs were shrinking in on themselves, and she couldn't help but notice the way everyone in the place was now staring at them. Seth Jr. looked ready to leap over the bar and play bouncer, and she wanted to tell everyone to stay back—she honestly worried about anyone who dared to take on Cam right now.

Unfortunately, she was the one who needed to. "Cam, please calm down."

"Oh, I don't think I'll be calm this time. Last time I was calm, and apparently you've taken that as a sign that you can jerk me around."

Pete was hunched over, flinching with every word.

"Hey, what did I say about Brantleys and the Triple S not mixing last time you came in," Trevor, one of the bartenders, said as he wrapped his hand around Cam's arm. "Let's just fast-forward to where you're permanently kicked out like your dad."

Cam spun, fist cocked, and Emma shot to her feet and grabbed his arm. "Cam. *Stop.*"

He glanced at her, and while his stony expression didn't change, he did lower his fist. Emma took advantage and tugged him toward the door of the Triple S. For years she'd been the quiet girl who walked the line, and with everyone staring, she missed the anonymity. Missed being the boring one.

As soon as she managed to get Cam outside, she opened her mouth to explain, but he cut her off. "You told me nothing was going on with Pete."

"Nothing is," she said, throwing her hands up in exasperation. "I mean, except the job offer, which—"

"I don't need this. I came to get away. All I wanted was to run the lodge and get away from everything." His hard footsteps as he paced the wooden walkway in front of the Triple S punctuated his words. "Now I'm here in town causing a scene, on the verge of getting banned from the bar for life, and for what?"

Hurt rose up and settled deep in Emma's chest. "Well, things didn't turn out like you expected, did they?"

"No. This wasn't what I wanted at all."

Tears sprang to her eyes. "You think *I* expected all of this?"

"Too bad for you I came home, right? Or you could've kept lying to everyone."

She moved into his pathway and crossed her arms. "So much for you saying that you forgive me. And I told you that I didn't need your help. You chose to get involved."

"Hey, we all make mistakes. Or do you just want to be forgiven for yours, but when it comes to other people, you expect them to be perfect?" He raked both hands through his hair then shook his head, resentment and rage practically wafting off him.

Swallowing didn't dislodge the lump in her throat, so she forced herself to talk through it. "I barely got the job offer today. I tried to talk to you about it, but then your dad got hurt, so I didn't have the chance. After reading over the contract a couple of times, I still had some questions, so I came to talk to Pete so I'd have all the facts before you and I talked about it."

He just kept shaking his head, muttering about how he should've known better.

"This is a great job, the kind of job I've wanted for as long as I can remember, and I could provide a better life for Zoey. I have to think about that, Cam."

"And what I could provide for Zoey wouldn't be enough?" he snapped.

"I'm not saying that! She needs you. Of course I want you to still be in her life."

"Oh, I will be." He leveled her with a cold glare, none of the affection that he'd shown her the past few weeks, and she swore she could feel her heart crack, the jagged pieces cutting deep before it split in two.

"Is that really what you think of me? That I'll try to take Zoey away if you don't play nice?"

"You kept her from me for two years, Emma. Toe the line, you make all the decisions, and you don't need me — I got the message loud and clear."

"So that's what the past month and a half has been about? Toeing the line so you can see your daughter?"

He didn't even look at her, more like through her. "I need to get back to the lodge. Back to the life I've worked for, so I don't lose my temper here and undo all the hard work Heath's done to restore the Brantley reputation."

"Yeah, don't let me and my impending difficult decision about my entire future keep you from escaping everything." Wiping at the tears that'd spilled over and run onto her cheeks seemed like accepting defeat, so she let them fall unchecked.

"We both know you've already made your decision. I'm not going to sit here and fight with you until things get really ugly."

This wasn't really ugly? It felt devastatingly ugly. A couple of people had started out of the Triple S, only to backpedal to give them space. Usually she would've ducked her head and backed away, unable to deal with the confrontation, and especially unable to deal with people witnessing it. But she didn't want to look back and think she should've fought harder for Cam.

"I'll make sure to schedule touring trips around when I have Zoey," he said, his voice completely monotone, and the missing warmth chilled her to her core. "Divorced people manage to raise kids all the time, so I'm sure we can figure out a way to deal with each other when we have to."

He started toward the parking lot, and she almost let it go at that. But each beat of her broken heart sent more misery coursing through her, and with it came a burst of anger edged with desperation. Anger at herself that she'd let him in so quickly and that she'd fallen for him so hard, desperation that he was going to walk away and she'd forever feel the emptiness that was spreading through her, taking over the spot where her heart used to be.

"So that's it?" she asked, following after him. "You're happy to walk away and just forget about us?"

"What us? Who were we kidding?" He shook his head and strode away, never looking back at her, and she wished she had let it go.

A minute or so later—she wasn't sure, because time had ceased to register or make sense—Cam's truck sped past…

Leaving her alone in the parking lot where they'd had one steamy night, and making it clear that all he'd ever see her as was the girl he'd settled for before one of his deployments.

Chapter Twenty-Five

After the scene she and Cam had caused at the Triple S, she'd still had to go back inside to retrieve her purse—it had her keys, and she'd made it all the way to her car before realizing she couldn't drive away like she desperately needed to.

She'd received a lot of sympathetic glances and questions about whether she was okay. The tear-streaked face had definitely been a dead giveaway, but she'd answered that she was fine, even though she was nowhere near anything resembling that word.

Pete had walked her out, waving off her insistence that he didn't need to, and he'd told her that he'd finish up everything at Mountain Ridge and check in with Mr. Strickland. As much as she didn't want to be the girl who couldn't go to work because of a breakup, she also didn't want to be the girl who burst into tears while having to work near her ex.

Besides, she'd see the property at the stupid picnic auction at the end of the week that she still had to attend, and she hoped that after four days to recover, she could fake her way through it.

Emma tried to be strong, and for a few days she even kept Zoey home from day care. Her heart remained broken, though, and it broke a little more each time Zoey asked about her daddy.

By the third day, she didn't feel any better, but she decided to drop Zoey off at day care and force herself to appear like a person who had her life together. No doubt people in town were talking and wondering what was going on, and she figured the sooner she could get her life back to normal, the sooner it might feel that way.

Normal.

Boring.

Lonely.

With all those words swirling through her head, she collapsed on the couch the second she arrived back home and let herself shed the tears she'd held at bay for two days. Well, she'd cried plenty the night she'd returned home from her big fight with Cam, but she'd told herself that she'd only allow herself that one breakdown.

The problem was her heart ached, and she didn't want to move on and put on a brave face. She wanted to wallow and cry. She didn't want to have to be strong anymore, and how could she be, when she couldn't even make a solid decision about her future?

If it were only hers, then it'd be easier. But she had to think about her career, about her responsibilities as a provider, about how moving away from Cam would affect Zoey long-term, and a dozen other things that completely overwhelmed her, especially while nursing a broken heart.

On top of all of that, someday, somehow, she needed to have a conversation with Cam and talk logistics of what their custody agreement would look like if she took the job in Salt Lake City that he'd already been so sure she'd take.

Custody agreements and lawyers and all the things that'd

terrified her that first day Cam had opened the door and reentered her life.

A heavy dose of guilt rose up. Over not telling him she was pregnant in the first place, that she was considering moving away right after he'd connected with Zoey, and that he'd had to find out about the job in Salt Lake in the worst way possible.

I tried to explain, though. Tried to get his input so I could make a decision about this huge opportunity and whether or not it was worth leaving Hope Springs.

More than that, she'd fought for him. Something he obviously wasn't willing to do for her.

As much as that fact hurt, making it clear that he'd been with her mostly out of convenience or obligation—either way, something she wouldn't settle for, even as her heart screamed it didn't care, because it wanted Cam anyway—she told herself it was better to know now.

She closed her eyes and reminded herself of the hurt that'd flash across Mom's face when Dad made it clear he was only with her because of Emma.

No, she wouldn't settle for that.

It took him all of six weeks to bring up the past and use it against me. I can only imagine how many times it'd come up if we tried to work things out. Her accidental pregnancy and the fact that she'd withheld it would always be between them, ammo used in every fight.

At least he wants Zoey. My main goal has always been to ensure she feels wanted. She'd have two families, basically. More love. It'd be…

Pain radiated through Emma's chest. She'd find a way to work out the whole coparenting thing for her daughter's sake. Even if it meant that eventually Cam would move on and find a woman he wanted to be with.

It'll be some beauty-queen type with no complications, too, who he'll make so many plans with that it'll take every ounce of my strength to not try to sabotage them all.

Ugh, why does she get plans and I don't?

And now she was feeling irrational hatred for someone who didn't exist. *Yet.*

The knock on the door made her jerk upright. She froze, hoping and praying whoever it was would believe she wasn't at home.

"Emma." The knocking grew louder. "It's Quinn and Sadie. Please let us in."

Emma wiped her eyes, knowing that there'd been too much crying for her to pull off a person who had her life together. As much as she hated for anyone to see her like this, she needed her friends more.

Sadie and Quinn took one look at her and then enveloped her in a hug.

They'd heard enough details to get the gist of what happened, and Emma filled in the rest. The tears flowed freely as she rehashed her and Cam's fight, and she didn't bother stopping them. "He didn't want me."

Quinn shook her head. "That's not true. I saw it—he cares about you, I know he does. He's just…ridiculously stubborn. And maybe a bit lost."

"I bet *he's* not sitting at home crying," Emma said, giving Quinn a look that challenged her to contradict the statement. The tiny part of her that'd been clinging to the shred of hope she couldn't quite let go of desperately wanted her to contradict it.

"He…left. Took off into the mountains. He's been up there for three days."

"I bet he's up there crying," Sadie said, patting Emma's knee, and in spite of everything, she laughed, even though a sob came on the heels of it.

"I doubt it. The ability to escape into the mountains was

what he wanted. I got in the way. Me and Zoey—but at least he doesn't regret Zoey. He's willing to give up time in the mountains for her."

Quinn dug into her bag and brought out a bottle of tequila. "Now, before you say you can't drink this with us, just…don't say it. We'll drown our sorrows for an hour or so, and then you'll have time to sober up before you go get Zoey. Promise."

Sadie produced three shot glasses. "Yeah, and I'm leaving in a little over a week, so I need a last hurrah."

Emma winced at the hard liquor as she tipped it back, not sure how much she could stomach. "If I end up taking the job, this might be my last hurrah here, too—the picnic basket auction certainly won't be hurrah material. More like shoot me now, with a side of an awkward date."

Quinn poured everyone another. "For the record, we don't want you to move. *But* we also understand following your dreams and doing what's best for your family and all that jazz. So, while we let the buzz work its way through our systems, why don't you tell us all about this new job? That way, maybe we can help you decide."

• • •

The wind rippled the surface of the lake, sending Cam's fishing line drifting farther toward the center and causing him to tighten his jacket and hike his shoulders up against the cold. The late spring storms had brought a heavy dose of rain, and while that usually meant better fishing conditions, he'd caught all of one fish in three days.

If Emma and I were having a contest this trip… His heart snagged. *Well, I'd lose.*

It definitely felt like he'd lost—something way more than a contest, too. This sense of failure went much deeper, down to where it took root and grew stronger every passing day.

After their fight, he'd realized he'd let his temper get the best of him again. Instead of facing up to it, he'd packed his gear, thinking once he headed into the mountains, he wouldn't feel so lost. That he could clear his mind and figure out his next step.

Even though he'd taken an obscure trail he'd only been on a few times in high school and hiked to a different lake than the one he'd been to with Emma, every damn thing reminded him of her. In an epically stupid move, he'd brought as much alcohol with him as he could carry, and he'd already burned through most of the beer and a bottle of vodka. He'd thought it'd make the long nights better, but in truth, all it did was make him feel just like his dad.

Not even the new-and-improved version who stubbornly refused medical treatment—the past, horrible version that had nothing going for him.

Which had only made Cam want to drink more. He'd thought of a hundred different things he should've said to Emma. Like, *don't take the job. I want you to stay.*

I want you.

I think I'm in love with you, and it scares the shit out of me.

Instead he'd yelled. Turned it all on her and then walked away, undeterred by the catch in her voice and the tears running down her face.

What scared him—and what he couldn't stop thinking about, though—was that he'd wanted to hit something so badly. That Pete guy would've been nice. Trevor the Prick, who'd compared him to Dad... Forget that he'd been acting like him that night, as well as ever since.

Emma's touch had cooled his temper just enough, but not enough to prevent him from ripping into her when they stepped outside.

As he'd driven away, his anger quickly morphing into self-loathing, he'd thought that the best thing for her, as well as for Zoey, was to get away from him.

He told himself the same thing now. *They're better off without me. They can go live their lives in the big city, and I can finally live mine the way I'd planned, without all these complications mucking it up.*

A form of panic he'd never felt before seized him as the reality of what his life would be like without his girls sank in. A lot of emptiness and regret. No more teasing back and forth with Emma, no more having Zoey run into his arms as she yelled, "Daddy!"

He pressed a hand over his tightening chest. It felt like someone had punched a hole through him and taken everything that mattered. He'd never survive complete ostracism from his girls, and not seeing Zoey wasn't an option.

Conjuring his daughter's image made his heart fill to the brink with the love he had for her. He hated the thought of her being too far away for drop-bys, of all the milestones and little moments in her life he'd miss, but he refused to subject her to the way he'd been raised. With the lodge's future so iffy, Emma was probably better off with a stable job in Utah.

Only seeing Zoey on weekends here and there is going to be torture.

It'd also be torturous to see Emma, because he knew he'd always want more, just like he knew she deserved a better guy. One who wouldn't snap, one who had his life together. So for the sake of everyone involved, he'd do his damnedest to figure out how to be good at coparenting. And during the times he had Zoey, he'd cut his work hours as much as he could and make every second they had together count.

A lump formed in his throat, and even though he'd just mentally worked through all of his revelations and resolutions for the future, that damned hollow hole remained in his chest.

Since he'd reached the sappy portion of the day, he reeled

in his pole, looked at the gray sky that threatened even more rain, and crawled into his tent.

Tomorrow was the big town picnic auction at Mountain Ridge.

Which meant he needed to stay in the mountains for a few more days.

Chapter Twenty-Six

Emma placed her picnic basket on the table behind the number Patsy Higgins had assigned to her. She twisted it so that the prettier side showed, momentarily disregarding the fact that she was fairly against this whole bid-on-a-woman's-baking-skills thing. Since Zoey had helped her pick it out late last night, when her procrastination had reached the critical, out-of-time stage, it was pink. In a sea of standard white and brown baskets and a lot of red-checked material, the color and tulle lining definitely stood out—it looked like several ballerinas had lost their clothes to make it possible.

Her already frazzled nerves frayed more as she glanced out at the line of chairs taking shape in front of the podium that'd been brought in. On top of not wanting to basically be an item for bid, Emma was also sure there wouldn't be a whole lot of interest in her basket, and then she'd get to experience humiliation on top of everything else, which her self-esteem could hardly handle right now.

It's for a good cause, it's for a good cause. Despite her best attempts to stop them, her eyes searched the faces of the people who were scurrying about the property, hoping to find one in particular. It made no sense after their ugly confrontation, but she'd had some time to think, and while Cam shouldn't have jumped all over her like that, she imagined finding out about her job offer the way he did would've made anyone lose their temper.

He still should've let her explain. Even if he didn't want her, they had a child together, and that meant talking out big decisions, whether he liked it or not.

That's why I'm looking for him. So we can have the big talk. Not because I miss his face and his voice, and the way he made me feel more adventurous and fun...sexier...

Her brain choosing to focus on all the things she missed about him when he clearly didn't want her the way she wanted him was a new form of torture.

Stop it, brain. We need to focus on the here and now. Get through setting up for the event, go on a date with—if she had any luck—a nice guy who would understand this was all a coerced, archaic ritual that in no way would equal a real date, and then go home and sign the contract so she didn't throw away an amazing opportunity for nothing.

While she still felt she owed it to Cam to have a conversation about the job *before* she signed the papers, she also felt that if she waited much longer, Pete might take offense and withdraw it. Cam was the one who'd decided to flee and hide instead of deal, which wasn't an option for her, even though she could certainly understand the allure.

She understood it even more as Patsy Higgins strode toward her, arms swinging in that way they did when she was on a mission.

Luckily she strode past her, another target in her sights. Emma noticed Quinn in the middle of the melee and headed over to her. The property looked amazing, every cabin complete, the landscaping flawlessly done with a lot of touches of bright flowers. Since Emma hadn't been able to do everything she'd wanted to help with during her few days off, she'd shown up extra early this morning.

As soon as she reached Quinn, she said, "Put me to work."

They set up a couple more rows of chairs, and Emma mentioned how impressed she was by the property.

Quinn held her hair up in a makeshift ponytail and fanned her face and neck. "Thanks. Hopefully the state of the property will make up for the fact that my basket looks completely pathetic."

"You're lucky that you've got a sure bet bidding on you," Emma said.

Quinn dropped her hold on her hair, frowned at a chair, and wiggled it an entire centimeter to the right. "Yeah. Although Heath made a joke about how this might be his last chance to eat another woman's cooking, so I made a joke about how he could cook his own meals from now on, and I think we've reached a compromise."

"The compromise being that he's bidding on your basket?"

"You guessed it."

Emma laughed. Quinn's version of compromise was different than the actual definition. What it usually meant was that she tried to sway Heath to her side, and when she couldn't—like when it came to decisions on decorations or furnishings for the cabins—she ordered what she wanted anyway and told him he could choose all the camping gear and vehicles. Emma loved how easily Heath always went along with it.

Why'd I have to go and pick the stubborn brother?

Quinn craned her neck and looked around. "I've got to make sure to give Heath a signal when my basket comes up, because even though I showed him last night, they all look similar, and I want to make sure he knows it's mine." Her eyebrows lowered as she continued to scan the area. "Have you seen him?"

"No," Emma said. When she glanced around to see if she could help Quinn locate Heath—and definitely not so she could check and see if Cam was with him—Pete caught her eye and waved.

She nodded and attempted a smile. For some reason, she hadn't expected him to be here, and the fact that he was made her think that she needed to give him her decision before she left the property.

All signs were pointing to her not having a good enough reason to stay in Hope Springs, and the sooner she wrapped her head around it, the better.

. . .

Cam slowed at the sound of the motorcycle engine, and a moment later his brother came though the thicket of trees, the loud buzz growing louder as he neared.

Heath killed the engine, set the kickstand, and then climbed off the bike and hung his helmet on one of the handles. "Most of the town is headed toward our property right now, and I have to spend my time searching for your ass. We're supposed to be in this together, you know."

Cam readjusted the straps of his backpack, shifting them so they'd cut into his shoulders a few inches over from where they'd already rubbed against his skin for a good hour. "Yeah, well, I'm going through something."

Heath crossed his arms. "What? Screwing up your life? Well, I hate to interrupt, but I thought maybe you should…" He blew out his breath. "Oh, I don't know. Unscrew it up before it ruins everything, including our business."

"How long have you been working on that pep talk?"

"For a couple of days, and that's the nice version. But I'm not done." Heath took a few steps closer. "You had everything—I've never seen you so happy. Then you threw it all away. For what?"

Cam's gaze drifted to the meadow he'd been headed for—the trail diverged there, and he hadn't quite decided which way to take yet. "I lost my temper. I said things… awful things I'm not proud of. Which just proves that I was right to be worried about my anger issues. I have them, just like Dad does—it's always been one of my biggest fears, and while I thought maybe it was just the military bringing it out more, clearly it goes deeper than that. Before long I'll push everyone away, and I'll hurt them in the process. I'd rather push them away *before* it causes permanent damage."

"Then what?" Heath asked. "Hope that twenty or thirty years from now you'll get it together? Why don't you learn from Dad's mistakes instead of repeating them?"

"I liked the army, Heath. When the bad guys needed taken out, I volunteered. Who does that?"

"A guy who protects people." Heath closed the remaining distance between them, walking right up to him so he couldn't look past him anymore. "You think you've got anger issues, but you've got trust issues, and you've got a hero complex. You're a protector, Cam. You took the brunt of Dad's anger growing up so that I didn't have to."

Cam swallowed, hard. "You still got too much of it."

"He didn't hit me the way he hit you." Heath jabbed a finger at Cam's chest. "And it was you who made sure of that."

"He still hit you."

"Once or twice, and mostly when I was older. When I could take it better. How often did he hit you? Once a month at least—sometimes more."

Cam dropped his gaze, staring at the toes of his hiking boots. "I'm fine."

"You pushed away a woman who cares about you, one I can tell you care about, too. You're not fine."

This was way mushier than their usual talks, and Cam

didn't think he could handle much more.

"You know who kicked my butt into gear when I nearly lost Quinn?" Heath didn't answer his own question until Cam glanced up at him. "Dad. Yeah. It took him telling me about his life of regrets. He'd probably tell you, too, if you let him. Forgiveness is earned."

"I'm not sure I'm ready to forgive and forget. I haven't seen much earning."

"I'm saying *you* need to earn it. Prove that you're not like him. Don't wait until you've lost Emma. Till your daughter resents you because you weren't there."

The fight leaked out of him, and without it, he felt lost and hollow once again. "What am I supposed to do? Ask her to give up her dream job?"

"You at least need to tell her how you really feel. I know, I know, that's not Brantley men's strength by a long shot. We don't talk about feelings, and we pretend we don't have any. It's a good way to keep people away. Not a great way to keep the people we need most."

"What if working it out means I have to move to Salt Lake, too?" He'd been holding it back, trying not to think about what he'd have to do, telling himself that Emma was better off without him. But he knew that if he really wanted a shot with her, it might take that. Leaving behind everything he'd finally gotten his hands on.

And that doubtful, nagging voice in the back of his brain asked what if he lost everything and then she still decided that he wasn't who she wanted? Where would he be then?

"Then we'll manage," Heath said. "We might need a few months to find another qualified guide, but I'd rather see you happy than anything else. But I'll also say that Quinn and I talked, and we might have an idea to keep Emma here... I think it might work, but of course that's up to Emma, and if you don't fix things, we've got no shot at talking her into it..."

Heath quickly outlined his and Quinn's idea, and while Cam was afraid to hope, a spark of it caught and whispered that maybe he could have everything he wanted.

There was one person responsible for his fate, for controlling his temper, for making sure he was good enough for Emma and Zoey, and that was himself. He might not be able to offer her a fancy job title with a big salary, but he could help provide a good home for her and for Zoey, one where they could laugh and enjoy days living next to one of the most beautiful places on earth. He could promise that he'd do whatever it took to protect his family, because he'd die before he let anyone hurt his girls.

And he could offer Emma his heart, because it was all he truly had, and it already belonged to her anyway.

"So?" Heath arched an eyebrow. "Are you ready to pull your head out? Or do I need to keep spouting off more inspirational lines? Because I've been writing songs for Dixie Rush's next album and I've got sappy lines to spare."

Cam laughed, and after days without feeling even an ounce of joy, he wanted to hold on to the happiness and the hope slowly working their way through him. "Save something for the album, man." He glanced at his wrist out of habit, only to remember that he'd purposely left his watch, thinking that the lack of watching time go by would make it pass by easier.

It hadn't.

"What time is it?"

Heath took his phone out of his pocket. "Eleven forty—so about ten minutes past the time when Quinn threatened to kill me if I hadn't made it back to Mountain Ridge yet."

Eleven forty? That didn't give him much time to get back to the property and pull together everything he needed to.

But it was time to take his fighting skills and use them in a healthier way.

He just hoped it wouldn't be too late…

Chapter Twenty-Seven

The first auction ended, and Brianna and Dusty Brooks, who were engaged and set to be married in a couple of months, walked away arm in arm.

In fact, Emma was noticing that the majority of women involved in the picnic basket auction were already engaged. Meaning that if she did stay in Hope Springs, next year she'd be about the only single woman under the age of forty left.

Another point for moving, I guess, she thought as she shifted in her seat, but it only sent a pang of sadness through her.

Grandma Bev came over and bumped her hip into Emma. "Scooch down," she said, and so Emma and Quinn moved down a couple seats to make room.

"Which basket is yours?" Emma asked.

"The empty one with the big red flashy bow on top." Grandma pointed.

"It's empty?"

"There's no food, anyway. Just a paperback book and a bottle of wine. 'Cause if a guy bids on me, he should know that that's what I'll be making him for dinner every night. Nothing."

Emma and Quinn laughed, and Emma said, "Why didn't I think of that?"

"Vera Mae's going to bid on it, actually. Since she's moving in, we figured we'd make people wonder about us. Stir up a little controversy, you know."

Emma shook her head, and Quinn asked if she could adopt her.

Caroline Dixon's basket was next—although no one was supposed to know whose basket was whose, Emma had seen her placing it on the table. Not to mention most everyone in town knew already. It helped people in the same age range bid on the basket, so the dates were only semiweird instead of super-duper weird.

As the bidding started, Grandma Bev patted Emma's leg. "How you holding up?"

She put on the best smile she could. Last night she'd finally broken down, gone over to Grandma Bev's house, and told her everything. She'd been so sure she'd only hear *I told you so*, but she'd simply told Emma that if Cam didn't want her, he was an idiot, then she'd made peach cobbler, and they'd eaten it with ice cream while Zoey played.

"What I should've said to you last night was…"

Emma braced herself.

"That I think maybe I pushed you a little too hard, because I didn't want you to have regrets and for you to waste that big, beautiful brain of yours. But you're smart, and funny, and beautiful, and you're raising a smart, beautiful daughter. What matters is that you're happy wherever you are. And also, I'll come visit if you move, so you're not getting rid of me anytime soon."

Emma gave her grandma a side hug, resting her head on her shoulder for a moment. "Thanks, Grandma."

The nice widower who owned the feed store was declared the winner with a thirty-dollar bid, and while Ms. Dixon was clearly nervous, she smiled shyly at him, and they headed toward the tree line. Not arm in arm, but Emma thought she still noticed a spark.

Sadie's basket was next, and Cory and Royce had a bidding war that was more friendly competition and driving the price up than a real fight for Sadie—the three of them and Quinn had been really close in high school, always going everywhere together. In fact, Quinn had once said that if Cory wasn't too scared to settle down, she could almost see him and Emma together.

Speaking of Quinn, she was texting and checking her phone constantly.

"Everything okay?" Emma asked.

Quinn dropped her phone quickly—almost as if she were hiding it—and then she smiled. "Yeah. It's fine. Just checking on Heath."

Something weird was definitely going on, but right as Emma was about to call Quinn on it, Patsy Higgins lifted her pink basket in the air.

"Let's start the bidding at five dollars," Patsy Higgins said.

Pete lifted his hand.

Forrest Scott, the guy who ran the parts store, bid him up by five dollars—she wouldn't have a clue what to talk about with the guy, and while he might've matured since high school, her brain still held the image of the cocky jock who thought he was cooler than everyone else.

"Oh, no, not that kid," Grandma said. "He's dumber than a sack of bricks."

Luckily the noise of the auction was loud enough to cover Grandma's commentary—Emma certainly hoped so, anyway.

Pete raised the bid to fifteen, then he turned and flashed her a big smile.

Crap. She'd insisted to Cam that nothing was going on, but Pete *had* asked her out, and even though he'd claimed his offer was purely professional, now she wondered if there was more to the job offer than a job. With everything that had happened with Cam, she was far from ready to even consider another relationship. Not to mention it'd probably make working together weird.

Maybe in time… She tried to imagine it, because the thought of never dating again was depressing, but the image of her and Pete simply didn't fit.

Keith, one of the guys on her crew, bid next, and then Pete upped him.

Well, they could talk about how nicely Mountain Ridge turned out, discuss options for the resort in Park City, and at least it shouldn't be too horribly awkward. As long as he didn't expect more.

Either way, she'd done her part to raise money for the town, and that was something to be proud of.

"Twenty-five dollars. Going once…going twice…"

"One hundred dollars."

The entire audience spun as one. Cam stood in the back, a resolute look on his face. Her gaze met his and held. Every cell in her body pricked up, and her pulse throbbed behind her temples, each beat faster and harder than the next. Moving on hadn't seemed possible a few moments ago, but with Cam physically here, his presence causing that oxygen-stealing sensation it always did, she knew there was no fully moving on from a guy like him.

"Maybe he's not as stupid as I thought," Grandma said, elbowing Emma in the side.

Pete bid $110, and the muscles in Cam's jaw tightened. Emma scooted to the edge of her chair. This was ridiculous. Neither of them should be throwing money away like this. Cam's eyes remained on hers as he said, "Two hundred dollars."

A combination of gasps and loudly whispered, "Did he say two hundred?" went through the crowd.

"Here's the thing," Cam said loudly as he strode up the aisle. "I behaved like a jackass the other night, and I intend to make it up to Emma. So I'm eating whatever's in that basket, even if it's disgusting, or if it gives me food poisoning…"

Patsy's mouth dropped, her expression making it clear even the implication offended her, and in spite of the surreal situation, Emma laughed. Cam flashed her a smile, and her heart fluttered, slowly coming to life after days of dormancy.

"Not that, uh, Emma would intentionally make bad food," Cam said. He cleared his throat. "But like I said, I'm going to be leaving here with Emma and that basket, whatever it takes." His gaze flicked to Pete, and Emma could see how hard he worked to keep his expression civil. "So I suggest you back down now. Because I won't. *Ever.*"

Goose bumps swept across Emma's skin, and Quinn grasped her hand. "It looks like I'm not the only one with the sure bet today."

Emma was afraid to read too much into it all. This was just his way of apologizing. It didn't fix everything, and it certainly wasn't the same as declaring he wanted her.

He looked dang good, though, his rolled-up flannel shirtsleeves showing off muscular, tattoo-covered forearms, his unshaven face wild in a way that made her want to be a little wild, too.

"Two hundred dollars," Patsy Higgins said, and the entire crowd seemed to be holding its breath. "Going once…going twice…" The gavel banged against the podium, and Emma was officially Cam's.

Er, her basket and company were his. For the next hour or so.

Cam strolled up to the front, grabbed the pink basket that

clashed with his rugged mountain man look, then strode back down the aisle, a man on a mission. When he reached her, he extended his hand across Grandma, to her.

"Emma, I know this is a long way from making anything up to you, but if you'll hear me out, this is just the beginning of my apology. I'd rather not have to make the rest of it with the entire town watching, but I will if it comes to that. So? What do you say?"

With him so close, her fingers twitched, longing to reach out and touch him. The vulnerability swimming in his eyes nearly undid her, too—as if he wasn't sure she'd come along. The truth was, she'd walk to the ends of the earth with him as long as he stayed by her side.

"If you're not going, I will," Grandma said, tilting her head toward Cam in a clear *go already* gesture. "Although I also wouldn't mind hearing the apology."

"Emma's grandma, I presume?"

"Beverly Harris. You and I are going to have quite the talk someday."

"Yes, ma'am," Cam said, then he returned his attention to Emma.

She took his extended hand and let him pull her to her feet. With her hand in his, the achy, broken pieces of her heart started to bind back together, leaving her feeling whole for the first time all week. She tried not to let herself get carried away, because she knew they still had a lot to work out, but after feeling hopeless for days, the happy optimism tingling through her body felt too nice to shove away.

So she pushed logistics and worries about the unsteady future from her mind and let her heart take the wheel, hoping it wouldn't end up crashing and burning.

They walked toward the trees, and Cam kept on walking until they reached the spot where he'd first asked her not to go out with Pete and then kissed her. She'd wanted him so badly that day—ever since she'd first laid eyes on him, really—and she still did. *I just need him to want me. Please let him want me.*

She sat down on the large flat rock, and when her hands couldn't deal with having nothing to do, she tucked them under her thighs.

Cam lowered his big body onto the rock and then lifted the basket and spun it around. "Quinn texted to let me know which basket was yours, but I'd know Zoey's influence anywhere. She help you decorate?"

Emma was afraid talking would cause her to burst into tears—she was pretty close to doing so as it was—so she simply nodded.

Cam ran his hand through his hair. "I don't even know where to start." His gaze drifted toward the trees, and then he sucked in a breath and turned his blue-green eyes back on her. "I'm so sorry, Emma. I saw that contract, and then I saw you with Pete, and I just…I lost my temper.

"Remember how I told you that when I first got home, I felt lost? Without the military in my life, I'd lost my sense of purpose. And I was still dealing with blaming myself for that last bad mission, and everything inside me was all mixed up. I thought Mountain Ridge would be enough—I'd hoped so badly it would be, for months. That it'd fix everything broken inside me. But there was still something missing." He placed his hand on her knee and ran his thumb over the top, and her skin hummed, coming alive so quickly under his touch. "Then you and Zoey happened."

Emma attempted to swallow, but her throat vetoed it.

"You guys became my sense of purpose, and when I found out I might be losing it… Everything I cared about was suddenly slipping through my fingers, and I panicked." He squeezed her knee tighter. "Then I saw you with Pete and… well, you were there."

"I was," Emma said, the words scraping from her tight

throat. The reminder of that night brought back the pain she'd felt and put a dent in the optimism she was doing her best to hold on to. She glanced down at the rock, focusing on a silver fleck that caught the sunlight. "You told me that you came here to run your lodge and to escape everything, and that I was getting in the way of what you truly wanted."

He put his hands on either side of her face, gently tipping it toward his. "That's because I'm an idiot. I don't express myself well. Anger's my knee-jerk reaction, and sometimes it's easier than feeling hurt. But that's what I felt. Hurt." He looked to the sky and let out a long exhale before his attention returned to her. "Heath told me… But I… You see…"

Cam growled, frustration radiating off him, and she almost wrapped her arms around him and told him it was all okay. But they needed to have a real talk, to discuss everything and figure out where they went from here, before she knew if it would truly be okay.

That was the problem with falling in love. It messed up your common sense, and she didn't mind being without it if she wasn't there alone, but someone had to be responsible, and time had proved again and again that that was her role.

Oh, well. The happy optimism was nice while it lasted.

"What do you want, Cam? No matter what you say, or what you decide about me, I'll make sure you get a lot of time with Zoey. We can schedule visits, and I'll travel back to Hope Springs whenever I can, or even meet you halfway between here and Salt Lake. It's so important to her and to me that you're in her life. If you're not ready for more…for us, you and I can just put our relationship aside and focus on her. Because she's what's important."

Time seemed to stop, and tears were coming, and she didn't want to cry in front of him again, so when, after several eternally long seconds, he still hadn't said anything, she started to stand.

Cam caught her hand, holding her in place. "Please, don't go yet. I'm trying, I swear I am. I just might need a few attempts to get it right." He pressed his lips together and took a few deep breaths, then his eyes met hers again. "The mountains have always been my escape. When things got bad at home, I'd hike as far as my legs could take me. Sometimes alone, sometimes with Heath. When we didn't have food, I'd go hunting and fishing and make sure the freezer was stocked enough to get us through the winter months. I survived because of those mountains. Misery didn't touch me there. So after our fight, I grabbed my gear and took off into the hills, the way I'd done dozens—hell, hundreds of times before…

"But without you? I was completely miserable. And it was more than the rain and lack of fish." He reached out and dragged his thumb across her lower lip, and intense longing like she'd never felt before took over every inch of her body. "I couldn't escape missing you. Which made me think that I might be in love with you."

Hope flooded her chest, and for a second she forgot how to breathe.

"Zoey *is* what's important," he said, "but she's not *all* that's important to me. I thought I was in love with you, but now that I'm sitting here across from you, I don't have to think, and there's no *might* about it. I love you, Emma Walker. Every part of you, from the bold girl who took shots with me all those years ago—the side I know you don't think is you, but you underestimate how brave and strong you are—to the quiet girl who knows everything and raised our daughter despite being so alone.

"I want you, Emma, but more than that, I *need* you. It scares me, but it doesn't make it less true. I'll fight for you, and I'll protect you, and I'm sitting here begging you for a second chance."

It was everything she'd ever wanted to hear, and another

wave of tears was coming.

"And if you take that job in Salt Lake, I'm ready to be in a long-distance relationship. And if you decide that city life is what you want long-term, I'll find a replacement for my position at Mountain Ridge, and I'll move to where you are."

She stared into his eyes, stunned by the steely determination she saw there. "That's crazy. Mountain Ridge is your dream."

"And now you are. You and Zoey. I don't want to settle for raising her together and trying to remain friends. Everything I thought I didn't want…a relationship, a kid, a family. I want them all. Because of you. I want *you*." He leaned forward and brushed his lips across hers, and desire and relief washed through her. "And I want *us*."

His words echoed through her head, rattling around until they caught hold and sank in. He wanted *her*.

She'd waited for so long to hear that, and she almost pinched herself to make sure it was real. Slowly she lifted her hand and placed it on the side of his face. Then she ran it down his beard, the tickle of his whiskers against her palm sending zips of electricity racing across her skin.

Hope shone through his features. "Does that mean…?"

Emma nodded, and he planted both hands on her butt and hauled her onto his lap. His lips crashed onto hers, and she whispered, "I want us, too," as she wrapped her arms around his neck.

She kissed him deeply, letting herself fall into the kiss for a moment before dazedly pulling back to look him in the eye. "And if I'm telling the truth, I want us here. In Hope Springs. I didn't realize how much I loved this place until I had to think about leaving it."

"Well, that's a relief. Because I actually have a proposition for you—a couple, in fact.

"One, Mountain Ridge needs a business manager. Quinn

wants to take care of the guests, Heath and I want to do the tours, and we'll need someone to keep the books, make sure we stick to a budget, and basically keep us running. We can't think of anyone better than you, and we realized that if we cut a few corners, like buying used vehicles that Heath and I can fix up instead of brand-new ones, we'd have enough money to hire a manager. Especially now that the website is up and running, and the cabins are booking so quickly. But if you want to go another way, or keep your current job, I totally understand."

She thought about how much she already loved Mountain Ridge, and all the ways she could work to keep the place running as efficiently as possible. She'd let her ex convince her bookkeeping was a boring job, and maybe to other people it was, but she liked the challenge, and she even experienced a thrill when the numbers all added up, nerdy or not.

And if she got to do that while working with Quinn, Heath, and the guy holding on to her like he was afraid to let go…that sounded like the dreamiest job she could ever have. "You're sure it won't make things between us…harder? Like, you might get sick of me."

"Impossible. In fact, that actually brings me to my other proposal. I'm sick of coming home to my empty cabin after nights with you and Zoey. I don't want to do it anymore. There's this spot that backs right up to the trees on the east end that would be perfect for a three- or four-bedroom cabin. It's far enough from the lodge and cabins to not feel like part of them, but not so far that it'll take us much longer than five minutes to walk to work.

"I've got to tell you, I started picturing you and Zoey there, and well, I…" A muscle along his jawline flexed, and she could tell he was struggling to keep hold of his emotions. Then he cleared his throat. "Basically, the thought makes me nearly tear up. And if you ever tell anyone that, I'll…" He swept the hair off her face and locked eyes with her. "I'll kiss you."

"Wow, you need to work on your threats. That only makes me want to announce it to the entire town."

"Honestly, I'm going to kiss you either way." He leaned in and did just that, kissing her until she was rendered incapable of speech, thought, or anything but melting into his embrace and envisioning that cabin he'd mentioned.

Whereas her thoughts were cloudy any time she thought about moving to the city, she saw the future with Cam, living right here at Mountain Ridge, and she knew down to her bones that it'd be the best future for her and Zoey.

"Is that a yes to designing a cabin for us, or to the manager job, or just to me, or…?"

"I'll take the job," she said. "And I'll definitely take you. Did I tell you that I love you yet?"

Cam shook his head. "Not yet. I was kinda hoping that you were getting to that part."

With a smile, she ran her hand down the side of his face, and he tightened his grip on her butt. "Cameron Brantley…" She kissed one corner of his mouth. "I'm completely"—she kissed the other corner—"and totally"—she kissed him square on the lips—"in love with you."

He took control of the kiss, laying her back in the grass and tangling his tongue with hers.

If more of this was in her future, it was definitely one she could get behind. And somewhere down that road, she also saw the image of a few more little ones that were half him and half her running around, keeping them busy as they lived out their dreams together.

Epilogue

The two months since Mountain Ridge had opened had been nonstop craziness, but Heath had returned from a tour with Dixie Rush and told Emma and Cam to take a break. It was good timing, since one of their bigger parties had just left and they had a few days before another came in. Cam's friend Jay Torres was planning to come up and spend some time with them in the next month or so as well.

On top of everything else, Emma was also drawing blueprints for a group of cabins going up near Green River—thanks to her work on Mountain Ridge, she'd lined up a few freelance jobs, that one and a house for a retired couple with expensive taste and the money to back it up. It was turning out to be the best of both worlds, really, even if it'd also left her busier than ever.

So of course she and Cam had jumped at the chance for a break, packed their fishing gear, and brought Zoey to the reservoir for the afternoon. Rod, Sheena, and Oliver had driven behind them, too, and they'd headed to the other side to check the fishing over there and give one another some space.

Gradually Emma had gotten used to Rod's more callous actions and speech, and he and Cam had come a long way in mending fences. Zoey bridged the gap that'd formed between them in a lot of ways. She adored both of them, and both of them would do anything for her. All of them, including Quinn and Heath—when he was in town—and Grandma Bev, on nights she wasn't too busy with her hopping social life, had Sunday dinners on a regular basis now. Usually at the B and B, and often at weird times to work around their guests, but they were the kind of family events Emma had always wanted in her life.

Emma lowered her book and looked over the back of her fold-up chair, searching for the rest of her family. Cam had taken Zoey for a walk so Emma could finish her book. The last page had left her with a happy sigh and a longing for her own prince charming.

Just when she was about to go looking for them, she saw them crest the hill. Zoey saw her and ran full out, so quickly Emma worried she'd trip and face-plant. Cam rushed to keep up, one of his arms shooting out each time Zoey wobbled, but she made it to flat ground without needing to be caught.

As soon as Zoey reached her, she held out a mangled bouquet of wildflowers, a few with bent stems, and a couple that even had the roots intact. "Daddy and I picked flowers for you."

Emma looked over their daughter's blond head of curls to Cam, who winked at her. Tingly butterflies swirled through her stomach—four months together, and her reaction to him was still just as strong.

He held out a hand, extending a more carefully picked bouquet of flowers. Emma took them and added them to Zoey's. She made a big display of sniffing them, and when she caught a whiff, she couldn't help lifting them closer to her nose and soaking in the smell that perfectly encapsulated the mountains.

"Thank you, you two. I love them."

Cam nudged Zoey, and she turned her big blue-green eyes back to Emma. "And we need to ask someting else."

A dozen possibilities ran through Emma's mind, everything from swimming to fishing to Zoey's recent request for a pony—Cam better not have given in and promised their daughter a pony. They'd talked about how impractical it was, even though Cam had also mentioned they did have enough land and they could always use a few more horses for the tours. He spoiled their daughter about as much as he spoiled her.

But then Cam pulled something out of his pocket and dropped to one knee. He popped open the black velvet box, and sunlight glinted off the diamond in the center of the silver ring.

Tears rose, and the ring and Cam's features blurred.

"Emma Walker, I love you. I want to marry you and make you mine—and I want to make sure no one else can ever bid on your basket," he added with a grin. "So, what do you say? Will you marry me?"

Emma sniffed, finding it hard to speak through the tears clotting her throat, but she managed to push out a squeaky, "Yes."

"Uh-oh," Zoey said, her eyes going wide as she took a few steps back. "You made Mommy cry. You better give her a hug."

Cam pulled her into his arms and did one better than a hug. He slipped the ring on to her finger and kissed her.

Then Emma reached out an arm and pulled her daughter into the hug, too.

It was funny how the world-changing days started like every other day, and then, the next thing you knew, all your dreams had come true and changed every single thing in the most perfect way.

Acknowledgments

For some reason, this book decided to be extra challenging, and I had a few freak-outs while writing it. Luckily I had Stacy Abrams, my amazing editor, to help me figure out how to make it way, way better, and it wouldn't be what it is today if it wasn't for her. You can thank her for pushing me in a direction that led to adding Grandma Bev, who quickly became one of my favorite side characters. Not only that, but she always keeps me laughing through the editing process, and cares enough to text me a quick congrats when my team wins the Super Bowl. (Yes, I might've added that just to relive that glorious win. Hehe.)

Also, big thanks to Liz Pelletier, for talking out plot points when I was first brainstorming this book, and for sending me texts to warn me away from Voltage Mtn Dew, since it's apparently much stronger than our faithful standby, Diet Mtn Dew. LOL. Thanks to everyone on the Entangled Publishing Team. You guys are so good to me! Thanks to ninja Heather Riccio, Jessica Turner, Alycia Tornetta, my awesome publicist Debbie Suzuki, and the rest of the Bliss team.

Thanks to these awesome people who help me brainstorm, push me through writing sprints, and are amazing author friends: Gina Maxwell, MK Meredith, Carla Laureano, Evangeline Denmark, Brandy Vallance, Rachel Harris, and Melissa West. You ladies are the best!

My family has been a great support system through my writing career, and I appreciate them for all the encouragement, and also for not caring how I look by the end of the day, or if we have quesadillas for the third night in a row.

Big thanks to my readers, whether it's just reading my books, or sending me notes wanting to know who the next book is going to be about and when it's coming out—those things make my day and keep me going! Thank you so much!

About the Author

Cindi Madsen is a *USA Today* bestselling author of contemporary romance and young adult novels. She sits at her computer every chance she gets, plotting, revising, and falling in love with her characters. Sometimes it makes her a crazy person. Without it, she'd be even crazier. She has way too many shoes, but can always find a reason to buy a pretty new pair, especially if they're sparkly, colorful, or super tall. She loves music and dancing and wishes summer lasted all year long. She lives in Colorado (where summer is most definitely NOT all year long) with her husband and three children.

You can visit Cindi at: www.cindimadsen.com, where you can sign up for her newsletter to get all the up-to-date information on her books.

Follow her on Twitter @cindimadsen.

THE CIPHER SERIES

DEMONS OF THE SUN

Find your Bliss with these great releases...

UNEXPECTEDLY YOURS
a novel by Coleen Kwan

Derek Carmichael has harbored a secret crush on his best friend's older sister for years, but Hannah has always been out of his reach. Hannah is wary of Derek's player past and the rampant rumors connecting him to beautiful socialites. Still, she can't help but give in when their attraction reaches a boiling point. Trying to keep it a secret from her overprotective brother is one thing, but when Hannah finds herself unexpectedly expecting, her life is thrown upside down. She and Derek may be becoming parents together, but that's no basis for a happily-ever-after.

THE BEST MAN'S BABY
a *Red River* novel by Victoria James

Florist Claire Holbrook has *always* played by the rules her entire life, but breaks them to spend one night with sexy lone wolf Jake Manning. Six weeks later she discovers they created a bond that will last a lifetime… Jake has *never* played by the rules. Getting Minister Holbrook's daughter pregnant wasn't part of any life plan, but he won't run from his responsibilities. He'll step up and be the best man he can, even if he doesn't have a clue where to begin.

THE WEDDING WAGER
a *Weddings in Westchester* novel by Barbara DeLeo

Nick Katsalos has a foolproof plan to save his parents' floundering wedding venue. The last thing he ex-pects is for Erin O'Malley, the captivating daughter of his parents' biggest rival, to waltz in and charm the client who could finally get the family business back on track. When Erin and Nick enter into a wager to de-termine who will win the contract she prepares for the worst... and is surprised by the glimpses of warmth she sees in the man behind the numbers. But as the competition heats up, Erin and Nick must decide what's more important — winning or love.

THE WEDDING WAGER
a *Weddings in Westchester* novel by Barbara DeLeo

Nick Katsalos has a foolproof plan to save his parents' floundering wedding venue. The last thing he ex-pects is for Erin O'Malley, the captivating daughter of his parents' biggest rival, to waltz in and charm the client who could finally get the family business back on track. When Erin and Nick enter into a wager to de-termine who will win the contract she prepares for the worst... and is surprised by the glimpses of warmth she sees in the man behind the numbers. But as the competition heats up, Erin and Nick must decide what's more important — winning or love.

CPSIA information can be obtained
at www.ICGtesting.com
Printed in the USA
LVHW030122301120
672984LV00053B/1062